# WRITTEN IN THE MARGINS

Shaun Ledger

ISBN-13: 9798407526223


Library of Congress Control Number: 2018675309
Printed in the United States of America

Cover design: Tony Noble (www.tonynoble-artist.com)

*To Christine, my wife, without whose encouragement this book would never have been written.*

# CONTENTS

# Prologue

**Copy of manuscript delivered to *Ashton and Ashton of London (Literary Agents)*, and handed to Barney Granwell, Spring 2022:**

The Angry Sun by Zachary Munro
(5 - Red Rankin Loses His Final Game)
Revised by Tom Jefferson (2022).

**Valance Township, Arizona - 30 miles north of Tombstone - July 1882.**

The blazing Arizona sun was at its highest when the riders pulled up outside The Berger Palace, hot, thirsty, and bedraggled after a hard ride through the arid landscape. Scoot and Frenchie had been following Red Rankin for nearly two weeks now, determined to reclaim their losses and some of the pride they'd lost after the card sharp had made fools of them back in Tucson. Almost as embarrassing, the gambler had killed their partner Curly in a gunfight over the unexpected appearance of a seven of diamonds. Neither of them had actually cared for Curly, but fellers on the range knew he travelled with them, so now there was a debt of honour to be paid. They had been breakfasting in Tombstone when word had reached them of a fancily dressed gambler with red hair who was emptying the wallets of the gamesters in the nearby township of Valance. The cowboy who had given them the news had been taken aback by the speed with which they'd leapt from their seats. *Looks like somebody done somebody wrong*, he'd thought as he happily mopped up the plentiful ham and eggs they abandoned.

As they tethered their horses to the hitching post outside The Palace, a tall figure approached. He was dressed neither as a ranch worker, nor a bank clerk, but something in between, something that didn't belong in a frontier town. 'You looking for Red Rankin?' he asked.

Scoot eyed him up, suspicion creasing his forehead. 'What of it?'

The stranger smiled, the kind of smile that didn't reach anywhere near his blue eyes. 'Just trying to be helpful. He's inside, fleecing a few more innocent lambs; he's not expecting you.'

Puzzled, Scoot glanced over at Frenchie, who answered with a shrug. 'It don't matter if he's expecting us or not, mister. If you've got your own feud with him, feel free to tag along.'

'Thanks, I will. I've been having a nose around. I figure if you two bring him out, I'll have the horses ready; this one belongs to him...' He gestured at the Palomino that was already tied to the post. 'We'll string him up down there, if that's agreeable to you fellers,' he continued, pointing in the direction of the churchyard.

'Sounds good to me,' Frenchie said, 'and what might your name be, mister?'

'You can call me Cassidy.'

'You been crossed by the son of a bitch as well?'

'You could say that.'

Satisfied that they now had a useful ally, they pushed open the swing doors and walked into the gloomy interior of the saloon. In spite of its name, the three storey Berger Palace bore no resemblance to a royal residence. A rickety staircase led up to some basic rooms, and the street level area was a single large space, with a long bar running down the wall opposite the entrance. Scoot gave a subtle nod towards a card game taking place in the corner of the room. Frenchie acknowledged the signal. 'I need a drink first. He ain't going nowhere.' They made their way to the bar. 'Two beers, two whiskies.' The barkeep eyed up the side arms that the newcomers were wearing, but if he was thinking about saying anything, he stopped when he took note of the intent on Frenchie's face.

After downing the whiskies in a single slug, and then taking a longer drink of their beers, the two cowboys left the glasses on the bar and walked over to take in the game. Red hadn't been hard to spot. He was wearing a shoestring tie and a bright crimson waistcoat that matched his name, as did the colour of his shoulder-length hair, and the extravagant Vandyke beard decorating his face. The three cowboys who were being taken for their trail earnings had, one by one, and with varying colourful expressions of dismay, thrown their cards onto the table.

'Come now, gentlemen,' Red spoke in a slow Texan drawl, 'am I to assume you have no confidence in your sporting abilities? Rarely have the gambling gods blessed me as they have today, and I -' he stopped talking when he felt the steel of Scoot's Colt pressing against his collar. Red smiled ruefully; he'd been expecting this, and spoke without turning. 'Thomas French, my old friend. I am most disappointed. Who'd have thought a full two weeks would pass before you tracked me down?'

Scoot cocked the hammer of his revolver. 'It's not Frenchie, Red, but he's here with me. You know who ain't here? Curly; he's filling a hole in the ground somewhere in Tucson, and you might say we ain't happy about that.' With a quick glance at Frenchie, he gestured at the pile of notes that were piled on the table next to Red's elbow. 'We'll take this as a deposit on your debt.'

'Deposit? Dare I ask how you intend to make up the balance?' Red asked.

'You still owe us for Curly, so I reckon you can guess.'

Red stretched for his black fedora and

placed it on his head, adjusting it until satisfied with its positioning. The watching audience parted to make way for the three men as they exited and stepped, blinking, into the sunlit street, where someone who Red didn't recognise was waiting with the horses.

Red turned to Frenchie. 'We going somewhere?' But it was the newcomer who answered.

'Not far. You see that?' Cassidy pointed along Main Street. A hundred yards away, a solitary Ash stood outside the churchyard. 'Locals call it The Mercy Tree. You know why?'

'No,' Red frowned. 'But I think I can guess.' Had he crossed this feller at some point in the past? It wasn't out of the question. Or had he joined up with Frenchie and Scoot somewhere out on the trail? Whoever he was, Red sensed he wasn't somebody to mess with.

'I'll tell you, anyway. It's how people such as yourself find their way into God's mercy.'

Red nodded his understanding and climbed onto the saddle of his palomino. The stranger and the two cowboys followed suit, and the group slowly headed towards the tree. When they reached it, the stranger produced a length of rope from his saddle bag. He tossed it to Scoot; one end of it had been fashioned into a noose. Scoot threw it over a branch, then pulled, testing its strength.

'Any last words?' Cassidy asked.

But before Red could answer, a loud shout

stopped proceedings in their tracks.

'Stop! Everyone stay where you are.' Sheriff Bill Gardner was cautiously making his way towards them, his left hand high, palm open, to show he wasn't looking for trouble. However, the cocked Colt 45 in his right hand sent the message that he was ready for it should it happen. 'Maybe you'd like to send Red over to me.'

'Bill, at last!' Cassidy said. 'I've been wondering when you were going to show up.'

'Do I know you, mister?'

'Maybe not now, but you will. The names Cassidy.'

'We don't want any upset, Sheriff. We're here on personal business; best you leave this well alone,' Frenchie said.

'If it's in this town, it is my business. We got rules in Valance, and you boys are breaking quite a few of them. If you're wanting a drink, there are saloons willing to accept your cash, as long as you hand your firearms in at my office. If you'd like to set this gentleman free, you can be on your way.' He turned to point out the Sheriff's Office, but before he could raise his arm, Scoot, who had been edging behind him, found the back of the lawman's head with the butt of his pistol. Bill fell to his knees, dazed.

Cassidy nodded his approval. He threw another section of rope towards Scoot. 'Might as well make it a double hanging.'

Scoot tied Red's hands together behind his

back, then moved on to do the same to the sheriff. 'Come prepared, eh? You always carry these around?' he asked as he tested the knots.

'Let's just say I like to be ready for all eventualities,' Cassidy answered. He pointed at Red, who had been watching the diversion. 'Get the sheriff up there, behind Rankin.'

A second noose was thrown alongside the first and, after a minute or two of swearing and cussing from Scoot and Frenchie, the unconscious form of Bill Gardner was balanced precariously behind Red on his horse. A noose was fitted over each of their heads.

Cassidy watched, satisfied. 'Red, I asked if you had any last words?'

After a brief pause for thought, Red spoke. 'I guess I would just -'

'I think we've heard enough of your philosophising,' Frenchie broke in. He slapped the rear of the Palomino, scaring it into taking off along the street. Red and Bill were left hanging by the neck, legs kicking out at the empty air. The last thing Bill remembered before darkness engulfed him was the burning hatred in Cassidy's eyes.

It was at that very moment that they heard the thunder. Frenchie scanned the sky, searching for any signs of a sudden storm, but saw nothing; the sky was clear. They realised it wasn't thunder when they spotted the approaching cloud of dust. Another group of riders, six of them, racing across the barren landscape towards town. The three would-be executioners sensed this wasn't any kind of welcoming committee. Without a word, Scoot and Frenchie saddled up and fled the scene. Cassidy took a moment to weigh up the situation before cursing and deciding it might be wise to follow them.

The new arrivals swept up Main Street, pulling up when they came to the swinging bodies. The two hanged men were lowered to the ground. A rider dismounted and removed the noose from Red's collar, then slapped him around the face. There was no response. The rider looked up at his companions and shook his head.

'What about him?' the leader asked, dismounting for a closer inspection.

Coughing and spluttering, his throat racked with pain, Bill regained consciousness just long enough to see the relief on her beautiful face.

*   *   *   *   *

# Chapter 1: London

Barney Granwell felt he ought to know this place. The comforting odour of stale beer and the laid-back groove of mid-seventies' Steely Dan that filled the surrounding air indicated a familiar setting, but something wasn't quite right. Slowly, the world drifting around him came into focus, and the pain in his throat calmed down enough for him to concentrate. Then it hit him – he was in The Wellington. The reason he'd struggled to identify the location was that he was seeing it from an unusual angle, laying flat on his back, facing the ceiling. Something appeared before him, blocking out his view. Now he was getting some practice, he recognised the bearded face of Robin, his best friend. He lifted his head a few inches and scanned the room. 'Has she gone?'

'Has who gone?'

'That woman. She was here a second ago.' And then, wistfully, 'She was gorgeous.'

Robin took hold of Barney's elbow. 'Let's get you up. That must have been a real bang on the noggin. This is The Welly, and there hasn't been a gorgeous woman in here since the nineteen sixties.'

Another pair of hands grabbed Barney's other elbow. These belonged to Trevor, the manager of the pub. 'A bit much, coming from an old fart like you,' Trevor said, offended by the remark.

'Sorry; but you know what I mean,' Robin said.

'Yeah, I suppose I do.' It was Trevor's turn to sound wistful. 'But whatever you think of the standard of my locals, you don't see them keeling over drunk, do you?' He stomped back to his position behind the bar.

'He's got a point,' Robin said. 'You've been drinking a lot more than normal lately. I mean, you were already pissed when I arrived, just in time to see you slither off your seat. You're lucky you didn't crack your skull open on the way down.'

Barney's hand reached for his forehead. He'd have a bump there in the morning, but at least the skin wasn't broken. 'But I'd only had a couple when you turned up...' he stopped talking as it became obvious that Robin wasn't convinced by his pleas of innocence. He couldn't blame him for being cynical. Barney *had* been hitting the bottle quite a lot in the last few months. Ever since Lucy had told him she was leaving him, in fact. Even more so after she'd recently announced three things: First, she wanted to formalise the separation by getting divorced from him; second, when the Decree Absolute arrived, she was going to marry Jonathan Carpwell-Higgins, the same man that she'd left Barney for; and third, that to celebrate all the above, she and Jonathan were embarking on a month-long Tour of European capitals. To top it all, he'd just undergone the most realistic out-of-body experience, where he'd been involved in a gambling feud in a Wild West town, and had only been rescued from being hanged by the Baddies by a posse of Goodies, led by one the most beautiful women he'd ever seen.

What.The.Fuck.

'Barney! You've gone again.'

'What? Oh, sorry.' In view of Robin's current perception of him, Barney decided it would be wise not to mention his hallucination. 'Actually, I've got something to show you. You say I've been acting odd lately; this might explain why.' He reached into his coat pocket and pulled out his phone. He worked through the menus until he'd found what he was looking for, then passed it over to Robin. On the screen was a picture of his soon-to-be ex-wife and her soon-to-be new husband, standing next to the life-sized statues representing Rembrandt's painting, *The Night Watch*, on Rembrandtplein in Amsterdam. Jonathan must have asked a passer-by to take it. Barney recognised the location because there was a similar printed image hiding in a box at the back of a cupboard somewhere at home. Only that one was of Lucy and himself, from ten years ago.

Robin sighed. 'You've got to get over this, Barney. It's been nearly a year since she left.'

'Yeah, but look at these.' Holding the screen so that Robin could see it, Barney flicked through more images. There were selfies of the happy couple, and some with just Lucy, always smiling into the camera, showing she couldn't be happier in her new life. Many of them had a famous monument in the background. 'They started in Paris,' Barney said, as he displayed a sequence of pictures. There was the Eiffel Tower, the Champs-Élysées and the Arc de Triomphe, Notre Dame Cathedral. Others had been taken in coffee shops and restaurants, usually with an almost empty bottle of wine on the table.

Robin furrowed his brow. 'Isn't this a good sign that things are getting better between you two? Why else would Lucy send these if -'

It was Barney's turn to interrupt. 'She didn't. It was the little shit that sent them.'

'Who? Jonathan?'

'I can't see any other little shit on these, can you? Of course Jonathan. He's been sending them since they left. I bet Lucy doesn't even know. Look at him.'

Barney pointed to an image of Jonathan and Lucy outside the Moulin Rouge, obviously just before they were due to enjoy an evening of Parisian entertainment. For once, Lucy wasn't looking at Jonathan, but gazing up at the huge red sign over the entrance. Jonathan, though - he was staring directly at the camera; through the lens and deep into Barney's eyes, mocking him. Now Robin had an inkling of some of what he'd been going through, maybe he would show a little understanding and sympathy? After all, they'd known each other for over thirty years now, ever since meeting on the first day of term at Leeds University, both studying Creative Writing. Barney now made a steady living from writing his fantasy and horror stories, while Robin had two early novels published. Both had received good reviews in the broadsheets, but neither sold sufficiently for him to consider giving up his job as an English teacher. However, Robin's life had its consolations, the main one being marriage to the beautiful Giuliana, and an equally beautiful daughter in Cristina, Barney's goddaughter. They'd each performed the best man's duties at the other's wedding, and had even moved to London within weeks of each other, along with their wives. But despite this shared past, sympathy from his friend was not forthcoming.

'Stop being an arsehole,' Robin said. 'Anyway, it's Lucy's loss, now that you're going to be a movie mogul. Speaking of which, tell me more about this deal that Mary's got lined up for *Seven Hells*. That's what I've come out tonight for, not to hear you snivelling.'

Barney was distracted by the sound of

high-pitched laughing, and knew who was doing the giggling even before he saw the culprits. A quick glance confirmed it came from Sandy and Denise, two of Lucy's workmates. They'd never liked him, and he'd always taken great pleasure in not liking them back.

'Oooh, watch out, it's the Thompson twins,' Denise laughed. Theatrically, Sandy looked around the room. 'Where's Tintin and Snowy?' she asked, straight-faced.

Hilarious. Robin and Barney had had to put up with this taunt for several years, after a fellow student referred to them one day as the cartoon character Tintin's hapless detective friends, Thomson and Thompson. This wasn't because they bore any physical resemblance to the sleuths, but because in their university days, one of them had often been mistaken for the other. Now though, while Barney was clean-shaven, widening in the middle, and enjoyed the same baldness as his father, Robin, under the stylish Italian influence of his wife, sported designer glasses and a neatly trimmed beard, and was always well dressed. Unlike Barney, whose daily decision of what to wear he still solved by putting on whichever jeans and polo shirt was closest to hand. He also carried a few pounds more than in his rugby playing years, but Robin was as lithe as ever.

Barney had a ready answer to the taunt. 'Actually, they're not twins. One spells his name with a "p".' He stopped when he saw he was talking to the women's backs as they sauntered off, having already lost interest. At least it made a change from *Barney and Robin, the Caped Crusader and his faithful assistant,* he thought.

Dismissing them from his thoughts, Barney answered his friend's request by telling him what little information that Mary - his agent - had entrusted him with about the potentially life-changing movie deal she'd lined up. As he did so, his feet began tapping along to the song now booming out of the jukebox.

It was *Highway to Hell*.

\* \* \* \* \*

# Chapter 2: London

He woke up the next morning on the couch in his front room, apparently in somebody else's body; somebody whose mouth wasn't big enough for his dry, swollen tongue, and whose skull didn't have the capacity to contain his painfully throbbing brain. Slowly, Barney sat up, then spent a good few minutes clearing his lungs. After this regular cleansing procedure, he reached for his cigarettes and lit one up. He remembered being in The Welly - laying on the floor, for some reason - then Robin turning up and giving him a bollocking over his drinking and general health, after which they'd had a conversation about the potential filming of *Seven Hells*. His next memory was of being outside on the street, waving Robin off as he climbed into a taxi. Judging by the way he was feeling, he must have returned inside to finish the evening off in style.

A large book was lying open on the coffee table. He leaned over and saw various images of himself and Lucy, both in their early twenties, laughing and in love. Even if Lucy hadn't been resplendent in a white dress, the fact that he himself was wearing a suit would have told him that this was their wedding album. Had he been in one of his drunken, maudlin moods again? The sort that led him to gaze dreamily at these reminders of the happy days when he'd thought they'd be together until death do us part, etc?

His phone was also on the table, and he remembered what had brought about this descent into despondency; it was Jonathan, sending his daily photo, with Lucy particularly joyful. Since she'd packed her bags, Barney had become used to the idea that she'd moved on, but her decision to appoint a solicitor and set divorce proceedings in motion had pushed him back a few emotional steps. It had been a case of out of sight, out of mind, but this series of unwanted pictures that kept appearing on his screen pulled his true feelings into the open. Yesterday, he'd called Jonathan a little shit. That description might have fitted Barney's jaundiced view of him, but he knew the reality was different. He forced himself to peer into the mirror hanging above the fireplace. Returning his gaze was a stooping, balding, fifty-year-old man who looked closer to sixty. Something to do with the booze, the smoking, the writer's desk-bound routine, the lack of exercise, and his poor diet, no doubt. He couldn't escape the unavoidable fact. Physically, Jonathan was all the things he wasn't; ramrod straight, shoulders back, six feet tall, tanned, glowing with good health, and full of energy. The only thing they had in common was what was on top of their head. But whereas Barney suffered from a pale, patchy scalp, Jonathan's baldness was more of the Yul Brynner type, or even The Rock, emphasising his masculinity.

His ruminations ended when the phone rang. 'Hello?'

'Barnaby Granwell, my number one client. How are you? I hope I'm not stopping you from writing the perfect sentence?' It was Mary Ashton, his agent.

'No, I was just thinking about having a fag.' So much for the perfect sentence. He could sense Mary's disappointment; she was in the mood for the kind of conversation she thought writers and their agents ought to have, but never did. Barney always enjoyed bursting her bubble.

'Well, no doubt you'll get around to it soon. I just wanted to make sure you're ready for tomorrow's meeting.'

'Of course. In fact, I'm in the middle of planning my presentation -'

'Don't you dare! I've already told you what to say; nothing, until spoken to. You do the writing, I'll do the talking. Arnie's flown over from Los Angeles especially to see us, so don't let me down.'

'Okay, miss.'

'And another thing. I know I can't persuade you to dress all Hollywood, but at least wear something clean.'

After a few more words of instruction, Mary ended the call, and Barney couldn't avoid it any longer. It was time to face up to the one thing he could remember clearly from last night - the frontier town of Valance, and his terrifying memory of almost being strung up alongside a red haired gambler. The most frightening part of the apparition wasn't even the realistic feeling of the noose tightening around his neck. It was the eyes of the cowboy called Cassidy. Blue didn't near enough capture the intensity of their colour, and more than that was the immense loathing that they'd contained; looking into them had been like looking into a waiting grave.

*  *  *  *  *

# Chapter 3: Whitby

Sally Steward paused as she approached the bridge that crossed the River Esk over to the older part of Whitby, and bent down to adjust the laces on her walking boots, grimacing at the sight of them. She made her way across and turned left onto Church Street. Past the time-worn pubs and the old Town Hall, the Jet work-shops and the tourist traps, before reaching the base of the mountainous stairs that led up to the ruined abbey. She craned her neck, looking up at the steps, all one hundred and ninety-nine of them. How many times over the previous few months had she placed a foot on the first step and started counting as she climbed, curious to know how many of them there really were? Always starting with the best of intentions, she couldn't ever recall getting beyond fifty before her concentration had faltered. After several failed attempts, she'd let the matter drop and put her in trust the guide books that claimed one short of two hundred. This was where Sally had arranged to meet Henry Hirst, author of some of her favourite novels about the living dead, be they vampires or zombies.

She glimpsed her reflection in the window of the tea shop across the street and sauntered over to check her outfit. She wanted to be sure that Henry recognised her as a true aficionado of the genre - a Goth Girl. Although she always dressed in the same style - black top and trousers underneath her black leather jacket, black-dyed shoulder-length hair, and black eye-liner, she'd made a special effort today and was also wearing her favourite brooch on her lapel. The one shaped like a skull and crafted from Whitby Jet, the darkest shade of black known to man. Henry had rolled into town this morning for two reasons. The first was to act as guest speaker at various events during the annual Goth Week (which tied in nicely with the publication of *The Devil Inside Us All*, his latest book) and, as a keen walker, to enjoy some fresh air on a section of The Cleveland Way. As part of the deal, he'd agreed to talk to Sally, giving her something for the on-line fanzine - *The Howling of The Wolf* - that she edited for the Goth community. However, his diary for the event being as full as it was, he'd suggested that she accompanied him on his walk, and to be interviewed by her over a cup of coffee in Robin Hood's Bay, his intended destination. Hence the walking boots that were clashing with the rest of her outfit. She was still assessing her image when a hand tapped her on the shoulder. A quick glance in the shop window reflection confirmed Henry's arrival. Smiling nervously, Sally turned to greet him, and was surprised to find that he looked younger and a lot fitter than he did in the photos on his website. She supposed it wouldn't do for a writer who specialised in the various forms of reincarnated evil to let it be known that he was actually the picture of good health, and obviously well exercised. He was properly dressed for the occasion, in top end weatherproof coat and trousers, and boots that appeared to be much more comfortable and lived-in than her own.

'Sally Steward?' Another surprise. He had a broad London accent. She had never heard him speak before, but had imagined that his voice would have a deeply sonorous Vincent Price quality. More Hammer Horror than Hammersmith.

'I am; and you must be Mr Hirst,' Sally replied.

'There's no need to be so formal. Call me Henry.' He took in Sally's appearance, examining her from head to toe. 'Is this rig for my benefit, or are you one of these local nutters I keep running into since I got here?'

Sally was taken aback. 'N-n-nutters?' she stammered, 'no, but I...'

Henry let out a giant roar of laughter, attracting the attention of several passers-by. 'Only joking,' he bellowed, 'where would I be without you and your tribe keeping me gainfully employed?'

*My tribe?* Before Sally could even think about being offended, Henry had moved on. 'I take it we're heading up there?' he pointed towards the Abbey Steps. 'Let's see if we can get the walk in before this place falls into the ocean.'

Sally decided not to bother boring him with minor details, such as the fact that the cliff's edge between here and their destination might well be crumbling, but Whitby itself wasn't going anywhere, at least not until global warming said otherwise, of course; and if it did happen, it would be swallowed by the North Sea, not the ocean.

'That's right. Have you been to Robin Hood's Bay before?'

'No. In fact, I've never even been here,' Henry looked around him.

'What? But Whitby's in almost all of your books, and you seem to know everything about it. How are you able to describe it so well?'

'Down south, we have this thing called the Internet. You can travel all over the world from the comfort of your armchair.' Henry stared at the ancient cobbles and then up at the equally ancient steps. 'Just wait until you get it up here. You'll wonder how you managed without it.'

'But...we *have* got it. We've always had it.'

'I'm pulling yer leg, Sal,' Henry laughed. 'Anyway, I like to squeeze a good walk in whenever I can, and I've been told that this one's worth a go.' He looked up at the route they were about to take. 'I once read that there's two hundred of these buggers.' He kicked the bottom step. 'So we'd better get cracking, eh?'

Sally decided it would be too pedantic to point out that he'd added an extra number to the actual figure.

Several minutes later, they arrived at the top. Henry had set a blistering pace, and Sally reckoned she'd have still been only half-way up if she'd been on her own. Breathing heavily, she sat down on a waiting bench, only just beating an elderly couple who had been heading for it. *They'll be alright,* she thought. *There are plenty of places in the church to sit down for a rest.* Henry came back and joined her.

'Blimey, Sal; you should be more careful. You're in danger of getting some colour in your cheeks.'

Sally laughed at this. She was beginning to enjoy the leg-pulling. She gazed over the red-tiled rooftops of fishermens' ancient cottages and across the river to the so-called new half of the town. She pointed at the enormous building dominating the hill beyond the harbour. 'So, do you know what happened over there?' she asked.

Henry's eyes followed her pointing finger. 'I'm not that daft, Sal. That's The Royal Hotel, isn't it? Where Bram Stoker's supposed to have written Dracula.'

'That's right; and just beyond it -'

'- is Royal Crescent, where he stayed at Mrs Veazey's,' Henry interrupted, now sounding annoyed, 'and that church behind us is St. Mary's, and over there's the Abbey and the route we'll be taking. As I said, there's always the Web. You've never been to the moon, but you know what it looks like, don't yer?'

'I'm sorry,' Sally apologised, 'it's just that you write about it so accurately, I'd assumed you'd been here, and then, when you said you hadn't, I suppose I thought -'

'Thought what? That I make it all up?'

'No, of course not.'

Henry frightened the seagull that had been waiting for scraps nearby with another of his huge-decibel outbursts. 'Don't be so serious, Sal. See, the thing is, I do make it all up, don't I? Doesn't mean I haven't done some research on the competition, though.'

Sally joined in with his laughter, hoping that he was joking when he referred to Bram Stoker, writer of the most famous vampire story ever written, as the competition. If not, he might need taking down a peg or two when she wrote her piece for the fanzine. They started on their way again.

'Have you read all my novels?' Henry asked.

'Not all of them.'

'Which ones, then?'

'Let's see. *The House of Countess Minova!*

Then there's the *Undead Saga* books.' In fact, despite regarding herself as a fan of Henry's work, Sally had only read *Minova!* - his breakthrough novel - and his *Darkness of the Night* trilogy about vampires fighting zombies for control of the world. However, a quick scan of his website and some on-line forums had provided her with the synopses and the general critical opinion of the rest of his published writing. Including the series named *The Undead Saga.* She reeled these titles off. '*Undying To Meet You, In The Undead Of The Night, The Undeadly Kiss.*'

'Quite a fan, I see. What did you think of *Sit Quietly By My Grave*?'

Sally ran through a mental tally of his novels, but nothing with a similar title came to mind. No, she definitely hadn't come across this one. Time to change the subject. She turned towards the ancient churchyard. 'I once spent a night camping up here. We'd had a bit to drink and thought we'd sample some real Goth atmosphere.'

'And did you? Sample the atmosphere, I mean?'

'Let's just say we never did it again.'

Henry scanned the gravestones, some of them leaning heavily, others cracked, a few fallen flat. He shivered, despite the mild temperature. 'I don't blame you. God, is this place creepy or what?'

Sally examined the sky. 'Anyway, we'd better be getting off. The weatherman said there's a possibility of sea frets later.' She strode out in front, setting a comfortable pace.

'Sea frets? What are they when they're at home?' Henry asked.

'It's a sort of fog that rolls in from the sea, really quickly. We don't want to be on a dodgy bit of the walk if one comes in,' Sally explained.

Henry stopped. The ruins of the Abbey towered over them on their right-hand side. 'Hold on, Sal; what do you mean by "a dodgy bit"?'

'That joke you made about things disappearing into the ocean? Well, the track keeps getting nearer to the edge of the cliffs, that's all. Because of the erosion.' She saw that Henry's eyes had widened. 'It's nothing to worry about. When it gets too close, that section is closed off and they divert it a few yards further inland. If it was dangerous, they wouldn't let people walk along it, would they?'

This last sentence seemed to reassure Henry. 'Let's get going, then. We both know what a Whitby fog brings with it, don't we?' He said. Sally was pleased that he didn't feel the need to explain this. He was referring to Dracula's arrival in Whitby on a foggy night, coming ashore from the wreck of the sailing vessel *Demeter* in the guise of a dog. She led the way over to the car park, through some fields and over a stile or two, until she could point to the clear path ahead of them.

'We're properly on our way now. Robin Hood's Bay, here we come.'

\* \* \* \* \*

# Chapter 4: London

Although Barney had made a decent living from his writing for the previous twenty-some years, there had been occasions when he and Lucy had to be careful with their finances. Relying on your imagination to make a living can cause all kinds of stress. For instance, was that last book he'd written actually the last, as in, not just the latest, but the final one? He knew that worse things happened at sea and down coal mines, but the strain of producing a novel each year had been wearing him down for a while now. In his chosen genre - fantasy, with a smattering of horror thrown in for good measure - he was forever having to create new worlds, strange creatures, fresh spells, and ever more imaginative ways to kill his carefully crafted characters. It was bloody hard work, regardless of what any sailors and miners might think; which was why today's meeting was important. The moguls over in Los Angeles had noted the ever-increasing popularity of the fantastic and the supernatural, with movies and TV series bringing in massive viewing figures, and had decided they wanted to try their hand before public taste moved on. Barney owned enough of a readership for his stand-alone novels to cover the mortgage payments as each of them was published, but the sales column showed a definite improvement when he'd followed the trail laid by the giants of the genre. Basically, this meant that the longer and more epic the story, the better. He'd thrown everything into inventing a universe that would keep readers happy over the course of a seven-part saga. 'Something they can get their teeth into,' as Mary said. So he'd started on the sequence of books called *Seven Hells*. The first three had proved to be a moderate success, sufficient for the likes of Artie Newfield, a Vice President of Kansas City Motion Pictures - also known as KCMP - to stake a claim in the growing global hunger for fantasy franchises. This was why Artie was at this moment deciding whether to make a play for *Seven Hells*, and either, A): produce a movie based on the opening instalment - *The Sleeping Moon Awakes* - and buy the rights to the following six, or B): not bother and move onto the next shiny thing his assistant brought to his attention. Today, it was Mary's job to persuade Artie that option A would be to KCMP's advantage, (and much more preferable as regards her own and Barney's careers and bank balances).

Barney gave himself the once over, to see if he was up to his agent's exacting standards. He knew she'd be disappointed that he was wearing his standard outfit of jeans, polo shirt (tucked in at the waist in honour of the occasion) and sports jacket, but at least they were clean, and he'd even given the ironing board a rare outing. Locking the front door behind him, he walked down the short path to what Lucy had always sarcastically called the garden gate, which led directly out onto the street (despite there being no garden, just a tiny concrete-covered space that separated the house from the prying eyes of passers-by).

At the time his first novel was published, Barney and Lucy were young enough to have had an appetite for adventure. Determined to survive on his talents, Barney had handed in his notice as a teacher, and Lucy successfully applied for a position as a medical secretary in a central London hospital, after which they'd decamped to the capital. They found a house south of the river, in the quiet suburb of Stockwell, just fifteen minutes' walk away from the nearest tube station. The price had been right, the neighbourhood on the up, and they'd possessed enough excess energy to do the upgrading that their new home needed. Nearly thirty years later, Barney was still there, but Lucy wasn't.

As habit dictated, he gave the roof of his Ford Fiesta a double rap with his knuckles, letting it know he knew it was there, parked patiently on the roadside. Barney had wondered for some time why he bothered with a car these days. Since becoming a born again bachelor, he could do all the travelling he wanted by bus or tube, and recently, the Fiesta had been used less than the iron.

Twenty minutes after shutting the gate, Barney was swaying along with the commuters on the 10:42 as the train rattled through the tunnels towards the city centre. He looked around at the crowded carriage. *Who are these people?* Most of them didn't appear to be tourists, so why weren't they already at work, leaving space for him to sit instead of clinging onto this pole with one hand and keeping a grip on his shoulder bag with the other? Despite the discomfort, Barney enjoyed travelling on London's Underground. The way everyone refused to interact with each other, apart from the occasional and accidental glance as eyes met for a fraction of a second, suited him down to the ground. This explained why his sixth sense went into overdrive when they left Elephant and Castle. He was busy sliding his gaze away whenever there was any danger of making eye contact with any of his fellow passengers, when he noticed an odd sensation.

The nape of his neck began tingling, so much so that he thought at first that someone was stroking it. *Oh God, please don't let it be some unhinged character trying to get a reaction.* The idea of confronting a stranger before an audience of onlookers was more frightening to him than the possibility that this might be a situation that could end with physical confrontation. He straightened his back and casually glanced behind. There was no-one within a metre of him. He relaxed again, but a moment later, the same irritating feeling returned. This time he twisted around, scanning the entire coach. Maybe forty travellers, each of them busy with their phones, books, newspapers, or fascinated by the maps of the London tube system positioned above the windows. And then he saw him, peering through the crowd. A man with a short grey beard, probably fifty, fifty-five, wearing a black baseball cap. The stranger realised he'd been spotted and turned away, flustered, disappearing into the next carriage. *Just another oddball*, Barney thought. *Could it even be a fan, someone who's recognised me from a back cover photo, but too embarrassed to approach me?* The train slowed to a stop at London Bridge and there followed the usual shuffling and repositioning as travellers alighted and others climbed aboard. Barney watched through the window as the exiting crowd drifted away, but there was no sign of his stalker. Must be still on board, then. He felt a little uncomfortable until he put things into perspective. Just one more passenger heading into the big city, the same as these hundreds of other people. *Stop being paranoid, Granwell.*

\* \* \* \* \*

# Chapter 5: London

He alighted from the train at Bank, and after a check over his shoulder to be sure that Grey Beard wasn't following him, made his way along Lombard Street towards Fenchurch and the building known to locals as The Walkie Talkie, among the tallest structures in London. Artie had booked a table for lunch at the restaurant that sat on top of the thirty-eight storey tower in the appropriately named Sky Garden. Mary was already waiting outside the entrance for him. She didn't hide her disappointment at how he was dressed and the cigarette dangling from his lips, letting him know how she felt by giving a little shake of her head and rolling her eyes. Barney took one last drag and threw the tab onto the pavement. As she ushered him inside, Mary repeated her instructions about him being a writer, not a talker. She handed their tickets over to the attendant and they walked together into the lift. Barney could tell she was nervous; this was set to be her biggest ever deal. Barney watched, fascinated, as the numbers illuminated on the panel kept climbing. A few seconds later, the doors opened.

Wow! Barney had seen photographs of the Sky Garden, but the sight that greeted him was more spectacular than he could have imagined. An enormous space, with the bright sun shining through the glass roof, floor to ceiling windows on three sides, and beyond them, open to the elements, a walkway for those needing to get a few feet closer to the view. He glimpsed The Shard - the *actual* tallest building in town - in the distance, as Mary led him through the crowd and up the steps towards the dining area. She approached the bearded youth waiting behind his lectern.

'We're here to meet Mr Newfield,' she announced. The young host checked his register, then called for a waiter to lead the way. Barney had assumed that there would be just three people present at the meeting, so he was surprised when the waiter stopped at a table occupied by a two men, one early sixties, wearing a dark business suit, the other in his late thirties. The one in the suit was checking his watch and drumming on the tabletop with his fingers. The other had a small laptop open, and was reading aloud something from the screen. As Barney and Mary reached them, the older head swivelled around, recognising Mary.

'Mary Ashton, great to see you,' he bellowed, giving her a bear hug, which Barney christened a Hollywood Hug, as it was obviously designed to attract the attention of everyone in the vicinity. Barney guessed this was Artie, because he couldn't have resembled a movie producer if he'd been Al Pacino hamming it up in the part of one. 'And this must be our guy. Barney, we're relying on you to make us all happy, son,' he said, taking Barney's right hand in both of his, and pumping it up and down. After squeezing all feeling out of it, he released the smarting extremity and introduced his companion. 'This is Charlie Fairweather, my scriptwriting genius.'

The younger man's eyes met Barney's for long enough to convey the equivalent of Mary's eye roll. Barney was relieved to note the brief look of annoyed embarrassment that passed over Charlie's face. If there had been any sign of smugness at being introduced this way, Barney would have had to fight the urge to make his excuses and leave. He knew how these things worked. Once contracts were signed, he'd be handing over the world he'd created in his series over to whichever scriptwriter Artie and the money men behind him chose. However, with that one facial expression, Charlie had set Barney's mind at ease. The forthcoming script might be good, it might be bad, but it wouldn't be written by a pompous Hollywood idiot. Not only that, but Barney couldn't help but notice the American was wearing the same outfit of jeans and polo shirt that he himself favoured. He doubted Mary would show any of the disdain she'd heaped on Barney for this, although he had to admit that Charlie carried off this casual ensemble a little better than he did. *Probably his tanned, athletic, Californian weight-trained body*, Barney thought. The two writers shared a brief handshake, and a mumbled 'Hi'. There was no point trying to say anything else, as Arnie was talking again, firing on all cylinders.

'Sit down, sit down, make yourselves comfortable. What'll you have? Waiter, bring these folks a drink.' Satisfied that his guests wanted for nothing, he switched seamlessly to business mode. 'Let's get the nuts and bolts out of the way, then we can all relax. Here's where we are. Mary, I want you to fix up an appointment with my people to thrash out the details, because we're definitely going ahead with this feller's books. Or at least the first one. My - I mean, our -' he placed a proprietary hand on Charlie's knee, '- our movie, *The Prince of Barbary* is due for release in a few days, so I've cleared the decks, you might say, and I intend making this my next project. I've persuaded Merv Douglas to come on board. Not only that, but - and keep this under your hats - he's bringing Teddy and Daisy with him.' Artie's eyes shifted between Barney and Mary, looking to gauge their reaction.

Barney's was short and sweet. *Wow,* he thought, for the second time in the space of a few minutes. He didn't have to be a movie buff to understand the meaning of that last sentence. *The Prince of Barbary* was KCMP's latest big money feature, and trailers for it had been doing the rounds on social media for months. Mervyn Douglas had directed, adding it to his bulging CV, which included several other box-office smashes over the years. And the cherry on the cake - Teddy Fleming and Daisy Trenton, two of the biggest names in movies, were going to be appearing as actual characters from his actual book!

Mary couldn't keep the excitement out of her voice. 'Artie, that's great. You won't regret it.' Realising she was being overenthusiastic, she switched back to her professional face. 'We'll have to check the figures, of course, but as long as they're as we've discussed...?'

'They are, don't worry,' Artie confirmed. 'Now the finances have been sorted, let's give the creatives some attention.' He turned to Barney. 'My understanding is that there'll be seven books in the series. Three are already out there in the stores, you're working on the fourth as we speak, and you've probably done the planning for the last three. Am I right, Barney?' Barney could feel Mary's eyes on him, willing him not to reveal the truth. She knew how he preferred to work.

'Erm, yes... I've almost finished the final draft of number four, *Death is the Currency*.'

'Exactly what I wanted to hear. What we plan to do, Mary, is stick to the offer we spoke about for the first book...*The*...'

'*The Sleeping Moon Awakes*,' Mary helped.

'That's the one. Anyhow, we'll make the terms for that one official, option the other six, and lock this feller up until he's done. Let's hear what Charlie has to say about things,' Artie said.

Charlie gave a friendly wave. 'Hi, guys. How're you both doing? Barney, I'm loving your material, but I just need you to send me your story arc for the entire series, right through to the end. I don't want to finish off some minor character that you have in mind to save the universe in the very last chapter of the seventh book.' Where Artie was Brooklyn, Charlie was softer spoken, more West Coast.

'No problem. I'll get it over to you.' *Oh shit.* Barney didn't even know himself how the saga was going to end. He always started writing when he found two compelling characters and put them in a situation that looked interesting, then took it from there. For the *Seven Hells* series, he'd begun by reading everything he could find about various mythical worlds - Greek, Roman, Norse, Indian, Chinese, whatever - then taking figures from one legend and dropping them into a different one, hoping that by putting them all together, there would be enough ideas to fill seven books. He never planned much further than the section he was working on. Mental note to self: spend the next few days brainstorming the plot until he'd got some kind of outline through to the end of the entire story. Note number two: try to stick to it for the three novels he'd yet to write.

Mary found her voice again. 'What do you think of Barney co-writing the screenplay?'

Artie wasn't impressed. 'That's not such a good idea, Mary. He can't be doing that and finishing the other three books, can he?'

Write the screenplay? Barney hadn't even given this any consideration, and he could see Artie's point of view. He wondered if it had only just occurred to Mary, or was it part of her strategy; give way on this to win something else further down the line? 'No, Artie's right. I need to get on with my side of things,' he said, trying to signal a *don't-go-rocking-the-boat* look with his eyes. Especially now that he had a story arc to dream up.

Artie pushed his chair back and stood up. 'Well guys, sorry it's being so brief, but we've got a plane to catch, deals to close, and scripts to write. You know how it is.' He handed a business card to Mary. 'Call Barbara, my assistant, on this number when you're ready. She'll be your contact from now on.'

Charlie leaned over and shook Barney's hand. 'Great to see you, Barney. I'd hoped we'd have had some time to sit down and thrash a few points out.' Once again, he was wearing a "sorry about this" expression. 'Any problems and I'll be in touch. I've got your number.'

Barney was about to mouth the usual formalities about how good it had been to meet the two Americans, but he was too late. Artie was already bulldozing his way to the lift, dragging Charlie in his wake. 'Anything you want,' Artie swung his arm about extravagantly, as though the whole of the London was in his gift, 'just put it on my tab. Enjoy yourselves, have a little luxury, hey?' With those parting words, they were gone.

Mary and Barney sat in silence for a while, lost in their own thoughts, until Barney felt a wide grin spreading on his face. 'Champagne?' he asked. Mary nodded, the size of her smile challenging Barney's own. As she signalled for the waiter, Barney turned and looked down onto the concourse below, watching Artie and Charlie make their way towards the lift through the crowds of sightseers. Then something else caught his eye. Standing at the bottom of the steps, looking directly at him, was the same grey-bearded, baseball-cap-wearing stalker who had been gazing at him on the train. Mary turned to see what had drawn Barney's attention.

'Isn't that Tom Jefferson?' she said as the mystery man turned and walked off.

'I've no idea. Who's Tom Jefferson?'

'Oh, I've worked with his agent on a few things and I've bumped into him occasionally at the office. Tom's an excellent writer. You could learn a thing or two from him.'

'Like what?'

'Let's see. For a start, he doesn't seem to have to wait for inspiration.' Barney let this little dig pass. Mary continued, 'He's Coffer & Houghton's go-to man when somebody else's work needs polishing. He can turn his hand to anything.'

'Like Westerns, for instance?'

'What?'

'Westerns. You know, Cowboys and Indians, gunfights, six-shooters.'

'I suppose so. Now you mention it, I think he helped Zachary Munro with his Wells Fargo series after Zach had his stroke. Why do you ask?'

Barney recognised the name. Before his death a few years ago, Zach could churn out a pulp western every few months. To say he had a successful formula was an understatement. His books always seemed to include at least one from a lengthy list of incidents - Cattle Barons hiring mercenaries to murder sheep farmers; wagon trains being attacked by pesky Redskins; mysterious Shane-like figures riding into town to dispose of the Baddie's hired guns; a cattle stampede.

Frontier Justice.

'I used to read Zach's books,' Barney said. 'They never seemed to bother much with the law in his stories, did they?' He tried his best ranch hand accent. ' "Feller's plum guilty. Let's string him up and have done with it." '

'Yes, well, there was a lot of it about in

those days, wasn't there?' Mary said, glancing at her watch, bored with discussing writers whose bank accounts she didn't have a stake in.

Barney looked down through the window, but Tom Jefferson had disappeared again.

\*   \*   \*   \*   \*

# Chapter 6: London/ The Margins - Casablanca, 1920

Two days after the Sky Garden meeting, Barney was finally confident about what would happen through to the finale of his imaginary saga. *Seven Hells* now had a beginning, a middle, and a notional end. He knew this framework was, in fact, nothing more than a series of linear events which were bound to change when he started the actual job of writing. What was it that a German General once said - No plan survives contact with the enemy? He wondered if Herr Whoever-It-Was had been an aspiring writer? He seemed to have known all about plotting a novel, anyway.

Then, with perfect timing, his phone rang. 'Hi Barney, Charlie, calling from LA. I didn't wake you up, did I?'

'Erm... no, it's no problem,' he mumbled, surprised.

'Are you alright, man? You sound frazzled. Still high from the meeting?'

'A little, I suppose.'

'You'll be fine. I'll make sure we don't ruin your work, and Artie'll take care of everything else.'

'Thanks, that's good to know. So, what can I do for you?'

'It's about *The Sleeping Moon Awakes.* I've sketched out the first draft and I'm planning ahead, still getting a feel for the entire project. I realise you'll be forwarding me the full outline -'

'It's ready; I was just about to press the button.'

'That's great, but in the meantime, there's something I need to know.'

'What's that?' Barney asked, hoping Charlie wasn't going to ask him about a minor character's motives.

'Does Tianma make it much further? I've been looking at the time-line, and we have to up the pace. Nothing's been killed for a while, so something's got to go. What do you think?'

Tianma was a flying horse that Barney had come across in an Oriental legend. It only appeared in one or two chapters of this first novel. He was fairly sure that it played no further part after its early involvement. *No problem. Let's do it in. Sorry, Tianma, but we can't have the punters getting bored, can we?* 'Do what you have to, you won't be treading on my toes. Just one thing, though; how are you intending to do it?'

'I haven't decided yet. Why - do you have a preference?' Charlie sounded puzzled.

'No, but make it quick, will you? No un-necessary suffering.'

There was a brief silence. 'If you want me to finish off something else...'

'Sorry, that was a joke. I'll leave it up to you.'

Another moment of silence, followed by a loud burst of laughter. 'You had me there. I thought you were going to be one of those bleeding heart Brits that I keep reading about. I've got a few blood-curdling ideas in my locker, so I'll be sure to pull out a good one.'

They ended the conversation. Barney couldn't help but think this might explain a few recent newspaper headlines. He imagined some sort of supreme being checking his calendar and realising it was time for more death and destruction. Why? Because there hadn't been any for a while.

Maybe he *was* a bleeding heart softie?

As he'd promised, Barney pressed the send button, and his outline was winging its way across the ocean. Then, as usually happened to him after despatching an important email, he was immediately filled with regret that he hadn't checked it thoroughly. He spent the next hour doing so, and was pleased to note that, apart from some unintended reincarnations - nothing he couldn't gloss over if Charlie noticed - everything seemed to make reasonable sense.

He switched off his laptop and glanced at

his watch. Twenty to seven. If he got a move on, he could fit in a swift pint in The Welly before meeting everyone around the corner at Casa Roberto at half past. This was for the get together that Mary had arranged following the encounter with Artie and Charlie, which she regarded as a success worthy of celebration. Mary and her husband Ivan would be there, along with whoever Barney wanted to invite. It hadn't taken him long to draw up his own side of the guest list. Robin, his wife Giuliana - even though she'd be reluctant to appear at any event that was on Barney's behalf - and Cristina, who was visiting her parents for a few days, taking a break from her middle management job at an Edinburgh bank. He splashed some water on his face, put his jacket on, and headed out of the house. From experience, he knew exactly how fast to walk in order to time his arrival at The Welly to coincide with the finishing of his second fag.

Trevor was standing behind the counter, reading a magazine. He didn't seem pleased to see Barney, who was puzzled by this attitude towards a regular customer until he remembered the last occasion he'd been in here. Not only had he blacked out, but Robin had told him that Trevor had said something about him drinking too much. *Never mind, I'm here now*, he thought, and ordered a pint of bitter. He was about to add a whisky chaser, but decided against it when he detected the warning in Trevor's eyes. He downed his drink in a matter of seconds but was still thirsty, so he strode to the bar and demanded a refill. It was as Trevor was pulling on the beer pump that it happened.

*The heat is unbearable. So is the noise of the crowd, the sweat pouring into my eyes, and the smell of fear in my nostrils. The Warlords have sent someone to kill me, and he's near. The Casablancan sun is noon-high and blinding. I race around corner after corner, but it's no good. I can't get away from him; he's never less than twenty yards behind me. Eventually, after rushing through a maze of streets and alleyways, I reach the souk and I believe I've shaken him off. I stop at a shop, pretending to study the baskets of spices that cover the stall, all the while searching for my would-be executioner. I see him! A hooded figure in a flowing Bedouin jalaba, with a scimitar in hand. He is a giant of a man, at least six and a half feet tall. I throw down the handful of cinnamon that I've been holding and set off running again, hoping to lose myself in the throng. After a few more minutes of breathless flight, there's another market square. I hope to disappear in here, find safety in numbers, but this is worse than before. Everybody – the stallholders, the buyers, even the few European tourists searching for souvenirs have turned into a raging mob, thirsty for my blood. Someone chants a name and soon the entire crowd has joined in – 'Khalid...Khalid'. I swing around, desperate for one last chance, but a human wall has blocked my es-*

*cape. I turn to face my nemesis. His eyes are as blue as the cloudless sky....*

Barney's mind returned to the pub. His breathing was coming heavy and fast, his knees shook, and he was staying upright only by clinging to the rail that ran along the under edge of the bar. Trevor slammed the fresh pint down, spilling beer on the counter top.

'Christ, Barney, you look terrible. I'll let you have this one, but after that, I think you should go home, alright?'

But Barney's thoughts were still thousands of miles away, somewhere in the shadowy alleyways of North Africa in what he guessed to be the 1920s. He needed some fresh air. Without speaking, he threw a note on the bar and left.

Bemused, Trevor watched him leave. He glanced at the abandoned beer, then back at the door through which Barney had disappeared. Shrugging his shoulders, he addressed the room.

'Anybody fancy a free pint?'

\*    \*    \*    \*    \*

# Chapter 7: London

Barney took the long route to the restaurant, giving himself time to recover from the terror he'd endured in the pub. He could still feel the dry heat of the Casablancan sun on his skin, and hear the chanting of the killer's name in the sounds of the evening traffic as he walked. And those eyes; they reminded him of the hangman in his Wild West hallucination.

It took twenty minutes and another three cigarettes before he considered himself in a fit enough state to meet up with Mary and the others. When he arrived, everyone was already gathered in the lively atmosphere of the restaurant, waiting to greet him. He then had to fight the impulse to turn around and walk straight back out, because as he was a about to sit down, they burst into a rendition of 'For He's a Jolly Good Fellow'. He had to stand, red-faced, until the song ended. The other diners must have thought it was his birthday, because they added to his embarrassment by applauding before joining in with a chorus of cheers, led by the grinning Robin. An exchange of glances told Barney who was the mastermind behind this painful reception. 'You bastard,' he mouthed across the table. A knowing smirk was the only response. Sitting on either side of his friend were his wife and daughter. Cristina gave him a cheerful smile. Her mother's greeting was distinctly cooler, as she still blamed him for breaking up their little circle, despite it being Lucy who had done the leaving.

'Looking overheated there, Barney! Here you go, a pint of lager to cool yourself down with. Shame you can't dip your face in it, though.' This was Ivan, Mary's husband and business partner, the other Ashton in *Ashton and Ashton of London (Literary Agents)*.

'Leave him alone,' Mary said, 'some writers don't enjoy being the centre of attention.'

Barney recognised this as a jibe at his reluctance to do any more than the minimum amount of publicity duties he could get away with. Book signings were akin to torture for him, the gratitude to those who had gone to the expense of buying his latest novel mixed up with the horror of having to talk to strangers. Even after half a lifetime of making a living based on the sales of his work, he still found it unfathomable that copies of them were in hundreds of homes around the world. Homes of people he didn't know, but who knew him, or thought they did. He brushed off the mild rebuke by pretending to study the menu. However, Barney's view was that food was fuel, not something that needed to be enjoyed for its own sake.

Robin came to his rescue. 'Don't worry about it, I've already ordered. Bruschetta and pizza be alright?'

Relieved, Barney accepted the foresight with a thankful nod. He picked up the pint that Ivan had provided and took a mouthful. Although he hadn't been looking forward to this occasion, he was grateful that it was taking his mind off what had happened in The Wellington. As the food was delivered and then the empty plates removed, glasses drained, then refilled, he settled into the evening, occasionally throwing in what little gossip he could provide. At one point, Ivan introduced a more serious topic. Having had enough of the tittle-tattle, he'd spent the previous few minutes peering at his phone. 'Mary, didn't you once have that French writer, François Garone, signed up?' he asked.

'No, not really. We spoke a long time ago, when he was looking for someone to represent him in the UK, but I wasn't interested because he was writing those existential novels, very Gallic, the ones that only teachers and other so-called serious writers read.' She glanced over at Robin as she said this. He gave her a wave, claiming ownership of the description. 'Of course, if I'd known he was about to produce those wartime blockbusters that keep making the Sunday Times' best-seller charts, I might have given him a little more consideration. It's a bit too late now though, I suppose.'

'You're right about it being too late. He's dead. Murdered, in fact,' Ivan said.

'What happened?' Barney asked. He only knew of Garone by reputation, but it still came as a shock to hear of this happening to a fellow writer.

Ivan read from his screen. 'Author François Garone was killed last night at his home outside Paris. The French authorities have revealed that Monsieur Garone was alone in his remote renovated farmhouse, when what police believe to be a World War Two F1 Hand Grenade was thrown through the kitchen window, killing the famous writer. He leaves behind a wife and three children. His family were visiting friends when the incident occurred.'

'That's odd, isn't it?' Cristina said.

'Is it? Probably some nutter with a grudge,' Robin said, 'they're everywhere these days.'

Cristina shook her head. 'I get that, but why do it with a hand grenade? It just seems a bit of a random way of killing someone.'

'I suppose that there's a kind of irony there, if you think about it,' Ivan said. 'It's like Mary says. Before he stopped with the philosophical stuff to write his war novels, Garone hardly sold anything. It wasn't until he started with the blood and guts that he really made it. So something used during the Second World War might be seen as a fitting weapon.'

'He who lives by the sword, dies by the sword, you mean?' Giuliana said.

'That's right,' Ivan answered, 'you should read some of the blurb on the covers of his books. Brutal hand to hand combat, soldiers blown to bits, villagers massacred by Nazis and so on.'

'You'd better watch your back then, Barney. You might end up being buried alive, or burnt at the stake by aliens.'

Barney checked to see if Giuliana had an amused glint in her eye when she said this, but wasn't surprised when he couldn't find one. She'd always felt that the genre he worked in was beneath her husband's more high-browed literary pretensions (at least as far as his writing went. Having frequently shared a room with him when they were younger, Barney knew that in other ways, Robin's tastes were no more elevated than his own).

'That's enough shop talk,' Mary said, sensing an unpleasant undercurrent beginning to flow. 'Let's move onto something more interesting.' She turned to Cristina. 'Now then, young lady, have you currently got a boyfriend clinging on to you adoringly? Found anyone suitable amongst our Pictish friends?'

At first, Barney was relieved that the spotlight had turned towards someone else, but soon realised this only gave him more time to reflect on his own state of mind. He excused himself and went outside for a calming smoke. When he returned, coffees were being ordered. Noting his reappearance. Robin brought the conversation back to the actual purpose of the occasion. At his signal, a waiter appeared with an impressive bottle of champagne and six glasses. When everyone had been supplied with some of the bubbly, he climbed to his feet, clearing his throat like a nervous father ready to make a speech at his daughter's wedding. Barney readied himself for more ritual humiliation. However, Robin kept it short and sweet, limiting the toast to raising a glass to 'the new King of Hollywood, the one and only Barnaby Granwell, Esquire. Let's just hope he doesn't forget his friends in England when he decamps to Los Angeles.' Barney responded by diverting the attention, warning those 'cigar-chewing moguls they would rue the day they tried to out-negotiate little Mrs Ashton.' Mary then took her turn, saying that, with Barney's books as ammunition, she'd been bargaining from a position of strength. 'But having said that, England's full of much better writers who don't have a movie deal, so I think I'm worth every penny. Anyone else want a go, or can we get on with the carousing?'

Carousing won the vote, and more wine was consumed until the waiters began hovering impatiently around their table, soon the only one in the room still occupied. The message was received, coats were fetched, and anecdotes finished as the party made its way onto the pavement outside.

'Oops, I almost forgot,' Mary declared, pulling out an envelope from her handbag, 'this arrived at the office for you today.' She handed the small package to Barney. He took it from her and read the address written on it.

'FAO: B. Granwell, c/o: Ashton and Ashton. Who delivered it?'

'I've no idea. It was shoved through the letter box, so if it's all creased inside, don't go blaming me.'

Barney removed the contents. There were five or six pages of white A4, filled with what appeared to be Arial 12 point, double spaced, set out in manuscript style. He read the title on the front page. *The Angry Sun by Zach Munro. Chapter 5 - Valance Township, Arizona. Red Rankin loses his Final Game. Revised by Tom Jefferson.*

Red Rankin. The gambler who was hanged during Barney's first episode in The Welly. He hadn't told a living soul about what had transpired, so how in God's name had it turned up on a document that had been hand-delivered to his agent?

'Well, what is it?' Robin asked, trying to get a closer view.

Barney replaced the pages in the envelope. 'Just some young writer, wanting an opinion from a master of the dark arts.' He suddenly wanted to be alone. He held his wrist up and tapped his finger on the face of his watch. 'It's getting late, so I'll be on my way, and I'll see you all later. Thanks for tonight, I've had a great time,' he shouted as he turned and hurriedly left for home, leaving his baffled guests standing by the roadside, mystified by his sudden departure.

*   *   *   *   *

# Chapter 8: Whitby

'I asked you before about *Sit Quietly By My Grave*, but you didn't answer, so now's your chance - did you enjoy it?'

Sally had hoped that Henry had forgotten all about this, as she'd never come across this book during her preparation for meeting him. Honesty being the best policy, she owned up. 'Sorry, I don't think I know that one; did you publish it under a different name?'

Another lung-bursting laugh. 'Well done, Sal, you've passed the test. You wouldn't believe how many journos have told me how good it is and nodded their heads when I've described scenes from it. The truth is, I've never written one called *Sit Quietly By My Grave.* It's a game I play during interviews; childish, but there you go. Anyway, you've bagged yourself a few brownie points; you've been honest with me, so I'll be honest with you when we do the interview.'

Sally smiled, hoping that these new points might let her delve a little deeper. 'You know you said you'd never been to Whitby, but use the Internet? Is that how you do all your research?

You put an awful lot of detail about vampire folk-lore in your books, I actually thought you'd been to Romania to see things for yourself.'

'Well, Sal, I'll let you into a secret. It's all done in my front room.'

'You have your own research library?'

'Nah... I have a DVD player. I watched every movie and TV series I could find about Dracula and vampires and the rest of it. I read a bunch of graphic novels, too.'

Sally was crestfallen. 'Oh... I assumed you'd made yourself into an expert by studying Vampire Lore.'

'I don't need to be an expert. I may not be the brightest, but most of my readers aren't either. They're not interested in any obscure facts about vampires...' he paused and gave her a meaningful look, '... not that they actually exist.' Sally pretended to be shocked. Henry continued, 'They know what they want and they expect to get it, so I'm not going to change anything, am I? All that stuff about having no reflection, can't cross running water, scared of crucifixes... if I come out with something different, I can forget about the next book because no-one would read it. It's all from the movies and the telly. Give 'em all that guff, make sure a truckload of inno-cent townsfolk are killed by the evil monster, and they'll keep coming back for more.' Henry had been gazing out to sea during this monologue. He turned towards Sally as she was pulling a notebook out of her rucksack.

'Woah, there,' he shouted, startling her, 'all that was off the record.'

'Oh, sorry. I just thought...'

'Well, think again. My agent would have kittens if you put that all over the Internet. You can get your pen out when we get to where we're going, and not before.' Seeing her disappointment, Henry patted her on the shoulder. 'Don't take it to heart, Sal. Let's get moving, eh? The sooner we're there, the sooner I can give you the official stuff. You happy with that?'

Feeling guilty now, Sally nodded and re-packed her bag. They started walking again. They were another half-hour further into their trek when Sally stopped and pointed at a tiny huddle of buildings in the distance. 'Almost there.'

It was then that she saw the fog rolling in, a sea fret, as had been predicted. The next section of the route looked to be the trickiest so far. At some points, it veered closer to the precipice than it had at any other point during their walk, and for yards at a time. There was a fence, alright. Unfortunately, it was on the landward side of the path, there to stop livestock from tumbling into the sea, not for the safety of people daft enough to take this risk. Exactly what they didn't want, with visibility about to be drastically reduced. The fret arrived sooner than she'd expected.

'Just keep your eyes on the track,' she shouted over her shoulder. Until a few moments before, walking for Sally had been an automatic process, one foot in front of the other, letting her mind drift. Now, though, with the reduced visibility, it was demanding all her concentration. She stared down at her boots; left, right, left, right. She stopped when she heard angry voices coming from behind her. There had been no-one else in sight before the fog had appeared. How on Earth had Henry found someone to argue with all the way out here? 'Henry? Are you alright?' There was no answer. Sally began to worry. The noises she was now hearing could easily be interpreted as that of two men fighting. There was some swearing, a lot of grunting, and the violent creaking of the fence, sounding as if somebody was forcing it back. Or clinging on to it. Then someone screamed, loud at first, but quickly fading away, falling towards the restless water two hundred feet below. Later, she would tell the police that she'd also heard a voice - not Henry's - shouting something that sounded like, "the killer". She stumbled, thrown off balance as the shadow of a tall man brushed past her. She fell to her knees and clutched at the grass beside the path with both hands, clinging on desperately as the ground beneath her tried to throw her off. Sally knelt, eyes closed, struggling to understand what had just happened. After a second or two, she felt able to open them. Once again, the air was warm, and filled with bright sunshine. The fret had disappeared.

But so had Henry.

She forced herself to crawl to the edge and peer down towards the heaving waves. Straining her neck, she could make out the shape of Henry's mangled body, lying on an outcrop of rock, waiting for the sea to come and claim it. Still dazed, she climbed to her feet and looked around. She had an unimpeded view of at least half-a-mile in every direction. Two hundred yards inland was a campsite, a field full of holiday makers relaxing and playing games in the sunshine, oblivious to the terrible events that she had just been a witness to.

Where was the running man, the shadow fleeing from his crime? There was no conceivable place for him to hide, yet he was gone. Melted away, like the fog in which he'd arrived.

\*　\*　\*　\*　\*

# Chapter 9: London

Barney suffered a restless night. He'd received such a shock on reading the title of the document that Mary gave him that he was almost sober when he'd arrived home, and had read it standing up at the kitchen table, without even taking his jacket off. What was happening to him? After blacking out in the pub while suffering a vision of being lynched in the Old West, he then finds himself running through a North African souk, chased by a sword-wielding giant of a man; and now this - a chapter from a book first published over thirty years ago, and then revised by a mysterious author who had been stalking him on the underground yesterday. The fact that the chapter described, in great detail, the lynching incident was more than a little disconcerting; strike that, it was bloody terrifying! He heard the pinging of his phone. Another photo of Lucy, with The Brandenburg Gate in the background. The love birds had reached Berlin, had they? So what; his mind was on other things, and any rage he felt against Jonathan would have to wait. He resisted falling asleep for as long as possible;

both of his episodes had crept up on him while he'd been awake, so who knew what spectres sleep might bring with it? But when it finally arrived, it was accompanied by nothing other than a few welcome hours of oblivion.

Now he was awake again, Barney reread the text. It was still the mind bending account of an incident that no-one else could have known about. An idea occurred to him. He turned to the title page. *Revised by Tom Jefferson.* In order for it to be revised, there had to be an original out there somewhere. He opened his laptop and began a search for Munro's books. The first result guided him to an online store, with a brief biography of the writer, and then a roll-call of his works that were available to download. There were a lot of them. Barney knew Zach had been prolific, but this was unbelievable; there were over a hundred titles! He scanned the list, then remembered something Mary had said about Tom helping Zach with his *Wells Fargo* series. A quick scroll brought up this sub-heading, beneath which were seven or eight novels. There it was, right in the middle - *The Angry Sun*. Barney took his credit card out of his wallet, and in less than a minute he had a copy of the book downloaded to his hard drive. He clicked on the cover, an image of a thirsty cowpoke suffering under the heat of the desert sun, and the Contents page appeared on his screen. He placed the manuscript on the desk so he could compare one against the other, pointed his cursor at *Chapter 5 - Red Rankin loses his Final Game*, and started to read.

It wasn't a long section, and the original, on screen, version was shorter than the printed copy he'd been given. A short scrutiny revealed why. Both stories told of the two cowboys seeking revenge, and the hanging of the gambler, but the revised copy included the addition of eight new characters - Cassidy, Bill Gardner, and the six members of the rescuing posse. Barney was now more confused than ever. He came to a decision; he could no longer keep this to himself, and there was only one person to turn to.

'Morning, Robin. You doing anything?'

When Barney arrived at Mandy's, Robin was already sitting at a table in the corner of the café that they regularly used as a meeting place. Barney had always thought the industrial sized coffee machine, steaming away behind the counter, was overambitious for such a small coffee shop, but he found the hissing and gurgling noises it produced oddly comforting, especially on rainy days such as this. He ordered a cappuccino and joined his friend, who seemed to be suffering the remnants of a hangover. Barney didn't waste any time. He took the manuscript from his shoulder bag and slid it across the table.

Robin read the title. 'Zachary Munro. I know that name. He used to write cowboy stories, didn't he?'

'Just do me a favour and read it,' Barney said. Robin picked it up and did as asked. When he'd done, he looked up, an enquiring expression on his face. Barney told him everything. Well, not everything. He described the happenings in Valance and being followed on the tube by someone who turned out to be the Tom Jefferson who wrote these pages. But not Casablanca; he was keeping that one to himself for the moment. With this manuscript in his possession, Barney at least had some proof of the first incident, even if he couldn't explain it. Yesterday's trip to North Africa would have to stay secret for a while longer.

Robin laughed. 'You don't have a fever or anything? Or have you being sprinkling crack on your cornflakes?'

'No and no,' Barney answered. 'I'm pretty bloody frightened by all this. If you're going to just sit there taking the piss, I'll talk to somebody else about it.'

'Come on, Barney, be fair. It's like something from one of your novels.'

Barney drew a deep breath before speaking. 'Jefferson followed me into town yesterday. Before you ask, I definitely wasn't imagining that part, because Mary saw him too.'

'Did you speak to him?'

'No, he kept his distance. Mary knows him vaguely, and mentioned that he'd done some work in the past for Munro, some ghost writing after Zach had fallen ill.'

'Let's assume you aren't having a nervous breakdown. What are you going to do about it?'

'God knows. I was hoping you'd tell me.'

Robin was saved from having to invent a strategy that didn't involve ruining their friendship forever because Barney's phone rang. Sighing, Barney took it out, expecting to see another taunting holiday snap, but there was no incoming number. Not only that, but the screen appeared to be faulty. It was taking on a 3D quality, becoming deeper and wider, stretching out until it filled the café and consumed everything in it. Barney stared into a void, empty, yet brimming with an alien energy. He was holding an entire universe in his hand, and gazing at galaxies beyond time and space, where there existed a fifth dimension, and a sixth...

'Barney! Barney?' Robin nodded down towards the phone. 'Are you getting that?'

At that moment, the ring tone fell silent as the attempted call was ended by whoever had made it, and Barney was back, having a cup of coffee with a friend.

'It's a good job you're not answering 999 calls. The house would've burnt down by the time you picked up. Who was it?'

Hiding the shaking of his hands, Barney returned the phone to his pocket. After Robin's negative reaction to hearing about Valance, he didn't want to make things between them any worse. 'Nobody. They'll call back if it's anything important.' He forced himself to concentrate. 'Give it some thought, and if you come up with any theories about this...' he held the manuscript up, '... let me know. All suggestions will be taken into consideration. One other thing; I'd rather you kept this to yourself.'

Robin was more than happy to agree to this instruction, and they left the café, each heading homeward in a different direction. Barney had only walked a few yards when he heard his name being shouted. He stopped and turned around.

'I'll call you,' Robin shouted, waving good-bye.

Barney responded with a nod of the head. He'd told Robin that whoever had called would ring again if it was important. Well, it was important, but he wasn't too sure that he wanted another one. As he'd been staring at his phone in Mandy's, a series of numbers and letters had appeared. The closest thing that Barney could liken it to was a murmuration of starlings, where thousands of the little birds appear to be controlled by a single mind, taking off together, wheeling right, left, up, down; totally synchronised, an incredible number of them in a small space, yet never one colliding with the next. There had been an infinite amount of those arbitrary digits, twisting and turning, fading into the distance before flying back and almost bursting out of the screen then gathering in random combinations, attempting to form a word or a sentence he might understand, until eventually, they'd arranged themselves in order to spell a name.

K.H.A.L.I.D.

\*   \*   \*   \*   \*

# Chapter 10: London

Satisfied that Robin was out of sight and that his hands had stopped shaking, he reached for his phone and checked the screen again, but now he saw nothing unusual. He was still staring at it, lost in thought, when it burst into life, causing his heart to cartwheel. This time, there was a notification - *Unknown Caller.* After what had just happened, Barney found the familiarity of these everyday words comforting.

'Hello?'

The speaker crackled and hissed, reminding him of one of those old war movies, when Bomber Command is struggling to contact the last plane home from the raid, and the radio operator's voice fades in and out as the signal bounces around the atmosphere. Eventually, an intelligible sound came to the forefront.

'Mr Granwell, my name is Smith. Please listen carefully. Khalid is only the beginning. Our enemy is growing stronger. You must prepare to face him in your own world. It is vital that...'

The voice faded to some unfathomable distance. Barney heard a shouted warning as someone barged into him from behind, knocking him off balance. He felt the blood drain from his face, followed by a wave of relief when he saw it was only a cyclist, shouting back over his shoulder as he rode off, 'Watch out, bloody idiot!'

Under normal circumstances, he'd be incandescent with rage at someone cycling on the pavement, but he was so relieved that it wasn't Khalid or a noose-carrying cowboy that he almost gave the rider a cheery wave goodbye. Once that short pump of adrenaline had dwindled away, his attention returned to the mysterious voice struggling to make itself heard through the ether. He shouted into the phone, 'Hello...hello...' But there was no answer, just a vacuum of silence.

He reached the garden gate out of breath and sweating, pausing only for the traditional double rap on the roof of the Fiesta. Desperate for a drink and a smoke, he was fumbling for his keys when he realised he didn't need them, as the door was ajar. Cautiously, he gave it a push and stepped inside. Ever since a spate of break-ins in the area a few years past, he'd kept an old cricket bat in the cupboard in the hallway. Lucy had found the thought of him fighting off burglars with a series of cover drives hilarious, and as the culprits had long been brought to justice, he'd never had the chance to use it. Until now? He held the bat using both hands, comforted by the weight. He pointed the bottom towards the ceiling, holding it baseball style, and slowly advanced, ears straining for the smallest sound of an interloper, yet hoping to hear nothing.

But then he did - the tentative footsteps of someone creeping down the stairs. There was sweat on Barney's palms, making him thankful for the rubber grip around the handle. He turned and walked back a few paces to the foot of the steps. His breathing became laboured as he waited for the intruder to reach the bottom. After what seemed like an age, the figure of a man came into view. The shape was striding towards the door before something made it stop and turn.

If they both hadn't been so nervous, Barney and Tom Jefferson might have found it funny, the way that they simultaneously stepped backwards while letting out a loud yelp of fright at the sight of one another. Barney was relieved to note that Tom was more afraid than he was. The relief quickly transformed into anger, and the anger into bafflement. 'What the hell are you doing here?' he snarled. Far from being a danger to him, Tom was a beaten man. Using the cricket bat as a cattle prod, he guided Tom into the kitchen and told him to sit down. Barney pulled a chair from under the table and sat opposite him.

'Let's start with an easy question. How did you get in?'

'I found a key under the big flower pot outside, the one with the hydrangea in.' Tom's voice carried the tinge of a soft Scottish burr.

Barney almost laughed at the thought that, even now, the writer within this burglar felt the need to be so precise about the identity of the plant concerned. When Lucy grew tired of answering his late night knocks - when he'd once again left his jacket with his key in it back at The Wellington - she'd come up with the tried and tested solution of the flower pot method. When he'd argued against it, saying how dangerous it was and that somebody would find it, she had replied that it was a risk she was willing to take if it stopped him interrupting her sleep.

'How did you know it was there?'

'I didn't; I hadn't thought any of this through. I suppose I hoped you might have left a window open or something. I was about to leave when I took a chance and looked under the pot. I couldn't believe my luck.'

'Well, your luck's run out. Tell me why I shouldn't call the police. What were you doing up there?' Barney asked, but Tom didn't answer. 'The police it is, then.' He brought his phone out and started punching the numbers in.

'Don't! No need to bother with that. I might as well tell you everything now. I'm a dead man walking, anyway.' A few days ago, Barney would have accused anyone who used a phrase such as "I'm a dead man walking" of being a drama queen, but this wasn't a few days ago.

'Did you read the manuscript I sent?' Tom

asked.

'Of course I did. Come on, what's this all about?'

'I'll tell you, but you won't like it.'

'Try me.'

'And I can also guarantee you won't believe a word.'

'I'll decide that.'

Tom's shoulders sank as he accepted defeat. He started talking. 'It began about a week ago, when he contacted me by phone, saying he had a job for me, a writing job. No problem. That's what I do, isn't it? I asked him to email the details over, but he wanted to meet me face to face. I tried to say no, I was too busy, but then my doorbell rang and he was standing there. He gave me this.' From his pocket, Tom produced a paperback book. It was a battered copy of *The Angry Sun*. 'He ordered me to rewrite chapter five, with some specific changes. Ordered. It wasn't a request. I said I had better things to do with my time and he should do it himself, if that was all he needed. That's when he made a call and put it on loudspeaker. I could hear someone sobbing and moaning, and it took me a second to realise it was my brother. He's a farmer, is Malcolm. Tough, lives alone outside Oban, in Scotland. Never been frightened of anything in his life, but he was frightened now. He begged me to do what they demanded, or they'd start on him again. He's all I've got these days, my only living relative, so I guess that's why they chose him. Anyway, if all I had to do to make sure he was alright was revise this bloody chapter, then I'm going to do it, aren't I? I had to create two new characters, Cassidy and Bill Gardner. Cassidy was to kill Gardner, and if I did it right, they'd set Malcolm free.' Tom lifted his gaze from the table top. 'Unbelievable, isn't it? But there was something about being in the same room as him, something that was making me do what he wanted; so I rewrote it there and then, complete with Cassidy hanging Gardner. You should have seen his eyes when I printed it out and gave it to him. It made me think I'd handed your soul over to the Devil. Yes, I'm aware of how that sounds, but if you ever meet him, you'll understand.'

'You keep saying *him*, but haven't given me a name yet. Who was it?'

'It was him,' Tom picked the manuscript up and pointed to a line on the page, 'it was Cassidy.'

'Okay...,' Barney said, lengthening the vowels to show his doubt. '... and did this Cassidy say why he wanted you to create a character with his own name?'

'I've told you why. To kill Bill Gardner.'

'I still don't understand. What has all this got to do with me?'

'Don't ask me to explain this, but somehow, Gardner was you.' With an eye on Barney, Tom let this sink in before continuing. 'He said he hoped I'd enjoy reading about Barnaby Granwell's murder, knowing that, by killing off Gardner, I'd played my part in it. He wants to see you suffer. At the time, I had this feeling anything was possible, and that my editing of this story really meant you'd die. In the copy I gave him, Bill gets hanged. I thought, maybe if I wrote it again, I might be able to change that, so I typed out another version. This one,' he took hold of the manuscript and held it up. 'The one where he's rescued.'

'How could that make a difference?'

'You're still alive, aren't you?'

Despite everything he'd said doubting Tom's revelations, an icy chill ran down Barney's spine. Was this a credible explanation for the way the story on these pages described what he'd experienced in his vision. Could there actually be some truth in this whole thing?

'Let's pretend for a minute that this isn't all in your head. Why did you send me a copy?'

'They'd let Malcolm go, and I persuaded him to leave the farm. I reckoned he'd be safe until I came up with a plan. Although it sounded as impossible to me then as it does to you now, I couldn't help feeling there might be something in it. I followed you into town -'

'I saw you.'

'Yeah, I'm not very good at that sort of thing. Anyway, I followed you. I'm not sure why. Perhaps I was weighing you up, comparing you to Malcolm, trying to decide who was in the most danger. I'd already asked around about you, and I couldn't see that you deserved to be killed by this maniac. I don't know what I expected to achieve, but...I...' Tom's voice became increasingly agitated until he almost shouted the last few words, '...I don't know, okay?'

Barney's grip tightened on the bat. 'Okay, stay calm. Having done all that, why have you broken into my house?'

'Because Malcolm rang me to tell me he was thinking about returning to the farm. I knew Cassidy would send his thugs again, and they might even kill him. If I could get this manuscript back from you before you read it, he'd never find out what I'd done.'

'Leaving me to look after myself?'

'I'm sorry, but that's how it was. Anyway, it doesn't matter now, does it? We'll both have to get ready for him.'

Barney's mind was spinning. He was in a quandary about what to do next. Despite his threats, he didn't want to involve the police, and would have been more than happy to throw Tom out of the house, grateful for another funny story to tell down at The Welly. But would it end there? Would this lunatic keep turning up with even more bizarre stories? Before he could decide, he heard a knocking at the front door.

Tom leapt to his feet. 'Who's that?' he whispered, his voice shaking.

'How the hell do I know? We haven't finished here yet, so don't think about running off, okay?' Barney waited for Tom to sit back down before he made his way down the hallway, still holding the cricket bat. He opened the door to find a solitary figure on the step.

'Hello Mr Granwell. We spoke earlier; the name is Smith. May I come in?'

*   *   *   *   *

# Chapter 11: London

Barney guessed Smith to be somewhere between sixty-five and seventy years of age. He was clean-shaven and wearing heavy framed glasses. The black Crombie overcoat and dark trilby hat gave him the appearance of an extra from a 1960s British movie about seedy spies and espionage of a most unglamorous kind. Taken aback at this new twist, Barney gazed at him in silence, then surprised himself with the calmness of his voice. 'You'd better come in.' Tom stood up as they entered, looking ready to make a run for it. Barney reassured him with a discreet nod of the head, then indicated they should all sit at the table before he began his interrogation. 'Are you the one that's been calling? How did you know where to find me?'

'Please, Mr Granwell. I will deal with your queries as well as I am able to, but it is imperative that we formulate a plan of action. I would also welcome the input of Mr Jefferson.' Tom's face took on a puzzled expression. 'Yes, I am fully aware of your own situation, and I hope that together, we can find a solution to it.' Barney had a thousand questions that needed answering, but he deduced that the quickest way of getting those answers was to hear out this stranger who had turned up on his doorstep. The stranger who seemed to know things.

Smith removed his hat, revealing a sparse covering of white hair. 'Mr Granwell, I'll begin by directing a question to both yourself and Mr Jefferson.'

'If things are that urgent, you could save some time by cutting out all the "Misters". Call me Barney; and I suppose you should call him Tom,' he added. The sooner they finished this, the sooner he could get these two nutcases out of his house.

'Very well. Here is my question. When you write your novels, from where do you summon your plots?'

'I've no idea. They start with a seed and then grow into something I can use,' Barney answered, frowning. He couldn't ever recall summoning anything.

'But where does that seed itself come from?' Smith persevered.

'Probably from books I've read or movies I saw years ago. Bits and pieces that I've half remembered and filed away somewhere in my head. One or two might even be my own original ideas.'

'I see; and what of the characters who enact the plot?'

'The same, I reckon; but I get the feeling you're going to tell me differently.'

'Yes. I'm from Ancilla, the world that has provided every character to appear in human fiction since your earliest storyteller told his first tale.' Smith was watching intently, waiting for a reaction. He didn't have to wait long.

'I think it's time for you to leave.' Barney stood, pushing his chair back.

'A few minutes more, please. If I can't convince you by then, Cassidy and his killers will be here and it will be too late, anyway.'

*Cassidy!* Surprised by the mention of that name, Barney sat down. Hearing the word "killers" hadn't helped, either.

It was Tom who spoke next. 'Wait a minute, Barney. Is this any weirder than what we were discussing before? Let's listen to what he has to say. What have you got to lose?' He was right. More than he knew, as he still wasn't aware of the other things that had happened, such as Khalid in Casablanca, and Smith's warning phone call.

'Okay. You've got five minutes, so you'd better start again. Where did you say you're from?' Barney asked.

'Ancilla.'

'And where is this Ancilla? Why have I never heard of it?'

'If you're asking where is it physically, I can't say. There are far more worlds surrounding us than you could possibly imagine, existing alongside both of ours; and yet, amongst these countless realities, Ancilla and Earth alone appear to share a particular connection. I appreciate your difficulties in accepting this, but are you able to explain how this...' his arm swept around the room, somehow taking in the whole of the planet, '... and all the different life forms that inhabit it, came into being?'

'No.' Barney kept it short and honest. The science and the philosophy of the beginnings of time and the universe had always been beyond him.

'Precisely, just as I cannot comprehend the mysteries of my world. I only know that it *is*, the Earth *is*, and somehow we feed off each other. You need us to populate your stories. We need you because it's possible that if we don't fulfil this function, there may be no reason for my kind to exist at all.'

'Let's pretend for a minute this is all true. Tell me how it works,' Barney said impatiently.

'Put simply, when you require characters for your fiction, there appears to be a mechanism by which your creative mind summons them from Ancilla.'

Tom was stroking his chin thoughtfully. 'So this place you're talking about is like a casting agency?'

'A very apt analogy, and a correct one. Picture it like this - you are the writer of the script, and we are the actors. Between the human writer and Ancillan actor, we both help to create the characters you use to further your plots, and once that is accomplished, we go back to Ancilla. However, if a particular story requires a character to die, the Ancillan involved does not return home. They simply cease to be, extinguished as completely as though they had never existed. Until recently, we accepted this as a necessary condition of our existence, what you might call collateral damage. But now there are those among who consider that too many of us are disappearing forever. They have named themselves Skeptics, and they believe you fail to value our contribution.'

'And this is where this Cassidy and Khalid come in?' Before Smith could answer, a thought occurred to Barney. 'Was it you who sent me the message about Khalid? Just before you spoke to me on the phone?'

'Yes, it was me, and in answer to your previous question, Cassidy and Khalid are Assassins - the group tasked by the Skeptic leaders with finding a way to Earth and executing those they perceive to be the guilty writers.'

*Executing!* Another word that gave Barney pause. 'And what about you? What's your part in all this?'

'I am a Warden, committed to maintaining the status quo. If I may, I have another question; your books - how many deaths occur in each of them? How many in all your years of writing?'

Barney was suddenly defensive in the face of this unexpected demand. 'Well, it's the nature of the beast, isn't it? I write fantasy novels, so my readers expect the occasional bloodbath.'

'Which you certainly give them. Let me be blunt; the events you have encountered are a result of the Assassins attempting to eliminate you, to stop you writing your stories and thereby ending your contribution to this carnage.'

Barney's blood froze. The apparitions he'd been having were one thing, but to hear it stated so bluntly that there was someone out there who actively wanted him dead - that was something else entirely.

'But why me? There are thousands of writers doing the same as me. Why am I the only one being attacked?'

'Oh, but you aren't. There are several other assassination attempts in progress, even as we speak.'

'But Tom said that Cassidy seemed to have some sort of grudge against me personally. What's that all about?'

'It would appear that you killed his wife.'

'What? I wouldn't know how to. I've never even been in a fight.' Barney was aghast, and his face expressed the shock of this revelation.

Smith raised an eyebrow, showing the tiniest measure of frustration. 'I can see that you're struggling to digest everything I'm saying.' He spoke more clearly, as if explaining something to a child. 'At some point in your career, you wrote a story which included a certain character; Cassidy's wife was chosen -' he held his hand up, forestalling the question Barney was about to ask, '- and no, we don't know the hows or whys of that particular part of the process. As I was saying, Cassidy's wife was...elected, shall we say, to help you in the creation of that doomed character.'

'Doomed?'

'Unfortunately, you ensured that her contribution concluded in a bloody ending, and she subsequently became a Lost One.'

'A lost one; you mean she never went back to where she came from?' Tom asked.

'Correct. This explains why Cassidy was among the very first to volunteer to be trained as an Assassin. Each of them has a score to settle, which is why they are so single-minded and cold-blooded. As Wardens, our brief is to warn those of you whose names appear on the Skeptics' Termination Lists.'

*Termination Lists!* In Barney's mind, those last two words deserved capital letters and italics.

'Obviously, the Assassins failed to kill you, but they've been experimenting. The approach they used with Tom - forcing him to revise a section of another writer's book - plainly didn't work, so they're exploring different methods.

Their attempts on your life so far have taken place in the Margins. However, it seems they've succeeded in creating a Channel in there, connecting it to Earth. As some of your colleagues have discovered.'

'First Ancilla, then Margins, and now Channel. What does all this gibberish mean?' Barney was becoming exasperated by the amount of new knowledge he was being presented with.

'The Margins lie in the hinterland between our two worlds. In there is the shadow of every single story that has ever required our involvement, a shadow created during character conception. It is not somewhere that can easily be explained.'

'You don't say,' Barney sighed. 'And who are these colleagues of mine you mentioned?'

'Other writers. The Skeptics don't intend to eliminate every writer who uses bloodshed as a tool, of course - even they are wary of how that might impact on Ancilla - but the ones that, like you, resort to high body-counts. I believe that another reason you're a target is because of the forthcoming adaptations of your novels into movies, which will double the number of deaths involved. Equally, the two people you met recently, Mr Newfield and Mr Fairweather, may also be in immediate jeopardy.'

'Artie and Charlie? And what do you suggest I do about that? Give them a call and tell them what you've just told me?' Barney said, his voice rich in sarcasm.

'Of course not. A Warden will contact them directly.'

'But if they got to him -' he gestured in Tom's direction, '- through his brother, should I be warning my wife...ex-wife, I suppose...to go into hiding? That wouldn't go down well.'

'Where is she?'

'She's touring around Europe with her new fiancé.'

'Are either of them writers?'

'You're joking. He's in finance; a banker of some description, and she's a medical secretary.'

'Then she'll be safe. The Assassins can't trace anyone who lacks the creative impulse.'

Despite his cynicism, Barney felt strangely relieved by this.

Tom interjected again. 'So it's not only novelists? This crusade includes movie script-writers and producers?'

'You are correct. The Skeptics regard creators of any form of this type of fiction as legitimate targets.'

'These colleagues you mentioned. Were you thinking along the lines of François Garone, for example?' Barney asked.

'Yes. Now that the Skeptics seem to have finally established a method of sending Assassins to Earth, Garone, Henry Hirst, and Samuel Allan have been amongst the first to be dealt with.'

'Sam Allan? He's one of Mary Ashton's clients. Mary's my agent, so I'm sure that she'd have mentioned if anything had happened to him,' Barney said, 'but Hirst - I think I've seen his name in the news somewhere. Let me check something.' He took out his phone and started a search. It didn't take long to find a result. He read aloud, ' "Author Henry Hirst was killed after falling from a cliff during a coastal walk in Yorkshire, from Whitby to Robin Hood's Bay. A heavy bank of fog was covering the section of the path where the event occurred, reducing visibility, which is believed to have had a bearing on events. The author was visiting Whitby as a guest of the town's Goth Week. He had been accompanied by a local journalist, who was later treated for shock. We understand the incident is being dealt with as an accident." There you go; he wasn't murdered, it was an accident.'

'If you could track down his companion on the cliff, you will discover they are of the opinion that Hirst didn't jump or slip, but was pushed. *He* was there.'

'Who was?'

'Cassidy.'

'But he only threatened me in some kind of vision. You're suggesting he could physically push Henry into the sea?'

'Yes, or one of his team. As I said earlier, in the two episodes that you've experienced, the Assassins were still experimenting, but now they're finding success in implementing the Channel. The next time they come for you, it will almost certainly be of a similar physical nature.'

Barney's head was spinning. 'Can we get this straight before I lose my mind?' He grabbed a sheet of paper and a pen from a drawer. On the left side, he drew a circle and wrote "Earth" in the centre. He did the same on the right, this time writing, "Ancilla". 'Show me how this all works,' he said, handing the pen over.

Smith took it and, in the space between the circles, he created the shape of a flattened oval which he labelled, "Margins". He penned a line connecting the Margins to Earth. At the side of this he wrote, "Channel".

'When the Skeptics identify a target, they send an Assassin to execute them. The Assassin enters the Margins and waits there, inside a chapter of their target's novel, until a Shadow Writer edits the same chapter, thus opening the Channel to Earth.'

Exasperated, Barney narrowed his eyes in bewilderment at the introduction of yet another type of character into this farce.

Undeterred, Smith carried on. 'Shadow Writer is the name we've given to any human who has been persuaded to perform this task. They must be another writer, one skilled enough to fulfil their requirements, such as our friend here,' he pointed at Tom, who shifted uncomfortably in his seat. 'The Shadow Writer will then revise the chapter. Doing this opens the Channel, enabling the Assassin to pass through and manifest on Earth, and thus able to carry out his mission; such as pushing Hirst over the edge of a cliff. One other thing we've noted is that the manner of the death of each victim relates to a method they themselves have used in killing a character in their work. I'm sure we'll discover a similarly violent death somewhere in Hirst's novels to match his own ending. We still don't know if this choice of extermination is necessary, or is simple vengefulness - that is, the punishment fitting the crime.'

'But the thugs who beat Tom's brother up? If they were... humans...' Barney struggled to accept the word in the current context, '... then obviously they're already here on Earth, so why don't these Assassins just use them to do their dirty work, instead of having to go through all the palaver you're talking about?'

'We suspect that initially, their plan was indeed to recruit a network of Earthly collaborators; the men who held Tom's brother prisoner were part of this early group of mercenaries. However, their recent progress has made this group at least partially redundant, although we suspect they may still use the remnants of their human organisation when circumstances demand. Probably for intelligence gathering or surveillance purposes.'

Barney absorbed this information as another thought popped into his brain. He hesitated to ask the question, but couldn't help himself. 'What about zombies, then?'

'What?' Tom sounded as though even he thought this was a step too far.

Barney ignored him and ploughed on. 'Zombies and vampires and werewolves, creatures like that. You say fictional human characters are from Ancilla, so do these others show up from the same place?'

Smith gave this some thought. 'I assume they follow a similar path, but from somewhere other than Ancilla. I'm afraid I don't have an answer for every question that you may ask.'

'Yeah, I'm beginning to get that. Here's another one - what about all the deaths in movies and books that are based on actual events? The Holocaust, for instance, or the sinking of the Titanic. Are incidents like these that really happened included in all this?'

'No. Situations such as those haven't been invented by the writer. Even the most fanatical Skeptic understands the difference between interpretation and imagination.'

'Hold on a second. You said they pick a target's own pieces of work to revise, but I've never written a western in my life. Why would they choose a lynch mob in a frontier town to get at me?'

'We believe they could only make random

connections at that time.'

'So you're saying that with Valance and Casablanca, it was a case of them getting me mixed up in somebody else's stories?'

'Possibly; but their next attempt will be based on one of the violent deaths from your own work.'

Barney's eye was caught by some movement on his phone screen. 'I've got a newsflash here. I don't believe it! It says - "Samuel Allan, author of several horror novels, has died after being savaged by his own dogs while at his home in Leicestershire. Details to follow." So, by your reckoning, Sam will have written a story that involved somebody being killed by a pack of hounds, or something like that?'

'Yes.'

Barney's mind was spinning. He needed to calm it down, so he asked the most mundane question he could think of. 'If you're not human, why do you look the way you do?'

Smith glanced down at his clothes. 'When we Wardens manifest here for the first time, we take on the physical aspects of a character that we helped to create somewhere in our past. We don't contribute to the end result.' Barney heard a little disappointment in Smith's voice. He could well imagine that, given the choice, Smith would have chosen to "manifest" in the guise of a skilled combat soldier rather than as an ageing bureaucrat.

During this lull in the conversation, Tom stirred himself. 'D'you think I could use your toilet?' Barney warned him again about making a break for it, then directed him up the stairs, second on the right. He glanced up at the clock hanging on the kitchen wall, wondering how long this was going to continue before he found a way of showing these two jokers the door.

\*　\*　\*　\*　\*

# Chapter 12: London

Smith listened to Tom's footsteps climbing the stairs, then leaned in closer to Barney. 'Though it's no fault of his own, I don't believe we can trust him, so I'll say this in his absence. I've been sent here for two reasons; not only to warn you but also to recruit you.'

'Recruit me for what?'

'The best way for you to help yourself is to take the fight to the Skeptics and their Assassins, by making Interventions in the Margins. You're already a target, so you've nothing to lose. We want to utilise your talents to combat them.'

Barney let out a cynical laugh. 'Do those glasses you're wearing actually work? I mean, look at me; I'm in no fit shape for any kind of fight. Why can't you take them on yourselves?'

'Because we Wardens do not have the ability to reach the Margins.'

'So who rescued me in Valance, then?'

'That was Taylor, one of my own colleagues, along with her group.'

'How did she get into these Margins if you can't?'

'Because she trained as an Assassin, as did those who accompanied her. She came to disagree with their methods and switched her allegiance. After we noticed some unusual activity in that particular chapter, which we now know was Tom Jefferson's doing, she was chosen to lead a scouting party to investigate.'

'But I still don't see what I can do. I'm not a trained soldier, in case you haven't noticed.'

Instead of saying anything, Smith stretched out his arm and touched Barney's forehead.

The kitchen, the house and the whole of London faded.

*At first, everything is dark. He is on a remote hillside, somewhere in the countryside. There are no stars in the sky, just an impenetrable blackness. And then the display begins. In the distance, he hears the rumbles of massive explosions; a great battle is being fought beyond the horizon. He's standing in the desert, under the blistering sun, watching teams of slaves being whipped as they drag huge carved stones towards the half-built pyramids. A wagon train is being drawn into a circle on the endless plains of North America, the weary travellers defending themselves against an attack from a bloodthirsty enemy enraged by these newcomers to their land. A Fire Spell flashes from the palm of a white-bearded wizard, and is parried by the defensive magic of his opponent, a Titan, three times taller than the magician. In a New York bar, a woman watches her husband as he walks to the restroom, then drops something into his glass, something that means the end of him, his final breath only arriving when she has left town with her lover. A blindfolded man in uniform stands against a wall, hands tied behind his back. He falls to the ground after the officer in charge gives the order to the firing squad. An alien fleet attacks an intergalactic transporter, which is carrying valuable minerals from a faraway planet. Somewhere within the Arctic Circle, an exhausted hunter, clad in furs, faces off against the hungry polar bear that has been stalking him for days, and is now closing in for the kill. In a flooded shell hole in the Western Front, a soldier drowns, crying out for his mother.*

*Kitchen Sink dramas, Palace Intrigues, mourners in a graveyard congregate in the rain, and yet, while all these images of slaughter and destruction are taking place, a series of more upbeat scenes are also filling his consciousness. Joyful births, happy marriages, peaceful deaths, passionate love affairs, victorious heroes.*

*Good overcoming Evil.*

*More exciting than these brief glimpses of an eternity of story telling, more enchanting than the wonder of being inside the creative minds of countless writers from every period of human history, is the thrill of recaptured youthful energy. A powerful strength surging through each fibre of his being. The aching knees; the lungs scarred by thousands of cig-*

*arettes; the weariness of age; these are all forgotten as he senses the life-force of imagination refuelling his body and his mind. He can see everything with a clarity he'd previously thought could only ever be experienced by ancient Zen masters.*

*He's the King of the World.*

*But all the time, his inner consciousness is ordering him to return to the place he knows and understands, before this assault on his senses becomes too much to handle, and with a jolt, he is back in the kitchen.*

By some trick of whichever universe he had just visited, each of these sights has appeared to Barney separately and simultaneously. Those and a thousand other tales. A million others, including some of his own, in a place that had been indifferent to his presence. There was one trend Barney couldn't avoid noting. The amount of bloodshed and violence far outweighed the happy endings. He wanted to tell Smith about it, but something was amiss - one more thing that didn't fit in with his world as he knew it; Smith was disappearing. As he did so, he inclined his head, as though listening intently to a distant sound. His demeanour took on a fresh urgency.

'They are near. You must go, go now. Trust no-one.' His voice became remote, fading to nothing, and then the rest of him followed, leaving a vacuum where he'd been just seconds before.

Barney sat with his mouth open, stunned by this inexplicable event. Smith had vanished right before his eyes, like a cloud of smoke blown apart by a gust of wind! If he'd needed any more proof that the fantastical story that this "Ancillan" had been telling him was the truth, this was it.

He was now persuaded that an Assassin from another world was travelling across space and time to kill him.

*   *   *   *   *

# Chapter 13: London/ The Margins

Tom hadn't planned on leaving until he paused at the closed kitchen door and overheard Smith's warning: "Go now. Trust no-one". That was the moment when he decided not to linger. He left the house and started hurriedly towards Stockwell tube station, intending to ride into the centre of London and disappear into the crowd. As he walked, he called his brother. If Cassidy was on his way back, it was more important than ever that Malcolm remained in hiding.

'Hello?'

'It's Tom. Where are you?'

'Where do you think I am? At home.'

'For Christ's sake, Malcolm. I told you to stay away from there. You need to get out, and now!'

'I know what you told me and I nearly did; but then I thought, what the hell am I doing? I'm not letting some thugs scare me out of my own house.'

'Mal, I'm begging you to go. It doesn't matter where. Give me a chance to sort something out with them,' Tom pleaded.

'I don't know what kind of mess you've got yourself into, and I don't want to. Those buggers took me by surprise; they caught me off balance, that's all. It won't happen again.'

Malcolm had never been one to take a backward step. As far back as Tom could remember, his brother had been the toughest person around. One day, after school, members of a local gang had waylaid him. Five of them, all older and bigger than him. He'd upset the younger sister of one of them, and received a good kicking for his troubles. He'd arrived home in tears, but wouldn't tell their father what had happened. Instead, he'd chosen the long view by enrolling at a boxing and martial arts club. One by one, each of those lads had taken back what they'd given, and a bit more in interest. What had impressed Tom the most about this whole incident was that the fifth and final one wasn't dealt with until three years after the beating; he hadn't let the passing months come between him and his revenge, but had waited for the right opportunity to repay each of his attackers. By now, he'd probably already blanked out the memory of how scared he'd been when Cassidy's thugs had taken him.. He'd have persuaded himself that it had been a moment of weakness, caused by being surprised and "caught off balance" as he'd put it. Tom knew that, no matter what he said, Malcolm would not be talked round, so he had to be content with warning him to stay vigilant, and telling him he'd be in touch.

Breathless, he arrived at the station. He bought a ticket and made his way to the north-bound platform on the Victoria line. His plan was to head for Green Park, and from there decide on his next move. He could tell he'd just missed a train by the number of passengers heading in the opposite direction to him as they aimed for the street up above. Never mind, there was another one due in eight minutes. Wary of being amongst a crowd of strangers, Tom walked through them until he was standing as close to the mouth of the tunnel as possible. From this position, he wouldn't need to watch his back.

He'd just found a suitable spot when the first gunshots sounded. Startled, he pivoted and scanned the area. He saw nothing out of the or-dinary, just the usual mix of workers and tour-ists milling about. No-one was the slightest bit perturbed, and yet the shots continued. Then he heard horses' hoof-beats approaching, getting louder and louder.

The Margins were taking him.

*He recognises this place. The scorching heat, the main street, the frightened faces peering out of the doorways. He is in Chapter 5 of The Angry Sun, riding next to Cassidy, driven out of Valance by the arriving posse. Tom looks back over his shoulder, searching for the chasing pack, but, after saving Bill - or Barney - the riders have turned and headed back towards the Mercy Tree. He can see the two victims laid on the ground beneath it, and knows that one will live, the other, the gambler, is already dead. That he is an expert in the saddle doesn't surprise him. He is now a character in a work of fiction, and he can guess the ending that is planned for him. He wonders who the Shadow Writer might be that has written him into Zach's story? He guesses that whoever is revising this part of the book is still learning their trade. No doubt they had intended to open the Channel and failed, which was why he is here and not being finished off on the streets of England by an Assassin.*

*Cassidy doesn't let the pace fall until he's sure they are no longer being followed. After a few miles of hard riding, he calls a halt near an isolated farmhouse, little more than a shotgun shack. He sends a silent signal to Scoot and Frenchie. They dismount and draw their pistols, having accepted him as their new leader. Scoot bangs on the door. From inside the cabin, an unseen hand pushes it open a crack. Frenchie kicks it all the way in, and charges through.*

*Two gunshots ring out and Scoot reappears. 'All clear.'*

*Cassidy climbs down from his horse. 'Bring him in,' he growls. Tom is frogmarched into the dark interior and shoved roughly down onto one of the two wooden chairs that, other than a table and a rickety bed, comprise the total of the furniture.*

*'Did your conscience get the better of you, Tom? Is that why you visited that bastard who murdered*

*my wife? Did you tell him I was coming for him? No matter - his suffering will be much worse than any-thing your brother went through; and he suffered al-right, snivelling and wailing and pleading until we shut him up. The thing is, we were willing to let him live. All you had to do was follow my instructions. So here's something to think about. He died because of you, nobody else -'*

*'I know he's not dead. I've just spoken to him!' Tom exclaims.*

*Cassidy leans in close. 'It doesn't work like that though, does it? We both know things happen differ-ently outside these pages. Time kinda plays tricks on you. He's dead alright.' He stands again, taking his pistol from its holster. 'And it's time for you to join him...'*

*Tom stares down the barrel of his fate, deter-mined not to look away. Malcolm wouldn't have wanted him to show any fear. Then, before the trig-ger can be pulled, Cassidy, Scoot and Frenchie, the cabin and its few meagre contents all begin to dis-solve, and from outside the shack, he hears a garbled station announcement, and then it becomes clearer, announcing that the next train will arrive in two minutes, and to step back from the edge...*

'You alright, mate?' Tom opened his eyes and realised that he was slumped against the tiled wall of the platform. He focused on the con-cerned face that was questioning him.

'I'm fine, thanks,' he said, pushing his shoulders back and shaking his head to clear it. 'I get these dizzy spells, but I'm fine now.'

'Just make sure you're not standing so near the edge next time, pal. A few yards that way -' his rescuer pointed towards the rails, '- and you'd have been down there.' On cue, the north-bound train thundered into the station. After a few moments of the usual confusion, with passengers arriving and leaving, the place was almost empty again, and the engine and its carriages had continued on their journey.

Without Tom.

Had Cassidy been telling him the truth when he'd said that Malcolm was dead? If he had been, this changed everything. He needed to find a signal. He rode up the escalator and walked out onto the street. As he searched in his coat pocket for his phone, he realised that there was something else in there, a piece of card. He pulled it out, and after studying it, bent over and vomited on the pavement. Oblivious to the disgust of the passers-by, he wiped his mouth, then rang Malcolm's number. There was no reply. Taking a deep breath, he held the card up and studied it again. It was a photograph, date and time stamped in small letters and numbers in the top right corner. If they were accurate, the photo had been taken in the last ten minutes.

He recognised the inside of the barn. Malcolm was nailed to the wall, in a position of crucifixion. They had stripped him naked, and bruises, cuts and gashes covered every inch of his body. It had to be a fake. They'd only spoken a quarter of an hour ago, and it must have taken hours to produce these results. He tried the number again and felt a surge of hope as this time, his call was answered.

It was Cassidy. 'Thomas Jefferson! Why, oh why, did we have to do this? If only you'd been a good boy...,'

But Tom wasn't listening. By some alchemy, the combination of the photo and Cassidy's hateful voice had produced an uncanny calmness in his mind. Whereas, for the last few days, he'd been in a fog of turmoil, he could now see, with pinpoint sharpness, the things he had to do.

He retraced his steps, heading for Barney's house.

* * * * *

# Chapter 14: London

The bang of the front door closing shook Barney out of his stupor. Realising that now was not the time for evaluation, but for action, he quickly made for the corridor. Too quickly, in fact, as the sudden movement caused his head to spin, and he had to hold on to the table until he regained his equilibrium. Whether Smith had hypnotised him or he really had been transported to some mysterious place that existed between two worlds, he didn't know, and at this moment, didn't care. It was time to decide between Fight or Flight. If he could only summon the same exhilaration, strength and power in his ageing limbs that had filled them while he'd been in the Margins, he might even choose Fight. Once the world stopped spinning, though, he headed upstairs.

He'd decided to take the Flight option.

He climbed the steps as fast as his legs would carry him, shouting out for Tom as he did so, but received no answer. The bathroom door was open enough for him to see there was nobody in there. Around the landing were another three rooms. He cautiously peered into each of them in turn, but Tom must have had enough. The slamming of the front door was probably him getting away from this madness, and who could blame him? He returned to his bedroom, took a suitcase from the wardrobe, and filled it with a spare set of clothes, then hurried downstairs, collected his laptop and placed it in his shoulder bag. Satisfied that he had all he needed, he left the house and ran down the path and through the gate. He opened the car boot and threw his case in. He was about to climb into the driver's seat when he realised he'd forgotten Tom's manuscript. Something told him he might be needing it, so he rushed back into the kitchen. There it lay, on the table. He picked it up and headed outside again. The door stood open, and he was stepping through it when yet another strange thing happened on this strangest of days.

In slow motion, right before his eyes, his little black Fiesta exploded with a mighty rumble, and he felt himself lifted off his feet by an invisible hand and carried back down the hallway.

\* \* \* \* \*

# Chapter 15: Movie Monthly

## The Prince of Barbary

*Review by Carol Everson for Movie Monthly,*
*October 2020*

Directed by Mervyn Douglas
Starring Teddy Fleming and Daisy Trenton
Produced by Artie Newfield.
Screenplay by Charlie Fairweather

*Score - 3/5. If you can stomach the all-too-realistic violence and gore, a reasonable effort at using an archaic template to make something more appropriate for modern tastes.*

An old-fashioned adventure story, brimming with Derring-Do, *The Prince of Barbary* is a nostalgic nod to the golden age of adventure movies, such as *The Sea Hawk*, and *Captain Blood*.

One almost expects Errol Flynn to swing down onto the deck of *The Dark Angel*, having spotted a Spanish galleon from the crows' nest, homeward bound and laden with gold from the Indies. Another similarity to Michael Curtiz's two classic swashbucklers is the lack of supernatural overtones, as in the more recent *Pirates of the Caribbean* series.

Of course, one thing that all of these movies shares is their disdain for the lives of anyone that gets in the hero's way. One flash of the cutlass and it's over. However, whereas the other three mentioned movies managed to soften the horror by presenting death as a cartoon event, harmless and amusing, in *The Prince of Barbary*, director Mervyn Douglas and writer Charlie Fairweather pull no such punches. Dying is no laughing matter, and the more gruesome the method, the better, or so it would seem. Particularly gut-wrenching is the fifteen minute scene wherein the entire crew of a captured ship is keelhauled. If they aren't dead after undergoing the lethal experience, Captain Tempest Read, the Prince of Barbary himself, finishes them off by taking pot-shots at them with his pistol. Very sporting.

Don't expect any insights into the human condition. Nevertheless, this is a good escape from the daily grind.

\* \* \* \* \*

# Chapter 16: Leeds - A Few Weeks Later

The area surrounding Barney's new temporary home was perfect for going to ground in. Row upon row of late Victorian terraces, each one indistinguishable from the next. The only obvious differences between them were the street names displayed on the cast iron signs attached to the end of each terrace. He figured he'd be able to stay under the radar in this student neighbourhood, as everyone around here was a stranger.

Miraculously, he'd suffered nothing more than a slight concussion and a few cuts and bruises from the explosion, along with the inconvenience of a police investigation. After the meeting with Smith, and his literal vanishing act, he wanted to disappear himself, but the investigating officers had arrived to question him at the hospital in full Good Cop/Bad Cop mode. He'd already decided not to mention anything about off-world assassins and rogue Scottish writers being the real culprits, if only for the sake of his own reputation.

'Been upsetting somebody, have we? Keeping a bit too much back for yourself?'

'Hold on, Terry. Can't you tell the gentleman's still in a state of shock? Let's be reasonable about this...'

'Nah, you're too naïve, Gordon. This feller's been around the block a time or two. You can see it in his eyes. A witness saw someone running off ten minutes before it happened. Who might that have been, I wonder...?'

'What Terry's trying to say is that we've been hearing things on the street about some disagreements regarding the supply of certain substances, and if you scratch our backs...'

Eventually, Barney made it through the thicket of innuendo and sub-Sweeney tough talk to realise that the two policemen were convinced he'd been targeted as the result of a narcotics deal gone wrong - a falling out among thieves. This was why they weren't treating him as an entirely innocent victim. He'd pointed out that drug barons don't generally drive to and from their clandestine meetings in a nine-year-old Ford Fiesta, and that there were less conspicuous ways of seeing off a rival than blowing him up in broad daylight.

Other than making that observation, Barney had kept his thoughts to himself. The knock on the head might actually be responsible for his memories, but he still had Tom's manuscript tucked away as proof that at least some of the events really had taken place. He couldn't tell them about Smith because Smith was gone. Had literally disappeared in front of him. And he wouldn't involve Jefferson, despite suspecting him, if not of physically planting the bomb, then of being what Smith called a Shadow Writer. If Smith's story had any truth to it, Tom must have enabled his would-be murderers to do their stuff. Barney wanted him to himself. How, he had no idea, but he knew he'd need Smith's involvement.

The following day, Gordon the Good returned alone, just as Barney was being discharged into Robin's care, to tell him their informant had confirmed he wasn't on any crime lord's radar, and that they were now pursuing a different line of investigation. Meanwhile, if he could let them know where he was staying, they'd be in touch to arrange some counselling.

On the drive from the hospital, he told Robin everything he hadn't told the police about Smith and Tom, but Robin was becoming concerned about what he was hearing. 'You've been through a traumatic event, that's all. The characters in your books come from in there,' he pointed at Barney's forehead, 'not from Planet Zog. You make them up yourself, simple as that.' Even Giuliana showed some compassion, making him feel welcome and offering him a drink. Robin said this softening might be connected to her just hearing her father had fallen ill at the family home in Rome, and she was feeling vulnerable. There followed a solicitous call from

Mary, shocked at the news, and enquiring after his health. Barney sensed that she'd been a few microseconds away from asking if this would delay his finishing *The Rustling of the Leaves*, before realising there'd be a more appropriate time for that kind of question.

He was surprised to receive a call from Lucy, who had heard about the explosion from Giuliana. Despite their recent troubles, his estranged wife was full of concern, worried that an ordeal of this kind might be the end of him. Barney had reassured her he wasn't considering doing anything stupid, and no, she didn't need to cut her holiday short and come back to check on him. He had to admit that Lucy's interest had touched him, and he hadn't even been too annoyed when, minutes after they'd finished, his phone had pinged, signalling another photo. Obviously taken during the conversation, it showed Lucy standing next to a Venetian canal, talking into her mobile with a genuine expression of concern on her face. Jonathan wouldn't have liked that.

It had been later that evening, when he was standing outside Robin's back door having his last cigarette of the day, that two thoughts came into his mind. The first was that, no matter how deep he dragged the nicotine into his lungs, it was leaving him unsatisfied. He now needed a stronger drug. He knew what that was, and where to find it. He was craving the thrill, the excitement, the *vigour* that he'd felt when Smith sent him into that other place. Whether it had been a genuine experience he'd undergone, or just Smith playing with his head, he wanted more of it. *Needed* more of it. The second thought was that, if these Assassins could make it across several dimensions to locate his car, then surely it wouldn't take them long to track him down now? He'd spent the rest of the night weighing up his options, and the next morning, he was up early, collaring Robin before breakfast. He'd considered hiring a car, but even the idea brought him out in the shakes.

'I need a favour. I want you to drive me somewhere.'

'No problem. Where?' Robin assumed a short trip to the ward for a check-up, or maybe the police station, to enquire after the investigation. He'd been wrong.

'Leeds.'

'Leeds?'

'Leeds.'

Robin took time to absorb this before asking the logical next question.

'Why?'

He'd explained that he was still in fear of his life, and if he'd thought about it earlier, he'd never have let Robin bring him home, because now he and Giuliana might be in danger. He intended hiding out near their old university digs, because where better to go to ground than a suburb of a big city with a transient student population, one where a newcomer wouldn't stand out? Despite his doubts about Barney being on his own after his trauma, Robin agreed to take him. If this was the only way to get these crazy ideas out of his friend's system, so be it. 'When do you want to go?'

'Now.'

'Now?'

'Now, and can you stop repeating everything? If we set off straight away, you can be back in time for dinner. I'll use my phone to find a B&B on the way, and then I'm out of your hair. Apart from anything else, we both know it won't be long before Giuliana wants me out, anyway.'

Robin found it hard to disagree with this last point, and after he'd cleared the decks for the day, Barney had loaded his new suitcase in the boot, and they'd begun the drive to Leeds. They'd talked of little more than the weather, the football results, and favourite albums from the 1970s, keen to avoid the notional elephant sitting in the back seat. When, after a few hours of motorway boredom, Barney tried to explain the reasoning behind his actions, Robin had changed the subject immediately, making a point of concentrating on the road ahead. Barney received the message loud and clear, and avoided the topic for the remainder of the drive. He could only try to persuade Robin of the truth so many times. He went back to searching on his phone for a place to stay, and hit gold with an estate agent who had been let down by a client. Better than a room in a B&B, he'd found an entire terraced house available to rent.

There had been one last task - making sure Robin understood how important it was not to tell anyone his new address. 'I know you think I'm going round the bend, but just do this for me. It's only for a short while and then I'll be back. Okay?'

'Okay.' Robin nodded his agreement as he'd climbed into his car. He started the engine and lowered his window. 'And you're right. I do think you're going round the bend.' Then, with a big smile, 'Weirdo.'

\* \* \* \* \*

# Chapter 17: Whitby

Sally zipped up her fleece jacket and adjusted her woolly hat as another late summer gust blew in from the North Sea. Although the sun was shining, and the air still carried a little residual warmth, the changing of the seasons was making itself felt up here on the cliff top.

'This is the place. The fog came out of nowhere. One second everything was clear, the next, you couldn't see for more than a few feet. I was standing right there when I heard them fighting.' Sally gestured beyond the fence towards a spot on the footpath, then turned to face Colin. He seemed reluctant to get any closer, even though there was a barrier between himself and the edge of the cliff. She studied him briefly; having contacted him by email and arranging to meet, her intention had been to walk the same route as on the day Henry died, so he could share the same experience. Without the dying, of course. However, whereas Henry had been younger than she'd expected, it was the other way around with Colin. When she'd met him earlier that morning, one glance at his creased suit and well-worn overcoat had persuaded her he wasn't dressed for a hike along the cliffs. Nor did his scuffed leather shoulder bag appear the kind to contain a change of footwear. She'd immediately decided it might be more sensible to drive down the coast and park at the campsite she'd seen after the fog had lifted. This meant they'd only have to stroll through the tents and over two fields to arrive at the place where it had happened. En route from Whitby, he'd revealed that he was sixty-seven and had been retired for three years. Journalism's loss was a gain for the investigation of the world of hidden intrigues.

'I reckon he tried to hang on to this,' she tapped a fence post, 'but he was dragged away from it and pushed over there.' She pointed downwards, towards the waves crashing into the black rocks that lay far beneath them.

Colin stared at the huddle of tents. 'And you say no-one saw anything from over there?'

'No, but they wouldn't have, would they? I mean, I didn't, and I was only a few feet away, and they wouldn't have heard anything, either, because it's like having a wet blanket over your head when the fog comes down as thick as it did.'

In spite of the opinions of the authorities, Sally remained convinced that a violent struggle had taken place in the depths of the sea fret that day. There had been three potential outcomes to the investigation: suicide, murder or accident.

Suicide? Could it have been a spur-of-the-moment decision brought about by some hidden depression, and the sudden bank of fog affecting his frame of mind?

Murder? The only thing to support this line of thinking was her own testimony, with not a shred of any other evidence to back it. *Have you seen the way she dresses? Not exactly a reliable source, is she?*

Accident? This seemed to be the best solution for all concerned. Henry had lost his bearings in the sea fret, stumbled off the path and fallen to his doom. No need to waste any more valuable police time.

Case closed, but not for Sally.

In the days following the incident, she'd annoyed the site owners by wandering amongst the tents, trying to find anyone who might have seen anything, keen to catch them before their holidays ended and they disappeared forever. She'd also re-walked the route, questioning any ramblers she met in the forlorn hope that they may have been on the same section of The Cleveland Way at around the same time, but had found no other witnesses.

Then one day in the works canteen, Sally had overheard two lads who worked in the office talking at the next table. They were discussing a random spate of authors' deaths and wondering how long it would be before some sensation seeking journalist linked them all up with some tenuous conspiracy theory. 'Probably win a

Pulitzer Prize when they do, as well', Billy from Stock Control said. They'd been flicking through a magazine called The Monthly Reader. Amongst the back pages were brief obituaries of writers, movie makers and playwrights who had died since the last issue. According to Tim, who was something in Accounts, the number of names printed this month was almost four times longer than normal. She'd waited for them to leave and, after retrieving the periodical from the waste bin, had turned to the relevant column. They were right. It did seem like it was a bad time to be a writer; there were murders, suicides, and unexplained deaths. She scanned the page and her heart skipped a beat when she saw Henry's name there, alongside one or two others she recognised.

And then she came to the last entry. '*Also, police believe that Barney Granwell, prolific creator of some of the best fantasy stories of recent years, was targeted by a car bomb, but escaped unscathed.*'

After work, a few on-line searches opened her eyes to the latent paranoia lurking out there. It didn't take her long to confirm Tim's forecast about conspiracy theorists. She found website after website, each of them run by suspicious and perpetually outraged people, usually men. Eventually, after sifting through endless pages dealing with the covert groups that apparently ran the governments of every major power, fake moon landings, mind-manipulating vaccines and Russian satellites that controlled cloud formations over East Anglia, she came across one that picked up on the writers' unusually high death rate. Henry Hirst and Barney Granwell were among the names mentioned.

The group running the site called itself TheVersusVirus, and after making a few enquiries, Sally discovered the founder was one Colin Naseby. She'd tracked him down, and after explaining her own involvement, Colin had been eager to add more meat to his website, and made the journey from his home in York to meet her in Whitby. Despite the extensive database that he and his world-wide web of fellow theorists had compiled, this would be his first chance to see with his own eyes the actual location where one of the unfortunate deaths had occurred.

He hadn't realised that he'd have to stand on the top of a tall cliff, so close to the angry North Sea.

*  *  *  *  *

# Chapter 18: Leeds

Mary was on the line. 'Hi Barney, how are you?'

'I'm fine. Just keeping things ticking over. One day at a time, as the song says.' He couldn't remember which song, and he knew she wasn't interested, anyway. Etiquette then demanded that Mary make a few polite enquiries about his health and state of mind before getting to the point of the call.

'I've got to ask, have you been writing at all? We don't want the grass to grow under our feet, do we?'

Barney hated to let her down, so he replied with a variation of the answer he'd been giving her for the last few days. 'I should have something to send to you soon, after I get a few things clear in my head.' Even as he said it, he realised there was no variation at all.

'Oh, well, never mind.' There was just enough in Mary's voice to show she understood his position, but that she wasn't happy, and he needed to get his act together. 'Moving on, there's a young woman keeps calling me, wanting to talk to you. I keep putting her off, but will you give her a ring for me? She says she's not a fan, which I know is a strange approach, but that she needs to discuss something important. If she could have the one conversation, she promises to leave you alone afterwards.'

Sensing a means of easing some of the guilt he felt about his obfuscating, Barney agreed to contact the young lady, regardless of her not being a fan. 'What's the number?'

Mary reeled off a series of digits. 'She writes for a fanzine, something on the Internet to do with Visigoths, I think. Ivan's heard of it, and he says it's quite well written and very popular. She insists it's not a business matter, but more personal. I've warned her you won't be answering questions about what happened in London. Her name's Sally Steward.'

Barney spent the rest of the day trying to think of a way to contact Smith. As far as he'd been able to find out, there hadn't been any more deaths since the car bomb, at least none that couldn't be put down to old age or illness. Had things been resolved on Ancilla? This would obviously be a good thing, meaning that he'd be free to live without fearing the sudden appearance of an Assassin. However, a significant part of him also worried that this would also rule out any more visits to the Margins, and he was already feeling the effects of withdrawal. Whatever was happening, there was nothing to do except wait.

While clearing up after his evening meal, he came across the number Mary had given him. He decided to call it, giving her one less thing to moan about. A nervous female voice answered, and he introduced himself, then listened as she rambled on for a few seconds, stopping and starting, tripping up over her words, and generally not making much sense. He was about to say goodbye, and thanks for getting in touch, when she said something that caught his full attention.

'... and even though they're saying it was an accident, and there were only the two of us there, I'm sure that someone pushed him off the cliff.'

'Pushed who off the cliff?'

'Henry Hirst. I'm convinced he was murdered, and I think there's a connection to you and the explosion, and to some other deaths as well.'

Henry Hirst! He was one of the authors who Smith had spoken of. 'I remember reading about this. Are you saying you were the journalist who was with him?'

Sally let out a sigh of relief. 'Well, I'm not exactly a journalist, but yes, I was standing right next to him and I *know* he didn't fall. Can I come and see you, face to face? There's something I'm sure you'll find interesting; it'll explain everything better than I can over the phone.'

Barney wasn't handing out his address to

any random caller. He gave her the name of a café in the city centre. Could she be there tomorrow? Sally said yes, Leeds was only a few hours' drive from Whitby. Would twelve noon be alright?

It would.

*    *    *    *    *

# Chapter 19: Leeds

Barney was about to leave for the bus that would take him to his meeting with the blog writer when his phone rang. Without looking, he guessed correctly that it was Mary; he hoped these early calls weren't going to become a daily habit.

'Why me? First, the bomb, and now this...', she moaned.

'What's happened?'

'Its Artie. He's dead; killed in a boating accident. I suspect he was already having to fight to get the movie made, so it wouldn't surprise me if they shut it down. It's always the same. You assume you're getting somewhere and then...'

*... and then your car blows up, or you fall off your boat, or whatever it is that's happened to Artie*. It shouldn't have surprised Barney that, although neither of these two incidents had involved Mary, in her eyes they were a sign that the gods had it in for her. She'd never been one for sympathy or other similarly unproductive emotions. 'Have you spoken to anyone about it?' he asked.

'I've tried, but nobody's giving me an answer, and they won't even put me through to somebody who will. So I was wondering if you'd call Charlie and find out the state of play? He might be a bit more forthcoming with you, writer to writer, so to speak.'

'We've only talked a couple of times, so I don't see him letting any secrets slip.' Then, before Mary could set off on another self-pitying rant, 'but I'll give it a try.'

After they'd finished the conversation, Barney couldn't help noting that she had wasted none of her valuable time on asking how he was feeling. Nevertheless, he'd made a promise so, true to his word, he dialled Charlie's number. The call went straight to voicemail, and he left a brief message. 'Hi Charlie. I've just heard the bad news about Artie. I'm sorry if this...' he paused as a thought struck him, 'I'm sorry if this seems cold, but Mary's been struggling to find out how this affects the movie. Do you know if it'll be going ahead, or will they pull the plug on it? If you could call me back, or email, that'd be great. Cheers.'

The reason he'd hesitated mid-sentence was the memory of his encounter with Smith, when he'd jokingly suggested warning Artie and Charlie that they were in danger. His blood ran cold as he considered that the producer might have been killed by the Assassins that Smith had talked about. He hadn't seen *The Prince of Bar-*

*bary,* but had read several reviews, all of which mentioned a brutal keelhauling scene aboard the ship. Smith had said there was some kind of tit-for-tat element in the method being used, so even though it was a stretch, the fact that Artie had died whilst on the water caused Barney some discomfort, but only for a moment. It was more likely a coincidence. But what to do about Charlie? He couldn't tell him of his suspicions without being thought of as insane, but he had to do something. He pressed recall and left another message.

'Hi, Charlie, it's me again. I know this might sound strange, but...just be careful. I'll talk to you later.'

Barney arrived at the café in Leeds city centre at 11:30, bought a cappuccino and an egg mayo sandwich, then found an empty table. He checked his watch every few seconds, curious to meet this blog writer who was bringing him some intriguing information. Each time the door swung open, he inspected the newcomers. He himself should be easy for her to identify. Anyone who had been pestering his agent for his number must have come across his image often enough on book covers and various websites. This theory was confirmed when a young woman came inside and spotted him. He wasn't an expert on the tribal divisions of the youth of today, but he recognised a Goth when he saw one.

The raven-black hair, black eye-liner, long black leather coat and black boots were a dead give away. He watched as she ordered a coffee, then squeezed her way between the tables, apologising to customers as they shuffled their chairs to make room for her to pass. He guessed her to be in her mid-twenties. If he had to describe her in one word, that word would be elfin. He stood to greet her. 'Sally Steward?'

'Yes, thanks for meeting me,' she said as she took a seat. 'First of all, Mr Granville -'

*There's that "Mister" again.* 'Please - call me Barney.'

'Oh, right. First of all, Barney, I just want to say how shocked I was when I read about what happened to you.'

'You and me, both. You seem to have been having your own adventures; it can't have been very pleasant to have been there when Henry Hirst fell over that cliff edge.'

'Well, that's the thing. He didn't fall.' Sally spoke quickly. Barney had the impression she was repeating a speech that she'd memorised, relating the details of Henry's death, the police's theories, and the evidence of her own eyes and ears, such as it was. Breathless, she came to the end of her story.

'And where do I come in?' Barney asked.

'I didn't mention this on the phone, because I was worried I might be taking a liberty, but I've brought someone who can explain things better than me. Is it alright for him to join us?'

Barney's first inclination was to get up and walk out. He was desperate to stay out of the public eye, and although he was interested in what Sally had to say, yesterday he'd almost called her straight back to cancel this meeting. To now find that someone was tagging along with her, doubling the chances of his whereabouts being broadcast, was disappointing. However, after only a moment's hesitation, his curiosity won him over. *In for a penny, and all that.*

'Do I have a choice?' he asked, hoping that the tone of his voice conveyed his annoyance. Sally turned and signalled to a tentative looking man who was standing out on the street, peering in through the window. The newcomer acknowledged her and came through the door to join them. Unlike her, he didn't bother with any apologies as he bumped his way through the room.

'This is Colin Naseby,' Sally said. 'I think you might want to hear him out.'

Looking at them as they sat side by side, Barney would never have put them together. Whereas Sally was a young Goth, Colin was neither young nor Goth-like. Elfin didn't work, either. He reckoned the interloper to be around the seventy mark, and the casual way he was dressed showed as little concern for sartorial elegance as he himself owned. He, too, was balding, but the small amount of hair he still had was unkempt and long enough to cover his ears. His eyes had that ethereal focus of the single-minded, as though only a part of his mind was focused on what was going on in the café.

'So you're the famous Barnaby Granwell, are you?' he asked in a loud voice, confirming Barney's suspicions. The single-mindedness often came with an apparent disdain for the social niceties. 'I've read all your books.'

'Thanks. That's good to hear.'

'Before you ask, I didn't think much about any of them.'

Sally was shocked, obviously taken by surprise. 'I'm sorry. I'd no idea he was going to do this.'

Barney waved away the apology, then checked to see if anyone had overheard Colin's statement. He didn't want this to turn into a situation where people sitting nearby caught the word "famous", then spent the next few minutes figuring out who in the room deserved that description. He didn't fool himself that he was a member of that rarefied breed, but the last thing he wanted was for somebody to take a photo and post it online.

'Now that we've got to know each other, how about telling me what you've got that I'll be interested in?'

Colin, missing the sarcasm in Barney's

voice, produced a laptop from his shoulder bag. 'Have you ever heard of TheVersusVirus.com? That's all one word, by the way.'

'No. Should I have?'

'What about TVV? Does that mean anything?' He pronounced the name tee-double-vee.

'Maybe you should start from the beginning,' Barney said.

Colin pointed to his laptop. 'This is TheVersusVirus website. We investigate all the things that governments and the establishment don't want people like you - i.e. the public - to know. We're a worldwide network of investigators, dedicated to uncovering the secret machinery that runs the system. The hidden hands that control everything that goes on in the world.'

Sally was fidgeting in her seat, looking a little embarrassed. 'Can you get to the point, Colin?'

'I *am* doing. When one of our team finds a pattern of events that nobody else has identified, they log it on our message board, and depending on which particular geographical area it's in, someone will investigate it. Then we put all our findings together and analyse them. A few months ago, someone spotted a higher than usual incidence of unexpected deaths of people from the creative industries. We've compiled a database, and included you, of course.'

'Me? Why?'

'Because we've assumed that you were a

target. One where they failed. For the time being.'

'I see. What else did your analysis tell you?' Barney said, trying to stay calm.

'We believe the spate of killings are connected, and that they're the work of a serial killer, or more likely a group of them working together. We don't know yet what their motives are, or who the controlling figure is, but it's only a matter of time.'

'Can I have a look?'

Colin pushed the laptop towards him. Barney quickly got the sense of the arrangement of the names and the other information on there. There were more than he'd expected, around thirty in total. The top row held the titles of the columns: Name, Country, Method of Death, and various others. Most of the cells below this had been filled in with relevant details, but some contained only a question mark. In the next section was the story that TVV had connected with the writer's demise, and other notes. 'There are more columns here. How do I get to them?'

Colin reached over and pressed a combination of keys. The hidden items came into view. 'This is why we think it's more than a coincidence. For every person murdered, we've found a book they've written, or a movie or a play of theirs that includes at least one character dying in the same way that the writer did. In most cases, we believe we've even pinned it down to the chapter or scene.'

'Let the punishment fit the crime, you mean?' he said, quoting Smith's words. He was becoming more intrigued with each revelation.

'Exactly.' Colin's fingers worked the keyboard again. He pointed at the screen. 'This is you.'

Sure enough, there was his own name. In the adjoining Method of Death column were the words "Explosion in car (failed)", and then a title: *The Wheels on the Bus* (printed in *Tales of Horror, Fear and Terror in the Twentieth Century*).

'What's this story? I can't remember this.'

'I'm not surprised. It's from an anthology that was published over twenty years ago and never been reprinted. Disappointing sales, I should imagine, as it's not very memorable. Some melodramatic twaddle about a school bus being blown up by terrorists, and all the kids dying in a bloodbath.'

Barney felt his stomach tightening. A bus full of children being massacred in a story he couldn't even remember? If what Smith said was true, this would go some way to explaining why he'd be considered a suitable target for execution, and also the use of the car bomb. He carried on scanning the screen, and saw Henry Hirst, Francois Garone and Samuel Allan mentioned. Then another name caught his eye - Tom Jefferson. At first, he assumed that this meant Tom had been killed, but against his name, though, were just a series of empty cells until the Notes column. Printed here were the words, "Unable to locate, but brother Malcolm murdered in Scotland. Is this relevant?"

Barney asked if they had any information about Malcolm's death. Colin brought up another page. There were a few images amongst the text. Sally held her hand up to her mouth. Barney thought she was about to be sick, and after seeing how the body in the on-screen image had been treated, he wasn't surprised. In what appeared to be the inside of a farm building, something was hanging from the wall, something that he assumed had once been Malcolm Jefferson. It was hard to tell that the misshapen collection of bloodied limbs, torso and battered face could ever have been a functioning human being. His eyes widened as they reached the final entry. It was Artie Newfield with *Prince of Barbary*. He moved the cursor to the Cause of Death column. His heart beat faster when he read what was written there - "Keelhauling in movie/Killed on boat."

'Where are you parked?' Barney was on his feet. 'I need to have a proper look at all this. We can go to my place.' His excitement at this breakthrough had overridden his paranoia about revealing where he lived. Sally breathed a sigh of relief. She'd expected to have received short shrift from the author, but he might be taking them seriously.

He *was* taking them seriously, but only

up to a point. A group of serial killers hadn't murdered these writers, as TVV believed. In the absence of Smith, he alone knew that it was the Assassins who were behind the killings, and why each of these victims had suffered the deaths they had. However, Colin and his fellow conspiracy theory geeks had made a connection between the murders. TheVersusVirus had done quite a bit of the heavy lifting for him.

\*　\*　\*　\*　\*

# Chapter 20: Leeds

'How do you two know each other?' Barney asked as they drove across town.

'It was me that found Colin,' Sally said, following Barney's pointing finger as he gave directions from the passenger seat. 'After Henry's death, I tried to dig up as much about it as possible. One day, I googled him again, and this time, there was a link to TheVersusVirus website. So I had a look, and saw his name, along with those other writers; including you. If I'd seen the site a couple of weeks earlier, I'd probably have thought it was just a bunch of conspiracy nutters.' She glanced in the rear-view mirror. 'Sorry.'

Colin shrugged off the accusation as though it were an everyday occurrence. 'Another few days and it would've been the other way around,' he said. 'When I heard the news about Hirst, I was going to contact Sally, but she got to me first.'

'Where have you both come from?'

'I live in Whitby. Colin's from York, which is more or less on the way to Leeds, so I picked him up this morning, and here we are.'

When they arrived, Barney led them into the living room. Since moving in, he'd converted this space into a study. He'd done this by taking the simple steps of buying an old table, a few bookshelves, and a corkboard, all from a nearby charity shop. An armchair and four wooden dining chairs were the only other items of furniture. He hadn't yet started writing again, but this was where he'd been spending most of his time, connected to the Internet, searching for clues that might lead him to Tom Jefferson or Smith. Colin used Barney's printer to produce three copies of the TVV database. He kept one, handed one to Sally and the other to Barney, who studied the names. He focused on the ones he'd discussed months ago with Smith. Henry Hirst, of course. As he already knew, Allan, Munro, and Garone were there. He looked across the page at the column containing the stories that related to the method of their demise. For Henry, it was *The House of Countess Minova, Chapter 6*, followed by a two word note: "The Killer?" For Samuel Allan, *The Final Fade, printed in The Cornucopia of Horrors, Issue 166, May 2003*. It identified Zachary Munro as dying from natural causes. Garone's story was *Panzer Tomb of Ice, Chapter 16*. He returned to the entry for Henry Hirst.

'What happens in chapter six of this book?'

'An English explorer goes to Countess Minova's castle - Minova's a vampire - looking for a friend who he's lost contact with, but he's too late. The friend's already been infected by her, and throws him over a balcony, killing him.'

'Seems to fit in, I suppose. What does this mean, "The Killer"?'

'It's something I heard. It wasn't clear, but I'm sure his attacker shouted it,' Sally answered.

'It's one of the reasons we've started calling them The Writer Killers,' Colin said, 'it'll look good on a headline when the press start to take us seriously.'

Barney decided not to comment on this statement, as he was deep in thought. *Killer. Sounds similar to Ancilla. It couldn't be, could it?* He ran his eyes further down the page.

'Who's Boris Zelesky, and why is there a question mark against his name?'

Colin peered at his screen. 'I remember him, because we haven't found a story that ties in with him yet. His body was discovered in his bed, in Moscow.'

'So why isn't he down as Natural Causes?'

'Because it wasn't. Unless you call suffering multiple broken bones and a cracked skull, and then climbing into bed, natural.'

'I don't get it. Do you mean somebody killed him, and then put his body in the bed?'

'Who knows? It's a proper Agatha Christie puzzle, this one. According to the Russian police report we got hold of, his apartment was locked from the inside, and the same with his bedroom. The authorities kept it out of the press, but...'

Colin tapped the side of his nose with his forefinger, '... we have our ways. We'll keep looking into Boris, and we'll find out what happened, don't you worry.'

Barney wasn't worried. Boris Zelesky could well be the victim of a real serial killer for all he cared. His dying might fit in with TVV's theories, but it didn't with his own. He dismissed Boris from his thoughts. 'All these titles in the last column. Do you have the printed versions, the actual books and magazines?'

'Yes. I've been putting together a collection of them,' Sally said.

'Any particular reason?'

'Just for my own peace of mind. I mean, as far as I knew, some of them could have been made up by someone at TVV with a sick sense of humour.' Sally glanced at Colin, worried again that she might have offended him. He brushed this second slur off with a shrug of his shoulders.

Barney nodded his appreciation. He would also feel happier seeing the proof with his own eyes. 'Can you bring them over here? Let me see for myself?'

Sally was only too pleased to be given the chance to show that she and Colin were on the right lines. 'I've booked the whole week off, so what about tomorrow?'

'That would be great. The sooner the better.'

Colin was packing his things away. 'We

ought to be going if we want to beat the traffic.' He looked at Barney. 'How about writing a testimonial to publicise TheVersusVirus? We could do with a semi-famous name attached. Every little helps.'

Sally glared at Colin, who had once again insulted their host. Barney, though, found it hard to argue with Colin's description of him, and tried to appear as though he was giving the idea serious consideration. 'Let see what I can come up with.' *Not a chance*, he thought.

'I've copied the file onto your laptop. I've named it TVV Database, so it should be easy enough to remember,' Colin said. He didn't notice the tightening of Sally's lips.

When his visitors had left, Barney made another cup of coffee, then sat down at his keyboard, ready to start his research into the book titles. He downloaded Colin's file and had just typed the first author's name into the search box when he heard a knock. He walked to the front door and opened it a crack. Recognising who was standing there, he pulled it fully open.

'And where have you been?' he said, taking a step back into the hallway, inviting Smith into the house.

\* \* \* \* \*

# Chapter 21: Leeds

Barney guided Smith through to his study and motioned for him to sit down. 'I've been waiting for you to show up. Where have you been?' Barney's questions came in a flood, the dam bursting after days of frustration. 'What's been happening? There haven't been more killings, have there? I've kept a lookout for any reports, but I've not seen anything lately. Neither have Sally and Colin.'

'Who?'

'Those two you saw leaving. I'll tell you about them later. I take it you turning up means it's all about to kick off again?'

Smith frowned, puzzled.

'I keep forgetting, you're not from around here, are you? I mean, is something bad about to happen?'

'I see. In that case, yes, I'm afraid it is going to kick off.'

Barney gathered himself, preparing to ask the one question that really mattered. 'And what about Cassidy? Is he still intent on killing me?'

'Very much so. In fact, it seems he wants

you dead more than ever.' Smith stared at him, ready to gauge his reaction.

Barney returned the stare, eyes unblinking, but in his chest his heart was thudding. 'Charming,' he said. 'And what about you? Why did you disappear?'

'I was recalled to Ancilla, as we had decisions to make. I've a question for you. I was concerned you wouldn't be welcoming, but you seemed pleased to see me when I arrived at your door. Why?'

*I need more of your Margins. I want to feel the way I did when you sent me there before, so I can cast off this weary body and be alive again, with the blood flowing, muscles flexing and senses sharpened, if only for a while. Will that do?* But Barney kept these thoughts to himself. 'Because attack is the best form of defence, and if I can save some other writers while I'm saving myself, then maybe I should try. I just feel I should do my bit,' was what actually came out of his mouth.

Smith nodded appreciatively. There was a hint of relief in his voice when he spoke. 'Good. We need the assistance of authors such as yourself.'

'Well, here I am, ready and willing, but I'm still not sure how I can help.'

'We want you to go to the Margins and prevent the Assassins from coming to Earth.'

'So you've said; but how would I do that?' Barney asked.

'By terminating them.'

'I see. But doesn't that mean they'll be gone forever? What was it you said...they become lost ones and never get to return to Ancilla?'

'You're correct, but these are the hard choices we have to make. It's us or them, and "us" includes you and your fellow writers. I'm asking you to fight and destroy the Assassins. If you have any moral qualms about doing this, I think I can reassure you of something - once you're in the Margins, it's probable that you will feel their lives are worth nothing more than the characters you dispose of so freely in your books.'

The Warden's sudden shift in tone took Barney aback. However, thinking about it, why should he be surprised? After all, Smith was asking him to collaborate in the destruction of some of his fellow Ancillans, regardless of them being his enemies. 'And what about Tom? Will you help me track him down?'

'I'll do what I can. What do you intend to do once you find him?'

'I'll have to think about that, but whatever it is, it won't be good for him. Anyway, that's for the future. When can we start?'

'Soon; first tell me about your two friends. Are they aware of our situation?'

'They're not friends. I only met them a few hours ago, and they don't know as much as they think they do. Sally was with Henry Hirst when he went over the edge of that cliff, and Colin loves a conspiracy. He's part of a group who have come up with their own theory about the killings. They were here because they'd made the connection between the car bomb that was supposed to kill me and those dead authors.'

Smith arched his eyebrows, but Barney dampened any expectations he might have had. 'Don't get too excited. They think it's the work of some serial killers - human ones - targeting writers. Which I suppose is the right answer, but the wrong workings-out.'

'Perhaps we could make use of their knowledge?'

'No, I don't want them involved in this. Sally might assume she has a stake in this, but she has no idea about what's really happening. It's alright them throwing a few theories around, but this is the real world,' Barney said, almost smiling at the irony. *When did this become the real world?* 'She's coming back tomorrow to bring some relevant books she's got together, but that's all. Anyway, never mind that. Let's get down to business.'

'Very well.' Smith leaned forward, ready to start. 'First, a brief refresher. As you already know, when the Skeptics choose a target for execution, their name will appear on a Termination List. This is delivered to a Shadow Writer, along with the title of the relevant book and a chapter number, and they are tasked with revising that section, following specific instructions from their Ancillan handler. This opens the Channel, allowing the Assassin, who will have been standing by in the Margins - inside the same chapter, in fact - to travel to Earth, to murder their target. We have ways of obtaining the List, so we intend to use this same material to enable you to go there. We call this an Intervention, and you will be a Scribe, a writer with the ability to enter the Margins and stop the Assassins before they reach the Channel.'

*A Scribe.* Barney could go for that. Made him sound like a member of the Knights Templar or some secret society. Which, in a way he would be, of course.

'As the Scribe, you become the interim author, and as such, you'll gain some of the abilities that exist within the internal logic of the narrative,' Smith said.

Barney considered this. 'You mean I could arrive in a Jane Austen novel as a skilled swordsman, but not as Superman?'

'Quite. To more practical matters. Previously, I sent you into the Margins simply by putting my hand on your head. However, using that method alone has its limits as regards the accuracy of it. For you to manifest in a specific chapter, you must be editing it at the same time as I touch you.'

'How does that work?'

'We suspect it has to do with the changes in your thought processes that occur when you write.'

Barney chose not to challenge the vagueness of this answer. He didn't need to know, and wasn't concerned by the mechanics of the operation.

Smith continued, 'You will find yourself within the fictional universe of the story. You may be lucky and find you are matched with one of the Assassins' newer recruits. Alternatively, you might come face to face with a more experienced operative. If that's the case, you could well die a virtual death, and your consciousness will return here. At which point we'll assess the situation, and either send you back in, or regroup and prepare for the next Intervention.'

Barney wasn't letting the possibility of a "virtual death" stop him now. 'So I'm in there, and let's say I've killed the Assassin. How do I leave? How do I get back here of my own volition?'

'Once again, I can't be more specific, but you'll just know. Ah, wait...' Smith tilted his head to one side, as though someone in the distance was calling his name, '...we have the first List.' He reached into his coat and pulled out a sheet of paper. After a quick glance, he placed it on the table.

'Did you bring that with you?' Barney asked.

'No. I received it a moment ago from home.'

'But if it's only just turned up, how come

it's printed out?'

It was Smith's turn to look puzzled. 'I have no idea.'

'For some reason, that makes me feel a little better about things.'

'Why?'

'Because it means I'm not the only one who hasn't got a clue about what's going on.'

\* \* \* \* \*

# Chapter 22: Leeds

While Smith gazed at the document, deep in study, Barney made a few notes - something he should have done a long time ago. As there was a distinct possibility he wouldn't come out of this thing alive, then whoever investigated his death, virtual or otherwise, might find a few words of explanation useful. He picked up a pen and found a blank sheet in the A4 pad he kept on the desk. Humans v. Ancillans, Wardens v. Assassins, Scribes v. Shadow Writers. It was all becoming a muddle.

He started with a simple diagram - similar to the one Smith had drawn back in London - of the four main components as he saw them: Earth, Ancilla, Margins and Channel, under which he made a few observations.

Good Guys:
1a: Wardens: Ancillans who want to maintain the status quo. They believe Ancilla may only exist to supply the writers of Earth with characters for their stories. If this ends, so might Ancilla.

1b: Scribes: writers recruited by Wardens to go into the Margins and prevent the Assassins before the Channel (the pathway to Earth) opens.

Bad Guys:
2a: Skeptics: Ancillans who are no longer willing to put up with the vast number of violent deaths in certain types of fiction.
2b: Assassins: the Skeptics' Extermination Squad
2c: Shadow Writers: writers recruited by Skeptics to revise the target's story in order to open the Channel.

Barney drew a line under his summary of the facts as he understood them. He read over what he'd written, then picked his pen up again.

3: I am now a Scribe
4: My job is to hunt down and kill Assassins, with the help of Warden Smith.

If an Assassin got to him and Mary came across this page amongst his papers, she'd probably assume they were notes for a new novel, and who could blame her?

Smith saw what he was doing and read what Barney had written. 'I see things are becoming a little clearer.' He handed the Termination List over. 'There are several more authors who have been targeted, but these are the ones allocated to the two of us. Obviously, we can only attempt one at a time, so we must prioritise.'

Barney's heart sank as he spotted the first name of the five. It was Charlie Fairweather, and the title of his work: *The Prince of Barbary*, scene 46. 'This is the new movie he wrote. I've read a few reviews in the papers. Can I start with him?'

'Do you have the screenplay?'

'Of course not.'

'Then you must obtain a copy.'

Barney pondered this, then fired off a message, telling Charlie he'd seen the movie and loved it. Not true, but more persuasive than, "I've read a few reviews". *Was there any chance he could have a digital copy of the shooting script?* He explained this request by saying he was considering trying his hand at screenwriting, and it would be a great help to study some of Charlie's work. He ended with, *Any news on our own project?*

'What of the other authors? Are there any we can proceed with immediately?' Smith asked.

'Let's see. There's Harald Mans, with *The Lost Palace of El Dorado*, Chapter 34. Alfie Lawrenson and *Stalag Tarantula*, Chapter 65. Then Helen Barron, and *The Worm in the Orchard*, Chapter 2. That rings a bell. Just hold on a second,' he said, disappearing through the door. Two minutes later, he was back, triumphantly brandishing a paperback copy of Barron's book. 'Whoever rented this place before me must have been keen on whodunnits, because they left a load in the bookcase upstairs. I thought I'd seen this. Bit of a coincidence, isn't it? Or is it?' He looked enquiringly at Smith, half-expecting him to admit to planting it there.

'I assure you that it is indeed a coincidence. No matter what you may think, nobody could have known you were moving here prior to your arrival.'

Barney sat down and carried on with the List. 'The last one is *Deadly Falls The Rain*, by Kate Mulholland, Chapter 14.'

'In summary, what do we have?' Smith said. 'Mr Fairweather should be sending you his script, and we have another of the named works already in our possession. How do we get hold of the remaining three?'

'I'll see if I can buy them online. If they exist as e-books, I'll download them. Do you know what an e-book is?'

'I do. We're well aware of your technologies.'

'Oh, right,' Barney said, feeling just a little stupid. This...person...he was having a conversation with had travelled across dimensions, and here he was asking if he knew what e-books were. To cover his embarrassment, he turned to the laptop again, and started searching for the three missing titles. He had no problem finding *The Lost Palace of El Dorado* (only 3 stars, he couldn't help noticing. Barney's last novel, *The*

*Rustling of the Leaves,* had received a 4 out of 5 rating. He smiled to himself at the thought that, even under these circumstances, an inbuilt competitive streak still reared its head). *Stalag Tarantula* was as easy to find (2.5 stars - ha!). He downloaded both and carried on searching for *Deadly Falls The Rain.* This was marked as unavailable in both hardback and paperback, and it seemed it had never been available as an e-book. He performed a more general online search. This led to a link to the author herself.

'According to this, Kate Mulholland's been dead for over fourteen years, so why is she on here?'

Smith frowned. 'The Skeptics wouldn't have missed that fact. I'll make enquiries.'

'Which brings up another question. What happens if the Shadow Writer can't find a copy of a book that's on the List? Not just this Mulholland one, but any of them?'

'There will be no reprieve for the target, if that's what you're asking,' Smith replied. 'If an author is tagged, it's not because they only have a single title to their name.'

'Good point. So what comes next?'

'Until we receive the screenplay, we have three potential starting points. Which would you rather begin with?'

'I've read the online synopses of these two that I've just downloaded. *Stalag Tarantula* is a science fiction novel, set in the future and on a planet ruled by giant spiders; *The Lost Palace of El Dorado* sounds like an Indiana Jones story.' Seeing the bafflement in Smith's eyes, he explained. 'He's a movie character, always having adventures in jungles, rescuing ancient treasures from Nazis and stuff.' This didn't appear to make things any clearer, so Barney continued, 'We'll return to that. Anyway, the point I'm making is that the location for *The Worm in the Orchard* is a genteel English village. I think this would be as good a place to as any to start, don't you?'

'If that's how you feel, then yes.' Smith picked up the book and handed it over. 'In which case, read Chapter 2 and familiarise yourself with this fictional world. When you've gleaned as much information as possible, we'll begin.'

Barney read the description printed on the back cover.

*"The tiny village of Heyton suffers from more than its fair share of dark deeds and mysterious goings-on. When five bodies are discovered up at Patford Manor, it falls to Inspector Laughton to make the now familiar journey from police headquarters to investigate the brutal murders. Once more, he has the helping hand of his unasked-for volunteers, Maude and Evelyn Gresham - spinsters, sisters, sleuths - to help and to hinder him. Can the detectives - professional and amateur - find the killer before he strikes again? As Seen on TV."*

He flipped through the opening pages. At the front were a map of the locale and a plan

154

of Patford Manor. Everything seemed familiar, and Barney knew why; it was because of the few times he'd joined Lucy in watching some of the endless reruns of *Death in the Village*, the TV adaptation of Barron's novels about the detecting exploits of the Gresham sisters. Barney skipped to chapter two and read about those dark deeds that had taken place at the big house. He let out a soft whistle. 'I can understand why they chose this. The stiffs are already piling up. Five of them so far, and it's only the second chapter. If the killings keep going at this rate, it'll be a ghost village by the end.'

Smith was not amused. 'It would be as well for you to remember the reasons for this situation we find ourselves in. Each of those "stiffs" as you call them, means one less of my kind, gone forever, and for what? To provide a few hours of amusement for your readers? They'll be forgotten about within minutes, and the reader will simply open another book, hoping for more dead bodies, because their appetite will never be satisfied. I've lost friends because of your fiction, and it's only by surveying the bigger picture that I've chosen to follow the path I'm on. Don't think that this fight we're engaged in is comparable to a game of chess, where those involved are either black or white pieces. There are many shades of grey involved.'

The outburst shocked Barney to the core. Until now, he'd understood the background of this conflict to be as simple as good versus bad. In the blue corner were himself, Smith, and the other Wardens; in the red corner were Cassidy, the Assassins and the Skeptics. Barney hadn't considered that Smith himself might harbour doubts about the cause he was fighting for. He had to remind himself that the Wardens weren't actually in favour of the fictional killings and the resultant disappearances of Ancillans, but that they knew that ending the association could mean the demise of Ancilla. They didn't care for the well-being of human writers, they had simply chosen the most pragmatic path towards their goal as they saw it.

'I'm sorry,' Barney said. 'It's just that...to me, they're made-up people, suffering made-up deaths. I realise it's not the same for you.'

'I understand.' Smith was calmer now that he'd made his feelings clear. 'Are you ready to proceed?'

'I think so, but there's one more thing I need to clear up. How will I know how to identify Assassin when I see him? Or her? I assume they'll disguise themselves as a character from the story?'

'The key clue may be their eyes. Something in their training gives them a bright blue colouring. Whatever form they take, you should have no difficulty recognising them for what they are. However, you must remember they will also recognise you as an outsider in the story.' Smith reached out and took the book. He flicked through the pages, reading them at lightning speed. 'I would assume that the Assassin will hide in the great house where these deaths occur.'

'So will I manifest there?'

'Possibly. Or it could be in the centre of the village. In fact, any location that exists within this segment. You may even find yourself face to face with the enemy the moment you arrive. As regards arming yourself, we now know from reading this section that there must be a shotgun somewhere on the premises, as one was used to commit the crimes. There is a kitchen, so knives are available. Also, you'll have noted that, in the description of the hall, there's a display of medieval weapons adorning the wall above the fireplace?'

'Er, I did, yes...' Barney didn't sound too sure.

Smith sighed. 'You should learn to study the stories so that you see everything in them that might be of use.'

Barney nodded, looking thoughtful. His confidence had just taken a knock. He'd thought he was prepared, but now he realised how little he knew. Before any more doubts could infest his thoughts, he opened *The Worm in the Orchard* at Chapter 2. The time for hesitation was past. 'Let's go,' he said, copying the words that Helen Barron had written, and preparing for the promised changes to happen.

'*The day after the annual fair, no-one was talking about the prize winners. Local chatter was all about the forthcoming return to Patford Manor of Peter Hemingway, Sir Archibald's estranged son...*'

Smith leaned across the table and touched Barney's forehead, sending him into the mysterious world of the Margins.

\* \* \* \* \*

# Chapter 23: The Margins
# - Heyton, 1974

... the sun is burning bright in the cloudless azure sky, birds are singing, and bees buzzing. Barney knows Heyton has always been like this, and always will be, at least for as long as Helen Barron writes the mysteries that she has set in this picturesque location. He is standing between the maypole and the duck pond. To his left, the postman whistles as he delivers letters and packages, and over on the right, a milk float cruises its daily round. Picture-perfect thatched cottages encircle the green. In amongst them stand The White Lion, The Kings Arms, and the village shop. He spies the narrow lane that leads up to Patford Manor. Having watched several episodes of the TV series, he recognises the setting. On the surface, everything has a faux-realistic quality. It is only when he looks again that he sees the small signs showing that realism has no place here. The village is alive with restless locals, all of them busy with their choreographed errands. No-one has registered Barney's presence. Heeding Smith's advice, he plans to start his search for the Assassin at the Manor. With his newly gained vitality, he sets off at a sprint, the wind blowing through his hair. Hair? Another welcome surprise.

After a hundred yards of effortless running, the big house comes into view. A grand Victorian mansion, Gothic in style, it comprises two floors and an attic and, as he knows from the plan, a basement below, containing the kitchen. He slows to a walk, pleased to note that he isn't even breathing heavily. A gardener walks around the corner, pushing a wheelbarrow. Barney steps aside for him to pass, and then moves onto the grass verge as a large motor glides up the drive, a Bentley. It pulls to a halt and a uniformed chauffeur alights. He opens the rear doors, first one side and then the other. An elderly couple climbs out; Sir Archibald and his wife, returning from a weekend in the country. Heathcote, the straight-backed butler, comes out to greet them, gesturing at a footman to take the luggage from the boot and to carry it inside. Then an open topped sports car appears, narrowly missing the Bentley and screeching to a stop. In the front seat is an outrageously glamorous young couple. This must be Peter, Sir Archibald's son, and his latest girlfriend. They swagger arm in arm past the frowning old retainer.

Again, Barney notes how busy the scene is. Everything here has to happen before the reader becomes bored and closes the book, or turns the television off. He's obviously arrived at a point in the chapter before the slaughter has begun. Sidestepping the commotion on the doorstep, he walks inside, into the entrance hall, which is brightly lit by the sunlight streaming through the glass roof of the atrium. Smith was right - hanging above the fireplace are the medieval weapons he'd pointed out. Swords, axes and halberds.

He starts with the first room on the left. The hinges of the huge old oak door squeak as he pushes it open. The curtains are closed, and all is in near darkness. He takes a step inside, then stops, allowing his eyes to adjust. He is becoming accustomed to the lack of light when he hears the creaking of a floorboard less than two yards away from him. Before he turns, his assailant is on him, punching him hard in the stomach. Barney reels backwards, gasping for breath. He covers his midriff, protecting it against the next blow, and realises he hasn't been punched, but stabbed. Even in the gloom, he can see his hands are coated in blood. His strength drains, and he sinks to his knees. The last sound he registers is of someone laughing with... what?... his befuddled mind searches for the word... scorn, that's it... somebody is laughing scornfully at him as the virtual life drips out of his virtual body and onto the floorboards of the virtual Patford Manor.

\* \* \* \* \*

# Chapter 24: Leeds

Back in the safety of his study, he forced himself to look down at his stomach, dreading what he might see there, and felt a surge of relief at the absence of a bleeding wound.

'How long was I gone for?' he asked.

Smith was eyeing him narrowly, waiting for him to recover. 'A minute or two,' he replied, 'how long did it seem to you?'

'Maybe fifteen minutes.'

'But did you succeed?'

'Well, I arrived in one piece, and at near enough where we'd hoped, so that part went alright; but I was stabbed in the stomach, so we'll call it a qualified success. When can I go again? The Assassin's in there, so we need to act fast if I'm going to stop him.' Hurriedly, he told Smith everything that had happened in Heyton. The adrenaline was still coursing through his body, and he was eager to return to the strange place that, up to now, had only existed in somebody else's mind. After years of living with the daily grind of the writer's sedentary lifestyle, he'd forgotten what it was like to have a young man's physical strength and fitness, and he wanted to experience it anew.

Smith looked relieved. He'd obviously been worried that Barney might say, *I've given it a go, thank you very much, but once was enough.* 'Good. The sooner the better. The Assassin has now been alerted, and you must return before the Channel is opened. Are you sure you're ready?'

In answer, Barney turned back to his laptop and deleted what he'd previously typed, and checked that *The Worm in the Orchard* was open at the right place. He started copying the words and leaned toward Smith, exposing his forehead to the Warden.

\* \* \* \* \*

# Chapter 25: The Margins
## - Heyton, 1974

Barney is on the green again, but this time he isn't wasting precious seconds taking in the sights. He sets off at a run, sprinting up the lane until Patford Manor appears. He ignores the gardener, who is still pushing his wheelbarrow around the corner. The Bentley and the sports car arrive as he pushes the front door of the house open, brushing by Heathcote, who is coming out to greet Sir Archibald. He makes straight for the fireplace and studies the display hanging above the mantelpiece. He pulls a hall chair over and climbs onto it. Stretching up, he realises he can only reach the bottom level, which means he has to be content with a battleaxe. He takes the axe from its position on the wall and jumps back down.

He starts in the same place as last time, with the room to the left of the entrance. The curtains are still closed. He inches forward, holding the axe high in one hand, using the other to feel along the wall, searching for the light switch. Finding it, he narrows his eyes against the sudden brightness and makes his way across the vast carpet, senses sharpened for anything that signals the presence of an Assassin. He arrives at the drapes and pulls them open. No-one there. He then conducts a more comprehensive search, kneeling to examine the underside of the large Victorian chairs and settee that fill most of the floor space.

Finally, he is satisfied that he's alone in here. He opens the door a crack and peers out into the entrance hall. As expected, this area is unnaturally busy with family members sauntering between rooms and servants forever going about their business. He watches closely, looking out for any telltale signs the Assassin might have disguised himself as a character from Helen's book. A few moments of cautious observation convince him that this isn't the case, and he steps out. He strides the few feet to the library and goes through the same procedure, with the same result. The only successful discovery is the gun cabinet in Sir Archibald's study. Like a player in a computer role-playing game, he upgrades from battle-axe to shotgun, loading his new weapon with cartridges that he finds in a drawer in the desk. After another few minutes of nerve-racking exploration, including the basement and attic, Barney is sure that his prey is no longer in Patford Manor. The outbuildings yield a similar result. Gardeners aplenty, but no Assassin. With the shotgun ready and cocked for instant action, he heads for the village, prepared to go through every room in every house if he has to.

Back at the green, he continues with the clockwise strategy he'd used up at the Manor. There are three cottages to his left, and then The White Lion. Beyond that are more homes, the shop, and The Kings Arms.

He reaches the first gate. Before unlatching it, he pauses, tuning in to the buzzing of bees as they make their way from foxglove to hollyhock in the garden. He walks down the path, the scent of roses hanging heavy in the air, and is about to test the handle on the door when it is pushed open from the other side. A little old lady appears. She bends down and places two empty milk bottles on the step, then calls out to someone passing by. Barney, although only three feet away, is invisible to her. He waits for her to return indoors and follows her inside. There is no vestibule, so he is straight into the living room. The old lady who had taken the bottles out is standing by the window, looking out. Her doppelgänger is sitting in the armchair by the fireplace. Barney realises these two must be Maude and Evelyn, the Gresham sisters - the amateur sleuths that solve the unfeasible number of murders that occur in this tiny community. Maude - or is it Evelyn? - is in mid-sentence. '... and that's four days running when Daphne Carpenter's put three empties out. Why would she need the extra bottle?'

Barney remembers reading that, for the TV series, the producers had scoured the casting agencies for months before finding actresses of a comparable age and appearance to play the spinster sisters. It occurs to him how easy writers sometimes had it. After describing one, Helen only has to type something along the lines of, "and her sister was identical in every way", to complete the picture. After eavesdropping on their conversation for a few seconds in the forlorn hope of picking up a clue, Barney gives up and walks past them. He sticks his head in the kitchen. There is nothing there that shouldn't have been, so he climbs the stairs. At the top is a small landing, two bedrooms and the bathroom, each of them as humdrum as they should be. He goes back downstairs. There doesn't appear to be a cellar, so that is the first house ticked off.

Ten minutes later, he's checked out the second and third, and is set to investigate The White Lion. This is a traditional pub, with two entrances, one signed for the Public Bar, and one for the Lounge. He steps through to the public bar. Nobody takes any notice of him as he walks over to the counter, where the landlord is busy pulling a pint. Three men are standing at the bar, chatting. The one closest to him has turned away, leaving his drink unattended. On a whim, Barney picks it up and tries a sample. The familiar bitter taste of British beer fills his mouth. The unexpected sensation prompts some other questions. If he stays here long enough, will he get hungry and have to eat? If he gets tired, will he need to sleep? And there's another thing - Smith said that when he is ready to return to his normal life, he'd know what to do. He's been into the Margins twice now, and on neither occasion has he made his own decision. What will happen this time? He'll be finding out soon, he supposes.

After the surprising result of the beer-drinking experiment, Barney tries something else. 'Has anybody seen any strangers around here lately?' he asks, then performs a double take when he hears his question being asked by one of the drinkers, each word emerging at precisely the same moment that he himself has said it. He is even more nonplussed when it receives an answer.

'Aye, there's a feller in there,' the landlord nods in the general direction of the other bar, 'that's been coming in for a few hours every day for about a week now. Never says a word, just sits there with an empty glass. I was going to ask him if he was here on business and, you know, have a laugh with him, but there's something a bit off about him. Then there's that other chap who was in here earlier, asking the same, about there being any strangers being around. I wonder where he's disappeared to?'

Barney tries again, not wanting to lose the moment. 'What did he look like, this other chap?' However, his proxy spokesman stays silent, and the question remains unasked. The landlord and his audience have already moved on to another subject.

He now has a lead, something that might save him from having to search the rest of the village. He needs to find this stranger that the landlord has mentioned. Holding the shotgun a little tighter, he crosses to the door that connects this area to the lounge. The top section is a window made of pebbled glass, decorated with the name and emblem of the pub. He is about to push it open when there is the deafening blast of a gunshot, and the glass shatters. Barney falls to his knees, yelling at everyone to get down, but nobody is listening. The invisible barrier between himself and this fictional world is fully operational again. From the other room comes the bang of the lounge's outer door slamming shut, followed by the noise of running feet on the street outside. Barney turns on his heels and leaves by the same way he'd entered.

There's the runner, twenty yards away, already building up some speed. If this is the Assassin, and all the signals suggest it is, Barney has to act now, and fast. He raises his shotgun and settles the butt of the stock into his shoulder. Before he can shoot, he hears the distant crash of a gun being fired from somewhere over to his right, and the running man falls, blood spurting from the entry hole that has suddenly appeared in the back of his head. Barney looks over to where the shot had come from. On the far side of the green, he sees the barrel of a rifle jutting out from an upstairs window. He watches, transfixed, as it shifts until it is pointing in his direction. He braces himself for the impact of a high-velocity bullet. There are two shots in quick succession, each from a different weapon. He feels a sharp pain and realises he's been hit in the upper arm, but not by the sniper. This shot came from behind him. Barney sees the rifle being pulled back inside the window, then turns around. The mystery marksman has added to his tally. The body of a second man is lying on the ground, victim of another head shot. His hand is clutching the still smoking revolver he's just used to put a bullet into Barney's biceps muscle. The dead man's lifeless blue eyes are staring sightlessly towards the sky.

*     *     *     *     *

# Chapter 26: Leeds

Smith was talking, his voice anxious. 'Barney. Are you alright?'

With a groan, Barney opened his eyes. 'I'm fine,' he said, rubbing his wounded arm; but there *was* no wound. How could there be, now that he'd left the Margins? And yet he felt a nagging ache in the spot where the bullet had hit him. He rolled his shirt sleeve up and studied the deepening bruise. Satisfied there was no lasting damage, he turned his attention to Smith.

'I had the Assassin in my sights, but somebody else got there first, somebody with a rifle. Then the same rifleman shot the one who was trying to kill me!' Barney saw the expression on the Warden's face. 'What is it?'

'We failed. Helen Barron died this morning.'

'How? I mean, I've just seen her Assassins die.'

'We've been outmanoeuvred. While the real Assassin came through the Channel undetected, decoys were sent to Heyton to throw us off the track. You say there were three of them?'

'Three, but only two of them were Assassins; or so I thought. The third one killed both of them both, so he must have been on our side, mustn't he?'

'I'll have to investigate, but it's very puzzling.'

'Okay. Tell me about Helen, then; how did she die?' Barney asked.

'She was in her bed, asleep, when an intruder killed her with a close range shot to her head.'

'What kind of weapon?'

'A shotgun.'

'That figures. It's how she wrote those killings in Chapter 2.' Barney told Smith everything. About the family and servants up at Patford Manor; how the locals never stopped to rest; that no-one seemed aware of his presence as he'd walked among them; the events in The White Lion, where he'd tasted the beer and received an answer to his question. Finally, the three-way shootout on the green.

'Did you know I'd be able to have a conversation?' he asked.

'No, I didn't. This could complicate things.'

*Complicate things? Damn. Just when I was beginning to understand everything. Not!*

'And you say you asked another question?' Smith continued with his interrogation.

'I tried, but by then they were ignoring me again.'

'Perhaps the inhabitants of the Margins may be of more use to us than we thought. However, this also means they could be utilised by the Skeptics as well. I'll attempt to discover the identity of the rifleman, as I'm quite certain that no other Scribe was assigned to this story.'

Barney assumed this meant that Smith would start his investigation after they'd finished their analysis of the Intervention. He realised he was mistaken; Smith was wearing that distant look, the one Barney was starting to recognise. It meant the Warden was about to disappear into the ether again.

\* \* \* \* \*

# Chapter 27: Los Angeles

The interloper first approached Charlie in *Jake's Coffee and Donuts* on Lexington Avenue, where he was waiting for Kayleigh. He'd assumed this intruder was about to ask for a handout, dressed as he was in an old knitted hoodie over a creased Hawaiian shirt, three-quarter shorts, and sandals. The unkempt beard and shoulder length hair hadn't helped his appearance, either.

'Hiya, Charlie. What's the coffee like in here?'

'Sorry? Do I know you?'

'The name's Newman. You got time for a talk?'

Charlie looked around to see if he recognised any of his friends that might be setting him up for a candid camera type fall. Failing to spot anyone he knew, he returned to his newspaper, hoping this pest would move on, but Newman used his hooked forefinger to drag the paper down, bringing his face back into view.

'This won't take long, Charlie boy.'

*Charlie boy! Who the fuck* was *this guy?* At that moment, Kayleigh appeared through the door, giving him the chance to escape. He picked up his coffee mug, aiming to meet her at the counter, but Newman blocked his path.

'I'll be in touch, Mr Fairweather, and soon. The speed the Skeptics are moving, we might need to get you somewhere safe pretty damn fast. Artie Newfield won't listen to me, but maybe you will.'

Charlie walked away. When he looked back, the intruder had gone.

The second time was when he was taking a bus across town. The same unkempt stranger sat beside him, trapping him in his seat, and explained who he was; he was in LA for one purpose: to protect him, and, "was Charlie aware the characters in his scripts didn't come out of his head, but from some sort of super casting agency that existed in another dimension, and they weren't happy with all the killing and the dying, and the assassins are coming for you, and you'll be on a deadly list of names, so you'd better listen, or... and blah, blah..."

Charlie had squeezed past Newman and made a break for it, jumping off before his stop, content to walk the last few blocks. Since then, his stalker had left him alone.

Presumably he'd been caught and sent back to whichever asylum he'd escaped from.

\* \* \* \* \*

# Chapter 28: Leeds

Left alone, Barney had eventually given up on trying to figure out why Smith had taken off without warning. Again. Did he decide himself, or was some other power calling him? He'd gone to bed, unable to sleep for more than an hour at a time. Too many thoughts were bouncing around in his head, ricocheting off each other in an agitated swirl. When morning came, he woke from his final few minutes of slumber tired, edgy, and in need of a smoke. There was no doubt about it. He wanted to be back in the Margins as quickly as possible. Despite having been stabbed and shot while in there, the exhilaration he'd experienced overcame any worries he had about the dangers it contained.

He was hungry for the next adventure.

Today ought to be a busy one; Charlie's screenplay might already be in his inbox, and Sally was due to arrive with the books and magazines she'd promised. However, Barney was now in two minds about this; he was no longer convinced he needed TheVersusVirus and their theories any more, as he now had his own experiences to fall back on, and what better proof of events could there be? He ought to consider whether involving her might put her in danger. If the Skeptics infiltrated the Wardens' system, they could be aware of Barney's partnership with Smith. Following on from that, it wouldn't be long before she was on the Assassins' radar as well. On the other hand, she, along with Colin's little group of misfits, had been the only outsiders to connect the circumstances of the writers' deaths, even if their reasoning was wrong. Could he afford to ignore their input? He wondered if Smith had solved the mystery of the identity of the gunman in the cottage window, the one who had saved his virtual life. Was it just a case of crossed wires? Had two Wardens mistakenly been assigned to stopping the Heyton Assassin, as a result of which a fellow Scribe had been present and able to recognise Barney's parlous situation at The White Lion?

Ten minutes after showering, Barney was sitting at his desk. He opened his emails and found fourteen unread messages, eleven of them digital junk mail. Of the others, two were from Mary, which he'd look at later. The third was the one he wanted.

*Hi Barney, good to hear from you. Sorry I never came back to you after you called about Artie, but things have been going a little crazy over here. He was the main man as regards getting the finance* together and now that he's gone, I have to say it's not looking too healthy. It's ironic that he died like he did in the same week his latest movie was released. Apparently, he'd got himself tangled up with a mooring rope, dragged overboard, and drowned. I say 'apparently' because he was out there on his own. No-one can understand how it could have happened, because he's had the boat for years, and he was an experienced sailor.

Puts the reviews for the movie into perspective, but I guess life goes on. RIP Artie. We were never what you'd call buddies, but he always watched my back. As I said, life goes on, so I'm glad you enjoyed it and I've sent you the screenplay. Just be aware that it won't tie in exactly with the cut that made it on screen. They never do, once the producers, directors, actors, editors, carpenters, special effects guys, and those fucking Wall Street suits have had their way with it (only joking), but the general sequence and the major scenes are all there.

If you've got any questions, send me a message, and I'll try to help with whatever it is you're doing. It'd be great if I was welcoming you to the Scriptwriters' Association! (Even though I may be leaving it soon. I'll be honest with you - it can be soul-destroying. You spend months/years working on something and then one of those suits decides you've wasted your time. It's funny that you're becoming interested in screenwriting just as I'm considering giving it up and taking my turn at producing The Great American Novel. Maybe we could *swap places!).*

*Stay in touch, Charlie.*

*P.S. You were asking if there'd been any strange incidents. As it happens, there's one weird guy who's been hanging around, enquiring if I'd ever been to some place where all these fictional characters hibernate between stories. He kept rambling on, talking some rubbish about pessimists, or sceptics, or something. I guess he's just another righteous junkie. This is LA, man, so it's probably not worth mentioning, but you asked!*

Barney opened the file attached to the message and sent it to print. When "Printing 1 of 134" appeared on his screen, he changed his mind and cancelled the operation. He knew from experience that the machine seemed to have been designed to run out of ink halfway through a job of this length. He scrolled down until he found Scene 46, then selected only the pages he needed. Having read the reviews of the movie, he'd already guessed what this scene was all about, but any satisfaction he felt at being proved correct could best be characterised as grim. As he'd expected, its subject was the infamous keelhauling episode.

*Great*, he thought. *Just great.* If his next Intervention was to take place here, he hoped he wouldn't manifest at the front of the queue of prisoners waiting to be dragged under the ship. He'd read enough *Boy's Own* stories about piracy on the high seas to understand what keelhauling was. However, he decided not to rely on memory and made an online search. He typed in the word "Keelhaul" and pressed enter. There was nothing there he didn't already know. The prisoner was tied to a rope, thrown overboard, pulled beneath the hull - and the keel, of course - and hauled back on board on the opposite side of the ship. Put like that, it didn't sound too deadly, if you could hold your breath for long enough, and if you didn't take into account the barnacles stuck to the bottom of the ship, ready to rip your flesh to shreds. If you somehow survived the ordeal, there'd be a good chance you'd die later from an infected wound. In this scene, Tempest Read, the captain, adopted this brutal method to execute the crew of *L'Atalante*, a French vessel that he'd captured. It had been sailing for Europe stuffed to the brim with gold and other valuables when *The Dark Angel* intercepted it and beat it into submission.

Barney finished reading the on-screen article, and he was studying the screenplay when Smith arrived. This time, he rapped on the study door before walking straight in.

'I don't understand,' Barney said. 'You can just disappear in front of me, so why can't you turn up the same way? Don't get me wrong, the last thing I want is for you to appear out of nowhere while I'm having a shower.'

'I see. Unfortunately, I'm unable to control

it to such a precise degree. I only know it will be in the general vicinity of my... subject. I'm as curious as you are as to the exact spot where I'll arrive.'

'Never mind. Any news about the mystery rifleman?'

'All I can tell you is that it was not the doing of my fellow Wardens.' Smith looked over Barney's shoulder. 'Is this the section of the story we need?'

'It is; but before we go over it, I've got a couple more questions. Charlie says that somebody's been asking him about Ancilla. Would this be the Warden you spoke about?'

'Yes, this is Newman. Mr Fairweather has been very antagonistic towards him.'

'I wonder why that is?' Barney said, sarcastically. 'Anyway, back to business. In this scene, the victims are keelhauled.' Seeing Smith's bafflement, he pointed to the screen. 'Here, read this. Does it mean they intend to kill Charlie by dragging him under a ship? Seems a bit of a stretch to me.'

Smith scanned the article in seconds. 'Probably not, but I'm sure water will be involved in some way. I understand that the producer died in a boating accident?'

'He did. So, do you think they used this same scene to get to Artie Newfield?'

'It would appear so.'

'And one other thing. How can we be certain the Assassins won't pull the same trick as in Heyton?'

'I assure you we've taken steps to ensure that our intelligence is accurate.' The cold way Smith said this gave Barney another glimpse of the iron fist that was clenched in Smith's velvet glove.

'Good. Anyway, I was scanning this before you turned up.' Barney tapped on his keyboard, and a new website appeared.

Smith read out the title. ' "*Spanish galleons of the early 18th Century*." '

'That's right. If I'm going to be wandering around on one, I thought it'd be worth getting to grips with the layout. I already knew about Heyton, and there was a map in the book, but I haven't a clue about these old sailing ships.'

Smith surprised Barney by telling him he shouldn't waste too much time doing this. 'Don't lose sight of the fact that these aren't historical situations we're dealing with, but figments of their creators' imaginations. It's more important that you're familiar with the source material as originally written by the target. As I've referred to previously, because you're writing yourself into the scene, you'll arrive there already endowed with an innate knowledge of the environment.'

'In that case, I won't bother with this.' Relieved to be told he wouldn't have to study any historical period that future Interventions might involve, Barney closed the web page. 'Shall we make a start?'

'Are you sure that you do not need more rest? Your encounters in the village must have exhausted you.'

'Do you seriously think I can sit here knowing that these bastards could come through at any time? I wouldn't feel too good if I found out Charlie had been topped while I lounged around here.'

Smith accepted this logic with a nod of understanding and reached out with his hand as Barney's fingers got to work on the keyboard.

*The Prince of Barbary, scene 46.*

*EXT. DAY. The Caribbean Sea, off the coast of Puerto Rico. The Dark Angel.*

*A few hundred yards to the rear, and receding fast, L'Atalante is listing badly and already sinking, having been boarded and scuppered by Read's crew.*

*On The Dark Angel,* **Captain Tempest Read** *is standing on the upper deck, watching events on the main deck below, where his crew are eagerly anticipating the forthcoming entertainment. The captured Frenchmen, led by* **Capitaine Julieaux***, are being escorted up from the lower decks, their eyes blinking against the bright sun. One of them sees* **Loxley** *with the keelhauling rope ready in his hands, leading the team waiting for them at the port rail, and guesses what is about to happen. He* *makes a break for it, but we hear a pistol shot and the fleeing sailor falls down, dead.*

*CUT to Read, holding the still smoking pistol. He smiles with...*

\* \* \* \* \*

# Chapter 29: The Margins - The Dark Angel, 1741

Tempest Read lowers his pistol and points at the dead sailor's body. 'Throw that shark bait overboard, and let's get on with things, shall we?'

Barney has manifested behind the captain, who is watching events down on the main deck. He steps back towards a quiet space closer to the stern. A solitary, scowling sailor, oblivious to Barney's presence, is manning the ship's wheel, stretching his neck, trying to catch a glimpse of the entertainment. High above, the sails hanging from the three masts billow in the wind. The ship sways, rolling in time with the white-flecked waves of the Caribbean Sea. Sailors are dotted here and there on the rigging, having climbed above their shipmates for a better view of the ongoing slaughter. He almost hears the stirring soundtrack of a Saturday morning pirate-adventure movie filling the surrounding air.

Now that he's gained his bearings, Barney performs an inventory on himself. He is sporting a neckerchief below a loose fitting and very uncomfortable canvas shirt. Below his waist is a wide pair of breeches that reached to just below his knees, held in place by a thick leather belt. He is barefoot, but in the circumstances, this doesn't feel odd. He notes that only the officers are wearing any kind of footwear. Boots might offer more protection, but he guesses that climbing the rigging and staying upright on deck during heavy seas must be easier in bare feet. Shirt, neckerchief, and breeches. That takes care of the clothes, but something else is bothering him, something other than the full head of hair he's grown. He is the proud owner of a pigtail. Also, his left ear lobe seems to carry a little extra weight. A quick examination with his fingers explains why. It is decorated with a gold earring!

Learning from his experience in Heyton, Barney decides that the first thing he needs to do is to arm himself.

Nearby, a set of ladders leads up to the poop deck, and behind them is a low wooden door. He bends down and goes through it, into the dim interior. The loudest sounds now are the creaking of the timbers and the lapping of the sea on the outer hull. This ship isn't huge, so it shouldn't take long to work from stern to bow and find what he's searching for. He is in a short corridor with three doors leading off it, and more steps heading further down. None of the cabins are locked. Two of these must belong to Read's lieutenants. The third is undoubtedly the captain's. It is twice the size of his officers' quarters, and with a touch of luxury to the furnishings and decorations.

He knows he can't linger here, so he heads further into the heart of the vessel, where he comes across another cabin, plainer even than the two upstairs. The bosun's, Barney thinks, digging up a memory from some old sea-faring novel he'd read years ago. If he remembers correctly, the bosun is in charge of the day-to-day tasks on board, which would account for him having his own space, on a lower deck than the captain's, on the same level as the crew's quarters. The only item of interest in here lies on the unmade cot. A scabbard, designed for a cutlass. Unfortunately, the sword itself isn't in it. Disappointed, he turns away and moved on along the corridor. He stops walking when, through the wooden wall, he hears the crash of something fall to the floor, accompanied by a loud curse. Judging by the odours, this will be the galley. Presumably all the killing will give the crew an appetite, and the cook is stuck down here preparing something to satisfy that need.

The next section of the corridor opens out into the crew's mess. Although their hammocks have been packed away for the day, one is still in place, visible in the far corner, swinging in sympathy with the rolling of the ship. Barney hears a small groan coming from that direction. Someone too sick to join in with the slaughter, he guesses. After satisfying himself he is in no danger from the stricken crewman, Barney's eyes light up as he spots something among the items under the occupied hammock. There is an assortment of clothes, a plate with some meat on, and a bucket. At the side of these are two that are of interest. A large wooden club, and a cutlass. He considers the club, then decides against it. When he finds his target, he wants to kill him, not send him to sleep. Sword now in hand, he works his way back towards the galley. The cook is still clearing up the spill. On the worktop is a selection of knives. He steps inside, taking care to avoid the kneeling sailor, chooses one that fits into his palm, and tucks it into his belt. He returns to the bosun's cabin and retrieves the empty scabbard. He inserts the cutlass and ties it around his waist.

After climbing the steps, he finds himself outside again, on the sunlit quarter deck. There is one major difference since he's been below - there are far fewer French sailors still on board. Barney feels helpless watching the massacre, but reminds himself that the only reason these characters exist is to die in this way. Charlie and Artie have seen to that.

He examines the group surrounding Read, studying them one at a time. Whatever emotion he'll experience when he discovers the Assassin, it isn't registering here. None of these seem to have what he wants. There's no avoiding it - he'll have to go down to the main deck and walk past the horrors that are taking place there. Barney is giving Read and his gang a wide berth on his way to the steps when he notices three things happen at once. There is a loud crash, audible even above the carousing; a tug on his breeches; and then the soft thud of a bullet hitting the boards beneath his feet.

He ducks behind the rail, and calculates the weapon must have been fired from somewhere above him, high on either the main- or the foremast. As the ship is in full sail, his attacker wouldn't have been able to fire an accurate shot if he'd been on the foremast. The billowing top- and mainsails would have blocked his view. Main mast it is then. Barney shields his eyes, squinting upwards. Silhouetted against the two huge sails are the figures of several crew members who haven't been invited to take part in the slaughter, but now have the consolation of watching it from a prime position. As he scans this grisly audience, a flash of light catches his eye; it is the sun reflecting off the barrel of a pistol.

He's found what he's come for.

The Assassin is already taking aim with a second weapon. He needs to find cover. If he can get down among the crowd of sailors, it will at least make him much more difficult to hit. He sprints towards the top step and takes the drop in a single leap, landing heavily on the wooden deck. Down here it is bedlam, as everyone has been drinking heavily. Barney fights his way past the indifferent crew to the base of the main mast. As he reaches it, he glances upwards, curious as to why he hasn't heard the crack of another shot. It is because there is a problem with the pistol, and the mechanism has failed. He uses this advantage by clambering up the rigging, desperate to get as close to his enemy as possible before being spotted.

Within seconds he's arrived at the level of the spar from which the largest sail hangs. The Assassin sees Barney's intention and throws the faulty pistol at him. He ducks and hears it whistle past him and hit the deck, twenty yards below. He looks up again. His enemy has turned away, climbing even higher. At some point, his foe is going to run out of rigging and will have no choice but to stand and fight. Now it is a question of manoeuvring to find the most advantageous position. He slows his ascent, giving himself a little more time to calculate his next move, when the Assassin surprises him by leaping into mid air, aiming for the undulating sail. He has a knife in his hand, and when he hits the sail, he thrusts the blade into the canvas, using it as a brake to prevent what otherwise would have been a deadly fall. Barney remembers seeing this manoeuvre in *The Prince of Barbary*, yet another scene that Charlie had pinched from those old pirate movies.

As he slides past, frustratingly out of Barney's reach, the Assassin glances over his shoulder and Barney sees triumph in eyes shining as blue as Cassidy's. He realises that, somewhere on Earth, at this very moment, a Shadow Writer is opening the Channel. If he doesn't act now, this killer will be through, with a free run at Charlie.

He takes out the knife he'd stolen from the galley and leaps onto the sail, trusting that the canvas will provide the same resistance to his blade as it did for his rival. It does, and he reaches the bottom safely, then jumps the last few feet. The Assassin is fading, preparing to leave through the widening Channel. Barney withdraws his cutlass from its sheath and takes a stride forward. He has never held a sword before, but via the magic of the Margins, he is more than comfortable handling one now. He has a practice stroke, swinging his arm in a figure of eight motion, even though he somehow knows this kind of action is more suited to a stabbing weapon such as an epee, and that this curved blade is designed for hacking. It doesn't matter. In his hands, in this place, it is just a tool for killing his enemy. The Assassin's eyes are already focusing on somewhere far beyond *The Dark Angel* and, without warning, he leaps forwards, shouting, 'For a free Ancilla!' The Assassin raises his sword and brings it down towards Barney's head. In defence, Barney lifts his cutlass, just in time to save himself from the oncoming blow. The impact reverberates along the length of his right arm, forcing him to drop his weapon. If he tries to pick the cutlass up, he'll be presenting his neck as an easy target. Then he spots the dagger lying on the floor. As he throws himself at his opponent, he scoops up the abandoned knife. They kick and punch, each determined to get the upper hand as their momentum carries them towards the short rail that runs alongside the edge of the deck. He can sense the Assassin's solid body melting as the Channel beckons him. With a sudden surge of strength, he thrusts his blade into his opponent's midriff. A brief shudder, and then nothing.

The Assassin is dead.

Exhausted, he looks around him, half expecting the crew to be gathered in a circle, watching this fight to the death that has just taken place amongst them, but not a single pirate has eyes for anything other than the keelhaulings. Some instinct tells him he shouldn't leave the body where it lays. He doesn't know why, but disposing of it seems the right thing to do. Groaning with the effort, he hoists the Assassin up against the rail, then struggles to lift the dead weight up and over it, into the waiting sea. His eyes flutter as he shuts out Tempest Read's wooden kingdom and its bloodthirsty crew, ready to begin the journey home. Little by little, the moaning of the wind and the waves recede, and there is a change in the atmosphere as he arrives in his study.

But something's wrong! He senses there is someone in the room with him, and it isn't Smith. Before he's fully returned, he feels himself being pulled back onto the ship by a woman's screams.

'Help me. Oh God, Barney, they're killing me!'

\* \* \* \* \*

# Chapter 30: Leeds

Sally put the cardboard carton down on Barney's doorstep and rang the bell. After a minute of agitated waiting, she tried again. *What if he's forgotten about her? Had he really meant it when he'd said he wanted to see the books?* She stared long and hard at her watch. Twenty past twelve, almost three hours since leaving Whitby. All that way for nothing. Sighing, she picked the box up and was about to return it to the car when the door opened a few inches. A suspicious frown appeared through the widening gap.

'Oh, hello. I'm here for Mr Granwell.' She double checked the house number pinned to the wall.

'You must be Miss Steward.' The stranger stepped forward, holding out his arms to take the box. 'I believe Barney is expecting these. My name's Smith; Barney and I have been working together and he's told me all about you.' Sally hesitated, but then, based on the theory that as this man seemed to know of her and why she was here, decided he could be trusted. Also, he seemed harmless enough. She handed it over, then followed him into the kitchen, relieved that it hadn't been a wasted journey after all. He pulled out a chair, inviting her to sit at the table. 'Barney's not available just now. He's just clearing something up in his study, but he should be free to see you soon. Help yourself to a drink.' he waved loosely in the direction of the kettle. 'Perhaps some music while you wait?' He turned the radio on and increased the volume until it was uncomfortably loud. The station was playing a rousing classical overture.

'No, I'm fine, thanks,' she said, almost having to shout. She pointed at the books. 'I'll just start putting these into some sort of order.'

'Good. Now, if you'll excuse me, I'll inform him you've arrived.' Smith left the room and disappeared through a door across the hallway. *Very formal*, Sally thought. At least she now knew he was in the building, and that she could relax.

Twenty minutes later, she was growing bored. She checked her watch again, working out how much time she'd have to spend with Barney before beginning the arduous trek back home. A long stretch of the journey between York and Whitby comprised miles of deserted moorland, and the daylight had dissipated well before she'd reached the end of the bleak emptiness. She hadn't enjoyed tackling the winding road alone in the dark, when the only illumination had been from her own headlights and those of the cars going in the opposite direction, each pair of passing lights blinding her momentarily. By the time she'd put the key in her door, the beginnings of a headache had taken hold. Today, she wanted to be inside her flat before the setting of the sun.

She switched the radio off and tried to discern any signs of a discussion taking place in the other room. These terrace houses were quite small, so at the very least, she ought to hear the low murmurings of voices, but there was nothing. Feeling like an intruder, she exited the kitchen and crossed the narrow hallway and stood still, listening intently. No normal conversation had silences that went on for this long. Had the two men nipped out for a quick pint? Annoyed now, she pushed the door open.

Barney was sitting at the desk, alone, facing his laptop. However, he wasn't actually looking at it. Sally knew this because his eyes were closed. The only movement was in his hands, which were palm down on the keyboard, jerking spasmodically.

'Barney,' she said, softly. There was no response from him. She looked down at his agitated hands and reached out to stop them from shaking. Her fingers touched his. Only for a second, but that was long enough for the Margins to leap up and claim her.

* * * * *

# Chapter 31: The Margins - The Dark Angel, 1741

The Assassin *might* have known his name, but he is dead, and besides, it is a female voice that's shouting. A young woman is being tied to the keelhaul rope, struggling against two of Tempest Read's men as they fasten their deadly knots. Then a bigger shock as he recognises the black outfit. It's Sally!

Barney sets off at a run in her direction. Expecting to move freely through the crowd of sailors, he is dumbfounded when one takes a step backwards, bumping into him and throwing him off balance. He is even more startled when the sailor turns and glares at him. Not recognising a brother buccaneer, the pirate faces up to him, a vicious-looking knife in his hand. 'Got one o' the Froggies here, lads, trying to stay dry!'

Barney is relieved to note he has returned here rearmed with both the cutlass and dagger. He pulls the sword from its scabbard. According to the unofficial rules that he and Smith had discussed, these pirates should not be aware of his presence. However, seeing the unmistakable gleam of bloodlust in their eyes, he decides this is a different game, with new rules. However, any inquiry will have to be saved for later. Right now, he is fighting for his life, and for Sally's.

One after the other they come at him, an endless stream of manic faces with swords and clubs swinging, seeking to find a weakness in his defences as he parries, slashes, and thrusts with his own blade, cutting them down one by one, their rough skills no match for his enhanced powers. The smell of gunpowder fills the air, as several of the pirates let loose with pistols, caring nothing for any of their shipmates who might be standing in their firing line. The blood of his opponents washes over the deck, but eventually, Barney tires. Over the heads of his attackers, he sees that Sally's captors, having been sidetracked for a few moments by the appearance of this madman who wants to fight the entire crew, have returned to their grizzly task. The situation has changed. Until a matter of minutes ago, he'd have assumed that, if Sally died here, it wouldn't matter too much, as she'd be fit and healthy again once she arrived home. He can no longer assume this to be the case; as there is now a genuine interaction between himself and the inhabitants of the Margins, it's possible that being injured or dying here will be mirrored back on Earth.

Not "virtual" any more.

Then Barney senses a change in the atmosphere. Another swordsman has appeared and is standing back to back with him, sharing his load. The crew's attacks prevent him from catching a sight of his comrade-in-arms, but whoever it is, he is skilled in the art of combat. Working together, they gradually gain the upper hand. He hears Sally scream again. They are about to throw her overboard. His new partner also sees what is happening. 'Go. Save her!' he shouts. Sensing Barney's hesitation, he repeats the command. 'Go, go now!'

Realising that she will perish if he doesn't act quickly, and that this mystery swordsman seems well capable of looking after himself, Barney forces one last effort from his flagging muscles, and with a few more primitive hacks, clears a route through the mob. He tosses aside his sword and jumps onto the deck rail, in time to see Sally's arms frantically waving as she disappears beneath the swirling waves. Kicking off the hands grabbing at him, he dives into the warm Caribbean Sea.

Barney has never been a keen swimmer, but at this moment, he belongs underwater. His eyesight is as good down here as it is up above. He spots Sally, fighting against the rope that is pulling her to her death. With powerful strokes, he swims through this green world until he's within a few inches of her. He draws the dagger from his waistband and cuts her free. The sight of her distressed condition gives another injection of strength to his weary muscles. With one arm around her waist, he heads towards the light shimmering above him, higher and higher, until they burst through the surface of the rolling sea, and he greedily takes in a lungful of the sweet air. *The Dark Angel* is already a hundred yards away. He can't see what's happening, but he guesses his erstwhile accomplice has sacrificed himself in exchange for Sally's life. *And mine as well*, he thinks.

But he has a more immediate concern. Sally is unconscious. He needs to get her home. He closes his eyes and prepares to leave the Margins.

Sodden Davey, watching from his perch in the Crow's Nest, is as baffled as every other person on the ship by the sudden arrival and abrupt departure of the two swordsmen who have been taking on all comers and beating them. One had dived overboard and rescued the young girl, while the other simply vanished, leaving the attacking mob slashing at empty air. Only Davey saw the girl and her guardian angel return to the surface together in the ships' wake   before they also disappeared. He considers climbing down and telling the captain what he's seen, but then he realises that Tempest Read is on the rampage, lashing out with his fists as he castigates his crew for their failure to kill the interlopers.

He fixes his sight on the horizon and concludes that some things should never be spoken of.

* * * * *

# Chapter 32: Los Angeles

While Barney was defeating the Assassin and rescuing Sally, Charlie Fairweather was in his apartment, waking from a nightmare. Shaken by its realism, he headed straight for his kitchen, desperate for coffee. He sat cradling the mug for a while as he gazed out onto the traffic on Santa Monica Boulevard.

In the dream, he'd been on the set of *The Dark Angel*, the one they'd used when shooting his screenplay for *The Prince of Barbary;* but it hadn't felt like a studio set, more an actual ship, complete with a real Captain Tempest Read strutting about the quarterdeck. Charlie often dreamt about his work, which was why he could be so sure that this episode was no such thing. He hadn't touched a drink or rolled a joint for over a week, so it wasn't the after effects of either of those pastimes. Although Charlie and Barney had only ever met face to face once - at The Sky Garden to discuss *The Seven Hells* adaptation - Charlie had *known* that the athletic character with the amazing sword skills had been the English writer. It was laughable; middle-aged, balding and overweight, a super fit swordsman Barney most definitely was not. But the most bizarre thing, and the most frightening, was to do with the man who'd been killed. He'd never been as sure of anything as of this one chilling fact; if Barney's enemy emerged victorious, his intention had been to hunt Charlie down and kill him. Not on a make-believe pirate ship in the Caribbean three centuries ago, but today, in modern Los Angeles.

He decided to give Barney a call and find out what he thought. He was still searching for his phone when he heard a rapping on his door. He opened it and his brow creased in a frown. It was his stalker from the café and the bus. Charlie wasn't in the mood. 'Listen, mister, I don't know what you're up to, but it's about time I called the cops.' He started to close the door, but the stranger blocked it with his foot. Before Charlie could say anything more, Newman reached out and touched his forehead.

*　*　*　*　*

# Chapter 33: Leeds

Barney arrived back from the Margins to find Sally lying unconscious on the floor. No longer endowed with any supernatural strength, he struggled to lift her onto the settee, where she was now sitting, safe in his study. Or as safe as she could be in the circumstances. He brought a glass of water. She took a sip and looked around, nervously seeking reassurance that she wasn't still on an eighteenth century sailing ship. Her accusing gaze returned to Barney. 'I think you've got some explaining to do,' she said.

Between them, they worked out a timetable of the events that had occurred after her arrival. 'You didn't see Smith again?' Barney asked after Sally had finished her contribution.

'No; and the kitchen door was open all the time, so I'd have seen if he'd left. I watched him walk into this room, and he didn't come out. Never mind him; what was that all about, all those pirates and the other stuff?' She held the drinking glass up high and studied it. 'There's no funny business going on, is there? You haven't drugged me or anything?'

'What? No, of course I haven't!' he said, shocked by the notion. 'I'll get to what's been happening in a minute, but first, tell me exactly what you did when you came in here.'

'You were sitting with your eyes shut, and I thought you were having some sort of fit. Your hands were shaking, so I tried to calm them down.'

'How?'

'I got hold of them.'

'You just touched me, that's all?'

'That's all. Then I was on that ship, and I'm sure I saw you, fighting with a sword. Only, it wasn't really you, but a version of you.' She peered at him again, closer this time. 'I think I'm going mad, but it *was* you, wasn't it?'

'Yes. Sounds impossible, but it was me, alright. One more question. Somebody was helping me. Could you see them?'

'No, there was too much happening.'

Barney sighed regretfully. 'I can imagine. Let's get down to it. I'll tell you everything I know about this whole thing.'

He now had a few more additions to the lengthening agenda of topics to discuss with Smith. First, where was he, and why had he abandoned the scene at such a crucial time? Second, did Sally cross into the Margins simply because she'd touched Barney's hand? Third, the ground rules within the Margins had changed again. Why, and by how much? Fourth, who was the swordsman? Could it have been the same individual who had saved him in Heyton? He needed answers to these questions, but he wouldn't be getting any until Smith returned. In the meantime, he owed Sally the explanation he'd promised. After what she'd been through, she deserved to hear everything, starting with the lynch mob in Valance, right through to her visit to *The Dark Angel.*

'I'll put the kettle on,' he said. 'This may take a while.'

\* \* \* \* \*

# Chapter 34: Leeds/ Los Angeles

He needed to tell his tale in such a way that he didn't lose any credibility in the first few sentences. However, the simple fact was that he couldn't come up with any narrative that didn't sound unbelievable from the very beginning. That being the case, he dived straight into his adventure in Valance, and was about to move on to his meeting with Khalid when his phone rang.

'Charlie, how are you?' he said, grateful for the interruption. He put the call on loudspeaker. No more secrets.

But Charlie didn't have time for any pleasantries, and his words arrived in a breathless torrent. 'This might sound crazy, but were you aboard *The Dark Angel* last night? Jesus, I can't believe what I'm saying. I had this fantastic dream. You were fighting like a madman to stop this sailor from killing me, and to save this woman who they'd tied up. I said it was a dream, but it wasn't. It was too lifelike; but if it wasn't a dream, then what was it? And I remembered those questions you've been asking, and now there's this mad guy that's been bothering me over here -'

'Whoa, slow down,' Barney broke in, 'I don't think it was a dream, either. There's someone here with me who's asking the same questions you are. If you call me straight back on video, I'll try to explain everything; it might be better if we can see each other.'

Charlie sounded frustrated. 'Don't you be disappearing on me. Not till I've got some answers.'

Within seconds, Charlie's worried face appeared on-screen. Barney introduced his two guests to each other before beginning his narrative again. 'You've heard this first bit, Sally. Let's see if it sounds any less strange the second time around - I was in the pub with a friend. Everybody was enjoying themselves until I sort of blacked out, and I was in a cowboy town, about to be hanged....' Thirty minutes later, Barney had finished talking. During his monologue, he'd given Tom's manuscript to Sally, who had scanned it and sent it to LA. He'd then shown them Zach's original Chapter 5, and pointed out the relevant differences. He asked Sally to relate her part of the story, and Charlie told of his meetings with the oddball who called himself Newman, and of his dream. The one that was too real to be a dream. 'So these Assassins kill people because of the stories they've written, and they murdered Artie because of the movies he's made?'

'That's right,' Barney answered.

'And my life's in jeopardy because I wrote the screenplay for a pirate movie?'

'Yes. Well, a very violent pirate movie, with a ton of deaths. Plus, most of the other stuff you've worked on. I've looked at your credits on-line, and there's nearly as high a body count as on mine. I know this is a lot to take in, but what if I talk to Smith, ask him to get Newman to contact you again? Maybe now you've heard my story, what he says might begin to make more sense?'

'Could be. There's one other thing I haven't told you yet. This Newman, he knocked on my door this morning, and I think he sent me to this place you're talking about.'

'The Margins? What happened?'

'He didn't say anything, just put his hand on my forehead, and I was away to Fantasy Island.' Charlie gave them a quick run down of what had happened.

Barney understood every word, because it was almost identical to what he went through the first time Smith had sent him there. Another writer - another human being - had shared his experience of that alien world! 'Can you see what I'm talking about now?'

'I'm beginning to. When I came round, I was alone again.' Charlie paused, a pensive expression growing on his face. 'Assuming there's something in all this, are you saying you risked your life to save me? Those are some balls you've got.'

But Barney wasn't holding back on the truth, not now. 'Sorry to disappoint you, but the fact is, I didn't think I was risking anything. Both Smith and I assumed I'd return unhurt, like I did after I was stabbed in the village. Even after I'd been shot there, I only ended up with a bruised arm, but things changed after Sally turned up there. When I returned to the ship, the crew could see me, and I knew that if I died this time, it would be the end for me. Sally as well; she was in serious trouble for a while.'

Sally nodded in agreement. 'I've never felt as bad; I thought I was dying. It was terrible.'

Charlie sat back, trying to take everything in. If Barney had called him twenty four hours ago with his story, he'd have slammed his phone down and made sure the mad English guy didn't come anywhere near him ever again. However, after his own experiences, he was already half way to accepting it before hearing a single word. He was now filled with a mixture of wonder and fear. The wonder came from the possibility of a new world opening up for him. That someone had been sent to execute him accounted for the fear, but these emotions were joined by a third one: outrage. He was incensed that a stranger had been en route to kill him - Charlie Fairweather, whose only crime was entertaining movie goers! So outraged was he in fact, that he wasn't prepared to put up with it, especially after taking into consideration the sheer high he'd enjoyed in this place that Barney called the Margins. He could do with some more of that. It had been better than any of the many drugs he'd tried over the years. He came to a decision; what had he got to lose? If this was a drug-induced fantasy, then let's go along and enjoy the ride. Also, if there was even a glimmer of truth in it, he wasn't hanging around for these murderers to show up in LA.

'I don't know why I'm taking this seriously, but something tells me I ought to. If this is all true, they'll keep coming for me, won't they? Do you reckon Newman can show me all the things that Smith showed you?' An earnest look filled Charlie's face. 'Say, do you reckon we'll be able to work together in there, like you and the mystery guy?'

Before Barney could answer, Sally had her say.'Me, too - I'm in as well!'

'Hold on a second. Whether he wants it or not, Charlie's implicated anyway, but there's no reason for you to be a part of this.'

'You can't tell me all this and expect me to go home and forget about it.' She'd listened as the writers had related their experiences, and realised that her own involvement was pretty mundane compared to what these two had been through. She could walk away from this right now if she chose to, and carry on with her life.

But things had changed. Going back to work in the supermarket and filling shelves would no longer be enough for her. She wanted to be involved, and nothing Barney could say would put her off.

The more Barney considered Charlie's proposition, the more he liked it. The thought of having a partner to share the load provided him with a thrill of excitement. Sally was another matter, though. She was only what? Twenty four, twenty five? He'd already been feeling guilty for asking her to drive alone across the country just to bring some old books - books that he was sure he'd have been able to find himself, given a little time. Did she truly understand the dangers involved? But, she was an adult, capable of making her own decisions. Who was he to prevent her from playing a part?

'Hello. LA calling Barney Granwell.'

Barney brought his attention back into the room. 'What? What were you saying?'

'We were speaking about Smith. Has he done this before? Disappeared for no obvious reason?'

'Oh, yes. Then he'll appear again when you're least expecting it.' He stopped talking because Charlie was open mouthed and pointing over Barney's shoulder. He was about to turn around to find out what was so fascinating when he heard a familiar voice.

'Hello Barney. I see you have company. I

believe I know who your two friends are. Am I to assume you've taken them into your confidence?'

*   *   *   *   *

# Chapter 35: Leeds/ Los Angeles/Whitby

It was Smith. Barney couldn't help but wonder if the Warden had been listening to them talk, biding his time somewhere in the ether, before manifesting in the room. 'You're back! And yes, I've told them everything. Obviously, that doesn't include why you disappeared during an Intervention.'

'I'm sorry about that, but I'll explain shortly. First, I must tell you we should leave here,' Smith said.

'Run away again? Why?'

'There have been more changes on Ancilla. Cassidy has risen through the ranks, and his influence is considerable. He's taken your survival as a black mark against his personal reputation, and your ending is now a priority for him.'

Barney held his hands wide and raised his eyebrows. *So what's new?* 'If you're sure,' he said reluctantly, 'but there's something you need to know before we do anything.'

'What is it?'

'It was different in there this time. Very

different.'

'How?'

'Me and the Assassin fought, and I killed him. As you'd expect, nobody on the ship knew we were there, even though we were right amongst them; and when Sally appeared, it was different again.'

'What?' Smith was aghast. 'You were *both* in there? How did this happen?'

Barney related everything that had taken place since Sally's arrival in Leeds, and how the crew of *The Dark Angel* had become aware of his presence. He followed this by telling of the appearance of his mysterious ally, and then Charlie's nightmare.

'The accomplice who fought alongside you - could he have been the one who saved you in the village?' Smith asked.

'I didn't see either of their faces, but I got the feeling it was. I can't explain what, but something about him seemed familiar.'

'The Assassins are making more progress than we suspected. This only strengthens the argument for moving on.'

Barney wasn't going to argue; he knew Smith wouldn't be talking this way without good reason. 'Alright, I need to get out of here, but where? Big cities are the best places to disappear into, so maybe Manchester or Glasgow? Not London, at least not yet.'

'You could leave the country; go abroad.'

Sally suggested.

'No. I'd create too much of a paper trail, what with buying tickets and going through passport control. It'd be the same with somewhere remote. The Shetlands, for instance. Somebody new in an area like that's bound to attract attention.'

A brief contemplative silence was broken by Sally. 'What about Whitby? You don't have any connection to it, do you? And it's full of tourists, even in September, so you wouldn't stand out.'

'I suppose it might do until I figure out somewhere more permanent.'

'You shouldn't consider that anything in your life will be permanent for some time yet,' Smith warned.

'I'm beginning to understand that. Whitby's a possibility, then; but if it's so busy, will I find a room?'

'There are always some cancellations, and you could even stay with me if need be,' Sally said. 'Sleeping on the couch,' she added.

Barney smiled at her discomfort. 'Actually, I'm familiar with the place. We had a family holiday there when I was a kid. I always wanted to go back with Lucy, but we never got around to it.' Some long-lost connection with this childhood memory made his mind up for him. 'Whitby it is, then; and if I'm going to on the move, one suitcase will have to do.'

A metallic voice emerged from the laptop speakers. 'Hello...hello...anybody remember me?' It was Charlie. 'Where do I come in? Will they be coming after me again?'

Smith peered down at the screen. 'Yes, but not straight away. One of the few things we have in our favour is that, until their new recruits are fully trained, their resources are limited. However, it won't be long before they have a sufficient number, and when they do, I'm afraid some will be sent to seek you out.'

It sounded like this was what Charlie had been hoping to hear. 'Good. So when can Newman start my training?'

'Training?' Smith sounded puzzled.

Barney began to explain. 'These two both want to be involved. Now, before you say anything to try to stop them -'

'Stop them! Why would I do that? We need all the help that is available. It would delight me to welcome you both to the fight.'

'Great, the sooner the better. I can't wait to get in there and kick some ass,' Charlie said.

'Kick some...?'

Barney came to Smith's rescue again. 'It means he wants to give them a taste of their own medicine. Beat them at their own game.'

Smith was impressed. 'Very good. It's only by taking this attitude that we can have any hope of success.' He turned to Sally. 'And as for your involvement, we should discuss the options during our journey. I'm afraid we may have already lingered here too long, and now we must be away.'

Charlie signed off after being reassured that Newman would be in touch. Sally packed up all the paperwork from the desk, along with the books and magazine cuttings that she'd brought from home. Barney disappeared upstairs and returned with the promised single suitcase. When they were all out on the street, he locked the door, then pushed the key through the letterbox. He'd sort the rent out with the landlord later. In the meantime, he had things on his mind other than who was putting the rubbish bin out for collection.

Barney climbed into the passenger seat of Sally's car, while Smith struggled into the back.

'I take it you've never been in one of these before?' Barney asked, after noting Smith's awkward entrance. 'You'll get used to it soon enough. If I can adapt to everything that's been going on, you won't have a problem with things like this. So - what's the plan for Sally?'

On the journey, Barney decided it might be a good idea to learn something about his young companion. They were on the run from alien killers together, but he knew nothing of her background. He started by telling her about his own current, soon to be non-marital situation, then pressed her for a few facts about herself.

'I grew up in Middlesbrough. Youngest of

three sisters. The other two married well, as Jane Austen would say, and now one lives in Paris, and the other one's in London. They're both living the high life. There again, so am I, four floors up in a single person's flat in down town Whitby.'

'How did you end up there?'

'Goth Week, simple as that. I loved the music and the look. Me and a mate came down three or four years ago for it. Michelle went back, but I stayed, got a job in a supermarket. I just loved the atmosphere, and I fitted in. In Middlesbrough, I could tell everybody thought I was an oddball.'

Barney grinned, but not before checking that she was being light hearted.

By the time they arrived at the outskirts of Whitby, dusk was falling, and the three of them had reached a decision on Sally's involvement. They agreed she wouldn't be going into the Margins again. Her task now comprised researching the authors that were on the first List - other than Charlie and Helen Barron - to find out if anything untoward had happened to them. She was also charged with keeping a record of events. The more information they could pull together, the more prepared they'd be. Sally then made a few calls, and found her promised cancellation on the fourth attempt - a self-contained apartment in the old part of town.

'Will you be staying for a while this time?' Barney asked Smith as they drove into a car park near the harbour. Sally steered into a space and switched the engine off before turning to see why the question hadn't been answered. Once again, Smith had disappeared without warning.

'He's gone! But we haven't stopped for miles. Did he jump out when I slowed down, or...?'

Barney laughed. 'It's like I said to him earlier. You'll get used to it. This is just how it seems to work. I don't know if he has a choice when they call him back, but he doesn't always announce it. Don't worry about it, he'll reappear when he's ready. Anyway, how far am I from my new home?' He took his suitcase from the boot while Sally paid for a parking ticket. They walked side by side down the narrow cobbled lane towards The Porthole, the wine bar above which was the apartment. She helped him to steer through the holiday drinkers in the lounge area and introduced Barney to the manager. Getting to his room meant going back out to the street and up the small alley that ran alongside the building. They climbed the stone steps leading up to the first-floor flat, then said their goodnights, with Sally promising to return in the morning to give him the guided tour of the town. Barney waited until she was out of sight, then walked downstairs and into the bar. He was in need of a smoke and a beer to help him sleep.

\* \* \* \* \*

# Chapter 36: Whitby

He woke early but dry-mouthed, the result of several nightcaps. Nothing he wasn't used to, though. He felt better after his nicotine fix, taken outside the open apartment door. He went back inside and had a look around. A single bedroom, a bathroom, and a living area with a television, three-piece suite and a table. As usual, Smith had given no indication as to when he'd be returning, so Barney decided to take advantage of his free time by getting some fresh air before lunch, then making a start on analysing the List with Sally in the afternoon. Registering the day's first pangs of hunger, he dressed and left the flat. He was pleasantly surprised to find The Porthole had transformed from evening wine bar to daytime café, and that breakfast was available.

A busy waitress guided him to a table and handed him a menu, on the back of which was printed a brief account of its past. In a previous life, The Porthole had been a pub named The Barque. The owners seemed proud of the fact that, unlike some of the bars over in the newer part of town, many of which were converted shop premises, it had kept its ancient atmosphere simply by not messing with the layout. From the main entrance, a narrow corridor offered the option of drinking or eating in a choice of lounge, which also contained the only bar, or one of four tiny snugs. The early morning sounds of quiet conversation and the jangle of cutlery on plates had replaced the alcohol fuelled bonhomie of the previous evening. While he worked his way the through the huge fry up he'd ordered, he scanned the flyers that he'd found on a stand in the doorway. Several of them shared the same potted history of the town.

*Whitby is a fishing port with an intriguing past and a modern, flourishing tourist trade. There's something here for everyone. Separated by the River Esk, there are two distinct parts. On one bank lies the old town, complete with the towering Abbey ruins, which date to the seventh century, and the world famous 199 steps leading up to them. On the other is the more recent part (although even this area began to be developed for visitors as far back as the Georgian period). For traditional holidaymakers, the beach comprises three miles of golden sand, running up to the aptly named nearby village of Sandsend.*

*If it's frights you're after - why not give the Dracula Experience a go?*

*And after a long walk on the sands or over the many footpaths covering the surrounding country-*

*side, every visitor knows the correct way to refuel: Fish and Chips, made with the freshest cod or haddock imaginable!*

As the waitress removed his empty plate from the table, Barney asked her for directions to The Old Town Hall, where he and Sally had arranged to meet. They must have passed it last night, as it was only fifty yards away, back over the ancient cobbles. Outside, the narrow street was cloaked in the shadows of buildings that, according to the leaflets, had been standing there for at least two hundred years. As he walked, he examined the tourists who were meandering between the same shop windows they'd probably gazed blankly into yesterday and the day before, filling the vacant hours of their holiday by planning a trip to the beach, or deciding where they were buying today's fish and chips from. In his present frame of mind, it seemed to him that the Margins were more real than this.

The Old Town Hall didn't look like any civic building that Barney had seen before. Everything about it was modest, to put it kindly. Only two storeys high, he estimated it to be about ten yards wide by ten long, and even then, only the upper floor would have been of much use for council business, as the lower section was open to the elements and partly filled by thick columns supporting the room above it. Presumably, this extra space had been needed to accommodate more traders in times gone by, because the market square in front of it was also the smallest he'd ever come across. He was pondering the impracticality of such a small edifice in such a cramped place when Sally arrived.

'It's lovely on this side of the river, isn't it?' she said.

'Is it? I haven't seen anything yet; I've been waiting for your inside information.'

Barney was pleased he'd invested some time in reading the brochures over breakfast, as Sally's promised tour consisted of her pointing beyond the harbour and announcing that her flat was 'over there somewhere', before turning around to face the opposite direction, and saying, 'That's where the abbey is, at the top of the hundred and ninety-nine steps. You can see everything from up there.'

Barney suggested that might be a good place to start, but he was soon reminded of his earthly limitations; unfortunately, he'd brought none of the advantages he gained in the Margins home with him but had reverted to being an unfit, overweight fifty-year-old who had to stop and catch his breath after only a few minutes on the steps.

'Are you alright? There's a bench just ahead.'

'I will be. Just give me a minute.' Barney sat down and studied the vista. 'You were right; this is some view.'

Sally started to talk about the town's association with Dracula, but after a few brief moments, she wanted to move on. The memories of being up here with Henry were becoming all too real. 'Are you ready to go again?' she asked.

Climbing at Barney's steady pace, they reached the final step, and the grounds of St. Mary's church. After a quick circuit of the ancient building, Barney was eager to carry on. He spotted a footpath sign declaring Robin Hood's Bay to be six miles distant. He pointed up at the finger post. 'So it's somewhere down there, is it? The place where Henry was pushed off?'

'Yes; we were about two thirds of the way along when it happened.'

Now he'd managed the steps and gained his second wind, Barney gave some thought to a new plan. Six miles wasn't that far, was it? Only three hours, and they'd be in Robin Hood's Bay in time for lunch, and then catch a bus back to Whitby before starting work on the List this afternoon. He was about to suggest this to Sally when something in her demeanour stopped him. She was staring out to sea. He followed her gaze, curious to see what had caused her change of mood. Where a minute ago there had been nothing but an endless combination of clear blue sky and calm water, a giant bank of fog was rolling in.

'Where did that appear from?' Barney could feel the atmosphere around him growing cold and damp.

'It's a sea fret. They come out of nowhere.' There was still a distance in Sally's eyes. Her mind was in some other place, at some other time. 'I think we should go back now,' she said, turning towards the steps.

Barney took in the sign, the footpath, the incoming cloud and, understanding what had just happened, walked after her as she retreated from the memory of Henry Hirst's violent demise.

\* \* \* \* \*

# Chapter 37: Whitby

Back at his apartment, Barney picked up the first List, and they got down to business. 'Who's at the top?' he asked, before answering his own question. 'Actually, that's Charlie and his screenplay, but we know all about that, don't we? And we can also draw a line through Helen Barron for the time being. Next is Harald Mans. What's his situation?'

Sally typed Harald's name into the search bar of her browser. 'Oh God!' She leaned back, as though the extra distance between herself and the screen could lessen the impact of what she was seeing.

'What is it? Did they get to him?'

'Yes, it's awful. He was on a camping holiday with his brother, and one morning he wasn't in his tent. They found his body a mile away. He'd been hacked to death.' White-faced, she looked up. 'I'm sorry. Even after what happened on that ship, I don't think I've been taking this as seriously as I should have been.'

'Are you sure you want to go on?'

Sally wasn't sure whether Barney meant

going on with this exercise or with the whole thing. Either way, it was the same answer. She drew a deep breath, steadying herself. 'Yes, I do. Who's next?'

Next was Alfie Lawrenson, and it only took a few more keyboard strokes for them to discover that he too had died. This was after being bitten by a poisonous spider in his hometown of Melbourne in Australia.

'But couldn't it have been an accident?' Sally asked, still trying to avoid the terrible truth about the vengeful efficiency of the Assassins. Barney responded by opening a file on his laptop. He turned it around so she could see the screen. It was one of the e-books he'd bought when Smith had brought this List.

'Here we are. Chapter 65 of *Stalag Tarantula*. I can tell you what it's about. Alfie created this future world in another universe. Giant spiders are in charge, and humans are their slaves. This book's about the prisons on that planet, where they send any inmates who've tried to escape. Anyway, as part of the punishment, they're used in experiments to find the quickest and least messiest way of annihilating the human race. In this chapter, they inject some prisoners with a deadly poison they've developed.'

'So you're saying that's why Alfie died like he did? You don't think it could have been a coincidence?'

'Go back to the news piece about Harald. You said they hacked him to death, but can you find a report with more detail?'

Sally searched for Harald Mans again, and after one or two false starts, Barney saw from the expression on her face that she'd come across a site containing a more graphic description.

'Before you say anything, let me guess. Did they use a machete on him?'

She nodded yes.

'Was his head hacked off while he was still alive?' Another nod. 'And were the fingers on his right hand chopped off?' He didn't need to wait for an answer. 'I thought so. That's what happens to a party of explorers in the jungle in *The Lost Palace of El Dorado,* Harald's book. In chapter 34, to be exact. So, no, I don't think the way Alfie died was a coincidence.'

After waiting for Sally to gather herself, they made another attempt at solving the riddle of why Kate Mulholland was on the List, despite dying several years ago. Having failed to come up with either a solution or to track down a copy of *Deadly Falls The Rain* for sale anywhere online, they decided it was time for some food. They needed to refuel.

Walking across town, they passed three wine bars that must have been amongst the ones mentioned in The Porthole's potted history. They all had large windows that covered most of their outer wall, giving those inside an excellent prospect of the harbour, and anyone passing by an equally fine view of the diners. He wasn't in the mood to be watched while he ate. Was he being paranoid again? No. He hadn't appreciated that kind of modern design even before he was being hunted by trained off-world killers. They finally settled on a secluded pub, well off the tourist trail.

\* \* \* \* \*

# Chapter 38: Whitby

Smith was waiting for them when they returned to the apartment. Wasting no time on greetings, he confirmed he had the second List, and that neither Barney nor Charlie were on it. He said Charlie would probably be on the next one, when his turn came around again.

'What about me?' Barney asked.

Smith wasn't encouraging. 'After his failures with you so far, perhaps he is planning something special? Let's just be grateful that you aren't in immediate danger. You now have the chance to build on your experience, and be all the stronger when your time comes.' He produced three sheets of paper and placed them on the table.

*Planning something special; When your time comes.* Barney didn't like the offhand way that Smith had spoken, but he *was* encouraged by the thought of being stronger when it mattered. He looked at the pages. 'There must be thirty names on here. We can't be expected to deal with them all, surely?'

Smith reached over, separated the first

sheet and gave it back. There were only four lines on this one. 'These are ours. The rest are being taken care of by other Wardens. However, I wanted you to see the full scale of the problem that we face as the number of targets continues to grow. Also, as you've reported, conditions have changed. I've discovered that, if you die in the Margins, it will almost certainly mean you die on Earth. This being the case, I understand if you choose to reconsider your involvement.'

'I don't need to do that; I'm going to see this through. What the...! Why is Mary on here; and Robin? What's going on? She's not a writer, and I can't recall there ever being a violent death in any of Robin's novels. Certainly not in this one, *The Last Place We Look.* It's about relationships, and that's always been his subject.' He couldn't hide the anxiety in his voice

'I assumed you'd be alarmed by this. We're investigating this apparent anomaly. Also, as you may have noticed, Robin Wylder doesn't have an associated chapter attached; something else we're looking into. Also, note the title that is alongside Mary Ashton's name,' Smith said.

'*Deadly Falls The Rain.* But that was on the first List, wasn't it? Kate Mulholland wrote it, and we know she's already dead. What's Mary got to do with it?'

'It seems she's gained the rights to this novel, along with several other out of print works, and means to republish them in what she intends to call the *Forgotten Gems* range. As it will result in a fresh wave of Ancillans disappearing, in the eyes of the Skeptics, she'll be as responsible for their deaths as the original author.'

'Shit!' Barney frowned in disbelief. 'These other two, Patrick Lavery and Jack Burns; I recognise their names, but that's all. I don't know anything about them, so I'm not going to concern myself with strangers before my friends. But how do I choose which one to save first, Mary or Robin?'

'Because of the lack of a chapter for Robin Wylder, I believe we must focus our immediate energies on Mary Ashton.'

Barney nodded in agreement. 'I think you're right, but we still haven't got Mullholland's book. We searched online again, but couldn't find it.'

'You'll have to call Mary,' Sally said.

'What, and tell her to watch her back because these alien fiends are out to kill her?'

'No, to ask for the novel. Can't you persuade her to email a proof copy? Make up some excuse about how somebody told you she's publishing it, and you've always wanted to read it.'

Sally was right. If Barney was going to save Mary, he needed the book, and to get it, he had to give to Mary a good reason for her to send it. He made the call. After listening for five minutes as Mary gave him a verbal lashing for not getting in touch, Barney said he'd heard a whisper that she was planning a new series. *Forgotten Diamonds*, or some such, and that among the titles was one by Kate Mulholland.

'That's right; it's a gangster novel, typical Mulholland. Set in 1930s' Chicago, Valentine's Day Massacre, gang warfare, bent cops and all that. Hit men and slayings by the dozen. Why are you so interested?'

'Nostalgia, I suppose. I read it years ago, and it's stayed with me. I've got an itch to try it again, to see what was so special about it.'

Mary had already lost interest in his reasons. 'You can do a bit of proof reading while you're at it. And speaking of hearing a whisper, a little bird tells me you're thinking of dabbling in scriptwriting?'

'Where did you get that from?' Charlie must have mentioned it to someone in LA, and it had somehow made it all the way across the Atlantic and right into Mary's office.

'Oh, just the agent's grapevine, dear. I'm sure I don't have to remind you that you owe me another four *Seven Hells* books before you consider a career change?'

'No problem. I'll soon be back on schedule with them,' Barney lied.

Mary asked a few more general questions about how he was getting on before saying goodbye, but not before he made sure that she'd pressed the send button while she was still on the line. He opened the email, then the attached file. Fortunately, in addition to the text of the novel, Mary had included the notes that had already been written by one of her team of readers. At least he could now have a quick overview before concentrating on Chapter 14.

'Won't Charlie need it?' Sally said.

'He will.' Barney forwarded the file to Los Angeles, then looked at Smith. 'You said you'd ask your Warden friend to contact him. How quickly can you do that?'

'Newman has already seen to it.'

'Okay. How do we synchronise our arrival? What about the time difference between here and Los Angeles?'

'All you need to know is that Charlie will manifest at a similar moment to yourself.'

Barney accepted this without further discussion. If he asked for a detailed explanation of everything that was going on, he wouldn't have time to actually do anything. He sent a copy of Kate's book over to Sally's laptop so they could both get to grips with it. Two pairs of eyes might see something that one pair missed.

Before they started reading, Sally spoke out. 'I've been thinking. Maybe I should give Colin a ring, ask if TVV have found anything else out about the writers?' She looked to Barney for confirmation, which he gave with a slight nod of the head. *And three pairs are better than two*, he thought. She retreated to a quiet corner to make the call.

The reader's notes told them there wasn't much more to the book than Mary's terse description had provided. As she'd said, it was set in Chicago, not long after The Valentine's Day Massacre. Gang warfare and bent cops. She was right about the brutality; it was the story of the battle between two gangs, the Irish Boys and the Italian Family, for control of the illegal liquor market, and of the men-in-blue's struggle to stop the resulting bloodshed. Chapter 14 involved a raid on The Diamond Club, and the ensuing shootout. Kate Mulholland had imagined a gunfight in a speakeasy between a renegade police squad and cold-blooded killers belonging to the worst crime family in town. Barney could see what had attracted the Skeptics to this chapter. The shootout took place in a crowded room that was packed with politicians and the elite of Chicago society. It began with Sergeant Rafferty briefing his team. Rafferty was obeying orders from his real paymaster, Sean Kilbride, the leader of The Boys. The Family oversaw security at the club. If there was ever such a thing as a recipe for a high body count, this was it.

Sally ended her call. 'Colin's just been updating his database. He already had Alfie Lawrenson and Harald Mans on there, and now he's adding a few others. Can I have the full List?' she asked. Smith handed it over.

'According to TVV, four of them have been killed in the last two days. Colin and his team still believe it's the work of a gang of serial killers, though.' She marked the names of the newly deceased writers with a pen, then passed the sheet to Barney, who read them out.

'Andre Duras, Lee Sangwha, Tomas Garcia Juarez, Amrita Gupta. I think this means we have to get on with it. Smith, can you try to find out about Robin's missing chapter while I'm gone?'

'I'll do my utmost,' the Warden replied.

'Good. Are we ready, then? Let's crack on.'

Cassidy had christened him Bill Gardner when Tom had revised *The Angry Sun*, so that was the name he'd use for this Intervention. He now felt strong enough to decide on his character in the story, and how he'd be armed. He peered at Kate Mullholland's words on the page and started typing them out, immersing himself in her world.

*Deadly Falls The Rain - Chapter 14*

*Sergeant Rafferty hammered his lectern with the palm of his hand. 'Settle down and stop your chinwagging. You'll be needing all your energy, so don't be wasting it.'*

*The room quietened. An air of excitement replaced the nervous chatter of twenty hardened cops. They all knew the background. This wasn't any ordinary raid on just another illegal drinking den, because The Diamond Club was anything but just another drinking den. It was run by the meanest gang of mobsters in the state. Tonight, the place would be crowded with the cream of Chicagoan society and bigwigs from City Hall, most of them in the pockets of The Family, and every one of them blatantly ignoring the law for the sake of a few illicit drinks and a Sunday morning headache.*

*After this evening, The Family would lose their influence over the decision makers that ran Chicago. There would be a vacuum at the top, ready to be filled by The Boys' political puppets. Rafferty and his cops knew that, if they wanted to hold on to their bonuses, they had to make sure the raid was a success. Everyone in the room was cradling a Thompson submachine gun in their arms, a companion piece for their holstered pistol.*

*Bill Gardner was sitting alone, similarly armed, and ready for whatever the night threw his way.*

Barney could feel Smith's eyes on him as he typed this last sentence. Too late for explanations now, though, as the Warden's touch worked its magic, and Barney drifted away from Whitby, into the Chicago of 1930, and the precinct station...

\* \* \* \* \*

# Chapter 39: The Margins - Chicago, 1930

Sergeant Rafferty is outlining the plan of attack. Barney sneaks a downward glance; he is wearing the uniform of the Chicago Police Department. His peaked cap lay on his lap, and his Thompson machine gun is on the empty chair beside him. He senses the welcome surge of youthful energy tingling in his muscles. Because the real meat of this episode occurs at The Diamond Club, he is certain this will be where he'll find the Assassins, but he has no way of knowing where Charlie might turn up. He isn't in the squad room, anyway.

'Owens, McQuinn, O'Hara, Brennan, Pearson - you're the team leaders. The motors are out back waiting for us. We scare the bejesus out of the toffs, then smash the joint so bad they'll never open it again; and remember, no fireworks.' A dissatisfied murmur ripples around his men. With a cynical grin, Rafferty continues, 'But if you feel you have no choice, make sure those Italian greaseballs don't realise what hit 'em!' Barney wonders if he should join in the cheer that greets this battle cry. The place is emptying. Does he follow everyone out and try to slip unnoticed into one of the cars? The answer comes when the one called Brennan shouts out. 'Gardner, pull your socks up. We don't want to miss the fun and games, do we?'

Writing himself in here as Bill Gardner seems to have worked. He's arrived as a bona fide character within the story. He places the cap on his head, tucks the Tommy Gun under his arm, and follows the other policemen out of the station. Minutes later, they're speeding through the streets of Chicago, sirens howling, heading for the club.

The 18th Amendment of the Constitution of the United States, otherwise known as The Volstead Act, came into effect on the 17th of January 1920. The Act prohibited the manufacture, transportation, and sale of intoxicating liquor, in a vain effort at promoting the virtues of temperance. However, from behind the counter, where Charlie is busy serving copious amounts of said intoxicating liquor, it looks to him as if everybody is still partying like it was 1919.

He'd arrived in the Margins in a storage area, sharing a break with Butch, a fellow barman. He knows he is a drinks server because he's wearing the same outfit as his smoking buddy. A white shirt with sleeves rolled up to the elbows, bow tie, black trousers, and a waist-toshin apron. Neither of their aprons are as white as their shirts, covered as they are in the various stains that accumulate during a few hours of pouring out intoxicants in a busy bar. The Diamond Club is no back street operation. High and wide, this main room reminds Charlie of photographs he's seen of the First Class dining rooms aboard The Titanic. It is sumptuously decorated, with three enormous chandeliers hanging above the patrons, most of whom are relaxing in plush red velvet seats as they enjoy their illicit hooch. The customers themselves are as swish as the ornamentation. Many of the men are dressed in penguin suits, while their wives - companions might be a more accurate word - are turned out in the latest fashions. Flapper costumes and headbands are everywhere, and some of the earrings being worn almost match the chandeliers for sparkle. A female singer, backed by a four piece jazz outfit, is on the small bandstand in a corner, providing the accompaniment to the party.

Being here is everything Charlie had hoped it would be. As Barney had discovered, it was like being immersed in the most realistic video game imaginable, with his strength and vitality points topped up to maximum. He is woken from his reverie by a supervisor banging on the surface of the counter with his fist. 'Hey you! Stop staring into space. There're waiters with orders that need filling down there!'

'No probs. I mean, sure thing, boss,' he splutters as he sets off for the other end of the long bar. He's only half way there when the music grinds to a halt, each instrument in turn fading to silence. The reason for the change in mood is that a uniformed cop has climbed onto the stage. Fifteen or sixteen other representatives of the constabulary have taken up positions around the surrounding walls, all of them heavily armed. One of them is surreptitiously trying to attract Charlie's attention. It's Barney! They acknowledge each other with a shake of the head, indicating that neither of them has come across their target yet.

Sergeant Rafferty strides to the front of the stage, elbowing the singer out of his way. 'Good evening, ladies and gentlemen. I hope that you're all having a pleasant time.' The sudden realisation of what is taking place washes over the gathering. Several of the drinkers jump to their feet, knocking chairs over, and move towards the exits. No-one gets very far before being ordered back to their seats by members of Rafferty's squad. The noise is now louder than before, and Rafferty has to shout to be heard. 'Sit down! The sooner we clear this up, the sooner you all get to go home.'

Reluctantly, everyone returns to their tables. The air is saturated with a series of indignant clichés; 'Do you know who I am?'; 'Who's in charge here?'; 'I'll be taking this to the Mayor in the morning!' *You don't have to wait until morning*, Charlie thinks - Butch has told him the Mayor is playing poker with his cronies in a private place somewhere in the depths of the building. Once he can be heard again, Rafferty continues. 'If everybody stays calm and does what I ask, you can all be off to your beds.' The sergeant is enjoying his moment in the spotlight. A room full of toffs and wealthy citizenry hanging on to his words, and none of them will dare to complain to the Chief of Police tomorrow. And what if they do? They'll be in for a shock, as the brains controlling this entire operation is the Chief himself.

Ten or twelve men are sitting together in an alcove. Charlie has the impression this is a stag party, one in its very early stages, because it is the only section of the club with no women present. Nor are they wearing the shocked expressions that are fixed on the faces of most of the other patrons. They've been expecting the raid. They stand as one and push the tables over. They all then disappear behind the flimsy barrier before resurfacing, each of them now armed with a machine gun. They must be members of The Family, forewarned by some copper with a loose tongue, planted here ready to take action. Without a word of warning, they fire their weapons, spraying a salvo of bullets into the crowd.

The room that had been tight with tension explodes into chaos.

On the bandstand, Sergeant Rafferty's

body crashes to the floor, bleeding from the bullet holes that perforate his uniform. Policemen are now also shooting in all directions. Trigger fingers twitch, firing .45 calibre slugs, indiscriminate in their choice of target. Within seconds, the area is a hell-hole, filled with screaming men and women as round after round of hot metal thuds into the soft, yielding flesh of the cream of Chicago society. Before ducking down, Charlie scans the room for Barney, but can't see him. What if he's been killed in the onslaught? He's not ready to fight the Assassins alone, no matter what new powers he's gained. He's about to peer over the bar, desperate for a sight of his companion, when he feels a pull on his shoulder.

'Stay down! Do you want your brains blowing out?'

'Barney! How did you get over here in one piece?' They are both shouting, battling the barrage of noise.

'I put my head down and hoped for the best. I don't think the Assassins are in here. We'll have to go looking for them.'

'What about everybody out there? It's a massacre. Can't we do anything to stop it?'

'Like what? Remember, this is the only reason they even exist. Come on, let's go.' Still crouching, Barney leads the way. When they reach the hatch, he points at the door leading to the kitchens. 'We'll have to get through there and start searching the back rooms, so let's make a run for it. On three then. One, two, three!'

They crash into the corridor as breathless as if they've just won gold and silver medals in the hundred yard dash. Barney slams the door shut, then grabs a chair and jams it beneath the handle, blocking it for a few seconds at least. He helps Charlie to stand. 'That won't keep them out for long. Let's get moving before -'

'Granwell? Is that you?' A cop has appeared further down the corridor. It's Brennan, one of Rafferty's team leaders. 'We've got some of the Eyeties cornered. Get down here and help.' Although it sounds like an invitation, Brennan is pointing his Colt Official at them. Something else is also making Barney uneasy: Brennan had called him Granwell!

The policeman realises the mistake and his face takes on a different expression. 'Okay, let's cut the bullshit. Get in here.' He waves his revolver towards the room he appeared from. 'There's some guys in there want to ask you a few questions.'

Their hands raised, the Scribes walk in and are confronted by a pair of powerful looking men. Even if they weren't aiming revolvers at the two Scribes, their uncannily blue eyes identify them as Assassins. One is wearing an evening suit, collar and tie unfastened, for all the world a high-roller taking a break from the roulette table. The other is in a policeman's uniform.

'Sit down. We want some answers before

we kill you.' Evening Suit says this as casually as if he's interviewing someone for a job as a checkout assistant. There are two empty chairs in which Barney and Charlie are told to sit, and Brennan is ordered to tie their hands behind their backs.

'Because we *are* going to kill you,' the Cop says, 'but not until we get some answers. You'll be surprised by how much pain we can fit into the rest of your life - what's left of it. As for you, thank you for your assistance.' He looks over at Brennan, raises his revolver and fires. Brennan slumps to the ground, his dead eyes still wide open in surprise. Even under the circumstances, Barney can't help thinking that this Assassin has just done the very thing he's supposed to be fighting against, as yet another Ancillan won't be returning home.

Barney has known for a while that every visit to the Margins might be courtesy of a one-way ticket; he'd just hoped to inflict a lot more damage on the Skeptics' cause before making his last trip. 'How did you recognise me?' he asks, hoping to delay the inevitable moment when either he or Charlie gives Smith and Newman up. 'Tell me that first, and then I'll talk.'

'We're doing the asking, you're doing the telling.' The Cop is angry.

Evening Suit holds his hand up to his colleague. 'No reason for him not to know. You're near the top of our list of targets, Granwell. Did you seriously believe we wouldn't know you?'

Before he can say any more, another uniformed policeman appears, his machine gun spitting shards of death. The Cop goes down first and Evening Suit only gets a single round away before he falls alongside his partner. Barney closes his eyes, waiting for the searing pain of a lead slug in his back, but nothing comes. He opens them to see the newcomer kicking the Assassins' weapons out of their reach in the unlikely event that they aren't dead. Satisfied they're no longer a danger, he turns around.

It's Tom Jefferson.

Barney leaps to his feet again and steps towards him before remembering that his hands are still tied behind him. 'You! Have you got them out of the way so you can finish me yourself?'

Tom has a hand tight against his stomach. He holds it up, as if to show that he didn't mean any harm. He winces as he does so. There is blood on his uniform and on his hand.

'Well, well...what a shame; looks like you've taken one for the team,' Barney says.

'Just be quiet, will you?' Tom says. 'I'm pretty sure these are the only Assassins in this chapter, and now that they're dead, we can leave.' He glances down at his bloodstained shirt and winces in pain. 'But before we go our separate ways, there're some things I want you to know. Charlie - you *are* Charlie, aren't you? Come over here and let me free you.' Tom cuts through the rope with a penknife he's produced from his pocket, doing so without letting go of his weapon. 'When I've done talking, untie him.' His breathing is becoming more laboured, and he is struggling to focus. 'I don't want him to get his hands on me until I've said what I have to say.'

Barney's own breath is coming in short bursts, his anger and frustration taking hold of him. 'A wise move, Jefferson, but it won't help. I'm still going to -'

'For God's sake, just shut up!' Tom interrupts, holding his bloodied hand in the air. 'I might have got it wrong when I said we'll be leaving. I'm not going anywhere; I think he's done for me. I'd better make this quick; when you get back home, you'll get an email with everything you need in it, but I want to tell you this part face to face...it wasn't me that helped plant the car bomb...I wasn't the Shadow Writer...that was Boris Zelesky.' Tom's breathing is growing more laboured by the second. He's on his way out; there can be no doubt about that, even to Barney's untrained eye. As dying here now leads to the same result on Earth, why would he waste his final few breaths making a claim that Barney should be able to verify on his return home? Or is this just a deathbed confession, something to wash his soul a little cleaner in his last few minutes? But Tom's next words help to persuade him.

'Think about this...if it had been me, why

would I save you in Heyton...and then again on the pirate ship?'

Barney struggles to keep the shock from showing on his face. 'That was you? You tell me why; a guilty conscience?' He guesses that the gurgling noise that comes from Tom's mouth is a bitter laugh.

'I got way beyond feeling guilty about anything a long time ago,' Tom says.

'If it was you, why didn't you make yourself known?'

'How could I? You'd have tried to kill me the second you saw me. I decided that if I made it through this chapter...I'd reach out to you back home, but...' his voice fades as he slowly slides from the chair.

'Quick, untie me.' Charlie does as he's been told, and Barney crouches down, holding his fingers to Tom's throat. Feeling no pulse, he shakes his head. 'He's gone.'

'Do you think he was telling the truth?'

Barney shrugs his shoulders. 'God knows, but he was dying, and he knew it, so why would he lie?' Before they can discuss this unexpected turn of events, gunshot blasts sound in the corridor. 'They're still at it and getting closer. We'd better be leaving.'

'How? Newman said I'd know when it was time.'

'It's time now. Just stop hanging onto this place and you'll be alright.'

He stops talking as Charlie begins to fade away, and waits until he is sure that his friend has left completely before steadying himself for his own departure. He feels the beginning of the now familiar experience as the place he is standing in grows distant. He realises he hasn't escaped the clutches of Chapter 38 when the door is kicked open. 'You! Show your hands. Jesus! There's more in here, and three of 'em are cops. This bastard must have killed them.'

Before he can join Charlie in escaping, Barney hears the footsteps coming towards him and then feels the dull thud of a rubber cosh, knocking him unconscious at the very moment he is leaving Chicago in 1930.

*   *   *   *   *

# Chapter 40: Whitby

Eventually, Barney's eyes did their job well enough for him to be able to identify the faces hovering above him as belonging to Sally and Smith. 'Charlie...' he whispered, '...is he alright?'

'He arrived back in Los Angeles safely,' Smith said.

'Good. We got them. The Assassins...they're dead. Tom was there. He saved us, but one of them shot him. I had it all wrong...he wasn't the Shadow Writer who edited my story about the kid's bus.'

Smith's eyes widened. 'He wasn't? Then who was?'

Barney felt himself slipping back into the darkness, as the concussion he'd received in Chicago in 1930 caught up with him some ninety years later. 'It was Boris, Boris...I can't remember...somebody's sending an email...I have to go and save Robin...' His voice grew quieter and dimmed to silence as he drifted into a deep slumber.

He was out for fifteen hours straight, his exhausted mind and body deciding they'd been asked to do too much in too short a space. The next time he came round, the first thing he saw was Sally, sitting in a chair next to the bed, a worried expression on her face. He struggled into a seating position. 'Where's Smith?'

'He's just gone out for a while. He hasn't disappeared again, if that's what you're thinking. He said to tell you that you needn't worry about Robin. They're still not sure why his name was on a List, but the Assassins aren't coming for him. Not for the time being, anyway.'

'Thank God for that,' Barney said.

The door opened, and Smith walked in, a polystyrene coffee cup in one hand, a bag of bagels in the other. 'You're back with us! I've brought you some food. From the condition you were in on your return, I assume you took a blow to the head?'

'Yes. They came at me from behind, so I didn't see who coshed me.'

'Could it have been another Assassin? Do you need to revisit the same chapter and stop them?' Smith's voice conveyed his concern.

'No. There were only two of them, and they were both dead when I left. It must have been a character from the book.' Barney climbed out from under the sheets and discovered he was wearing jogging pants and a tee shirt. He went into the bathroom to clean his teeth. When he came out, he sat at the table and savoured a taste of his coffee. Sally described his missing hours as he tucked into his bagels. When he'd returned from the Margins, he'd been groggy, suffering from a head injury. After examining him, they'd found nothing serious, and had put him to bed. He devoured the bagel, then signalled his readiness to start the post-mortem of the Chicago Intervention.

'Sally tells me they're leaving Robin alone?'

'That's correct; they've removed his name from the List,' Smith said. 'However, the fact they even considered him means we should continue to monitor his situation. He may still be in danger, just no longer a priority.'

'Good; and what about Charlie? You said he returned in one piece, but has he been in touch?'

'Oh, he's been in touch, alright,' Sally replied, 'he loved it. Said it was the most exciting thing he'd ever done, and that he can't wait for next time.'

'However, Newman's spoken to him,' Smith said, 'and he now has a more realistic view of the dangers involved. We've received Charlie's report, but considering he's a writer, it isn't very clear at all. I believe the excitement of his first visit to the Margins has coloured his recollection. I would like to hear your version, especially about Tom Jefferson's involvement.'

Barney related everything about the Intervention. He began with Sergeant Rafferty's rousing speech, and ended in the back room of the club, with two dead Assassins and a what he now knew was a Scribe lying at his feet. 'Tom told me it was somebody called Boris who was the Shadow Writer for *The Wheels on the Bus*. Also, he said I'd be receiving an email that would clear a few things up.'

Sally joined in the conversation. Her laptop had been open on her knees, and now she passed it to Barney. 'Do you remember when we were at your house in Leeds, when Colin was there? And you pointed out something on TVV's database?'

Barney studied the screen. 'I knew I'd seen that name. Boris Zel...Zelen...'

Sally helped him out. 'Boris Zelesky. We wondered why there wasn't a book title against his entry, and how he'd died the way he had?'

'That's right. They found his body in bed, didn't they? Multiple fractures, and the door locked from the inside. A real life Agatha Christie story. We don't know any more about him, then?'

'No. Nothing we didn't a week ago, anyway. Perhaps this email you're supposed to be getting might help?' Sally said.

'Of course. Maybe it's arrived?' he looked about him, searching for his laptop.

'It hasn't,' Lucy said. 'You mentioned something about it the first time you woke up, so I've been checking. Don't worry, I haven't opened any of your messages. I bet they're just from people trying to sell you stuff, anyway, but I couldn't see one from Tom.'

Barney sighed. He wanted to be in the thick of the action, taking the fight to the enemy, not hanging around for a list of doomed writers and a digital message that promised to shine a light on a dark corner or two.

* * * * *

# Chapter 41: Whitby

Sally had some news; Colin had called to tell her about another dead writer. 'Some Scottish chap named Jefferson'. A neighbour had found him on the family farm in Scotland. Not only that, but his brother's mutilated corpse had also been discovered there just a few months ago. Because Tom's body was riddled with multiple bullet wounds, and his brother had been tortured before he'd died, both deaths were being treated as resulting from a gangland feud. Barney wondered if "gangland feud" was the police equivalent of TV archaeologists' "for ritual purposes", a phrase they seemed to use whenever they couldn't explain something they'd dug out of the ground. No doubt the investigators would be even more puzzled when forensics identified the weapon that had killed Tom as a vintage Thompson submachine gun. He opened his laptop and checked his inbox. As Sally had said, ninety per cent of it was marketing rubbish, but the most recent unread message was from a company called *Howick and Woodcock (Solicitors)*. His heart beat a little faster when he read the header - *The*

*Estate of Thomas Jefferson Esq.*

*Dear Mr Granwell - it is my sad duty to inform you of the passing of my client, Mr Thomas Jefferson. I have attached a file which he has instructed me to forward to you in the eventuality of these unhappy circumstances. Please note that, as per instructions received from the above named, neither myself nor any of my colleagues are aware of the contents of said file.*

> *Regards*
> *JP Rowland*
> *Howick and Woodcock (Solicitors).*

'You'd better make yourselves comfortable,' Barney said.

*Hello Barney; if you're reading this, I guess you made it out of Chicago alive and I didn't. Taylor - she's my Warden - tells me the Assassins have put a price on my head. I don't think I'll be around much longer, so I want to clear up some of the mess I've helped to create. I intended sending you a message a while ago, but events kept getting in the way. Now that time's ticking, I realise I'd better get on with it.*

*The first thing I have to say is that I wasn't involved in the attempt on your life, even though you assume I was. I couldn't contact you earlier because Taylor was worried it would alert the Assassins. I also knew if I showed my face, you might not wait to hear what I had to say before you acted.*

When I broke into your place in London, my mind was in a mess. They were holding Malcolm hostage on his farm, and I had some half-arsed idea that, if I took the chapter back from you, they'd set him free. I should have known better. After I left you and Smith, Cassidy dragged me into Valance. He was about to kill me when something went wrong, and I managed to survive. When I returned to London, he sent a photo of Malcolm's body to my phone. I knew then my life was over, but I was determined to take Cassidy with me. I was coming back to your house to ask Smith to help me travel to the Margins, but as I reached the corner of your street, the explosion happened and there was hell on, so I turned around and took off again. Later, when I found out you'd survived, I discovered I was a suspect. What could I do? If I came out of hiding and tried to prove my innocence, Cassidy would find me again and finish me before the day was over - unless you got to me first! So, I disappeared from view, moving from one place to the next. Then Taylor appeared.

She's not the same as the other Wardens. She's formed a splinter group who believe in fighting fire with fire - if the Assassins choose to fight dirty, then so will they. She has some inside knowledge of how they work. Whereas Smith and the rest just want to stop the bad guys coming through to Earth, Taylor and her team would happily kill them all: Skeptics, Assassins and Scribes. I had some misgivings about the last one, but I didn't need much convincing to join them. She's been trained as an

Assassin, which means she can go into the Margins, something Smith can't. She discovered a way of getting hold of the Termination Lists, which is how I could follow you into Helen Barron's village, and onto The Dark Angel; and Chicago, of course. She wasn't happy with me for doing this, as she reckoned I should have concentrated on working alongside her, but I thought that, if I tailed you, I might come across Cassidy, and have the chance to make him pay for all he's done. Also, I suppose I felt I owed you. Even though I had nothing to do with the bomb, I was still the one who wrote you into Valance. I told her that keeping an eye on you was part of the deal.

I figured out it was your story, The Wheels on the Bus, that the Skeptics had used to come after you. It took me a while to find out who actually revised it, but I got there in the end. It was Boris Zelesky. I'd never heard of him, and at first, I almost had some sympathy for him. If they were threatening his family, I'd have understood why he'd done it, but when Taylor looked into it, she found he had a different motivation - money. They'd taken care of his gambling debts, and for him, that was reason enough; and guess what? It turns out he was responsible for my brother suffering the way he did. Once I knew that, it was over. Taylor dealt with him.

I assume that Smith's told you why Cassidy wants you dead? You can't let your guard down for a second, Barney.

I'll finish now, and get ready to go into Deadly Falls The Rain, but there's one last thing - I keep *hearing rumours about somebody close to you. I don't know any more than that, but be careful about who you talk to.*

'At least this explains the missing information on Boris Zelesky's entry on TVV's database,' Sally said.

'That's right,' Barney said, 'the way he died didn't seem to have a connection with any of his stories. These rumours Tom mentioned; who could he have meant? Apart from you two, only Robin and Colin know I was in Leeds, but neither of them know I've moved on.'

Smith was pensive. 'The fact that Robin's name appeared on a List suggests he hasn't been involved in any subterfuge.'

'Colin, then?' Barney looked at Sally.

'I didn't mention anything about where we were when I spoke to him,' she said, affronted by the implication, '*or* what we've been doing.'

'I know you didn't. Don't worry about it.' Barney reassured her. He turned to Smith. 'We're stuck without the next List. Is there no way you can hurry your informant along?'

'No, but until we have it, we should ensure that we are ready for whatever we each may have to face in the future. I'll contact Newman. You can discuss strategies with Charlie, while you, Sally, should maintain the lines of communication with Colin. His organisation may yet be of use to us.'

With renewed vigour, they each set about their allotted tasks. If things didn't go as they hoped, they were determined that it wouldn't be for want of preparation.

*   *   *   *   *

# Chapter 42: Whitby/ The Margins

There were four names: Karoline Madsen, Gene Villiers, Jacob Goldsmith, and D.K. Fallows. Another video call connected Whitby to LA, and Sally downloaded the associated books while the two teams of Scribes and Wardens decided on the order in which to deal with them. Neither Barney nor Charlie was familiar with any of the writers, so personal preference didn't come into it this time.

Without further ado, they began this sequence of Interventions with Chapter 4 of *Dark Winter*, by Karoline Madsen. A scan of the blurb and some of the reviews gave them a taste of what to expect. Barney commented that those online critics could have saved a lot of energy by simply saying it was a typical Scandi-Noir thriller. He recognised the set up as being almost a check-list of plot points for many of the novels that fit into the genre, at least those that he himself had read.

Setting: Northern Scandinavia, the area around Tromso, in the dead of winter. Check.

Victim: The body of a blond teenage girl - who had been reported missing four months ago - is found halfway along the tunnel that connects the island of Tromsoya to the Norwegian mainland. Check.

Ritual: The corpse had been posed in an upright kneeling position, hands clasped in prayer. Check.

No witnesses. Check.

Twist: What little evidence is available points to the *modus operandi* of a serial killer last in action fifteen years since, but this same butcher committed suicide in prison a few months into his life sentence, which seems to let him off the hook. Check.

They decide to create the parts of journalists Bernhoff Lund and Tor Steinsvik, and take their place amongst the media crowd outside the Police HQ in Tromso, awaiting developments. Beneath their winter coats, they are each armed with a pistol. Barney has followed Charlie's suggestion that they go for the Walther PPK 7.65mm. He doesn't ask why this is his partner's preferred firearm. It isn't long before the word goes around that there's been an arrest, and a police van containing the suspect will arrive soon. It's during the excited melee caused by this rumour that Charlie tugs on Barney's sleeve, pulling him out of the scrum of reporters. 'Those two, climbing into the black Saab.'

Barney signals for a taxi and persuades the

driver to make himself scarce by treating him to a glimpse of the Walther. Charlie climbs into the driver's seat. A high-speed drive through the suburbs, out of town and into the snow covered countryside follows. After a few hair-raising miles, they're stopped by the sight of a tree blocking the road, felled by a winter storm. The Assassins jump out of their car and flee into the woods. A footrace through the trees and then a shootout in the darkness of a Scandinavian pine forest ensues. Result: Two more dead Assassins, one still living author.

Check.

Next, Chapter 25 of *The Curse of Mistress Goode*, Gene Villiers' tale of the terrors of the Salem Witch Trials. As Giles Bishop and Michael Nurse, they are forced to watch as two women are drowned on the ducking stool. To Barney's eyes, neither Sarah Redd nor Dorcas Willard appear to be the evil witches they are accused of being. The Assassins, hiding in the baying crowd of onlookers, are to meet a similarly unpleasant fate.

After that, they become embroiled in the Second Punic War, where they arrive as members of the crew of a Carthaginian Quinquereme in the process of ramming a Roman slave galley on the open sea, sending all on board to the depths of the Mediterranean. The casualties include a pair of Assassins. This is in Chapter 31 of Jacob Goldsmith's aptly named *Fortunes of Holy War*.

The even more appropriately titled *Infinity Ends Tomorrow,* Chapter 47, written by D.K. Fallows, is the last book of this quartet. Going in as ship's officers on the Space Ship *Magellan,* Charlie and Barney have a grandstand view of the dramatic battle between the huge Terran and Andromedan star fleets. Enthralled, they watch as both sides endure massive casualties, and countless spacecraft are blown to atoms. Shaken, they tear themselves away from the spectacle and conduct a thorough search of the *Magellan.* They can scarcely believe their good fortune when they discover the comatose Assassins. By some spectacular miscalculation, the killers have landed here in hibernation pods, each in the depths of an induced coma. Barney doesn't think twice before making sure they will never wake up.

'How are we supposed to carry on like this?' he asked when he arrived back in Whitby. 'We can't keep riding our luck forever. What's wrong? Why the glum face?'

Smith didn't answer, but silently handed over a document. Unlike previous Lists, this one wouldn't take too long to evaluate, as it only comprised two names:

Barney Granwell and Charlie Fairweather.

\* \* \* \* \*

# Chapter 43: Whitby

The same title - *The Sleeping Moon Awakes,* the initial instalment in Barney's saga - was printed next to each of their names. For him, it was the novel, for Charlie the screenplay. That they didn't have to waste time deciding who to save first produced a refreshing clarity.

'Has Newman received this?'

'Of course,' Smith replied.

'Can you get hold of Charlie, please?' Barney asked Sally. 'We'd better talk.'

But Charlie was already on the case, and his excited face appeared on Barney's screen. Newman was hovering in the background, but he wasn't looking very excited at all.

'Have you seen who they've picked, man? They're coming after both of us! This is getting exciting; kind of gives things an extra edge, don't you think?'

*That's one way of putting it,* Barney thought. *I suppose the knowledge that some Assassins are en route to kill us certainly gets the juices flowing.* They needed to get into the Margins. While he was here in this apartment, inhabiting this ailing fifty-year-old body, he was a sitting duck; only in there did he have any chance of evening the odds. He reached out for his copy of the novel. Things were coming to a head, and this book would be the saving, or the death, of him. As he studied the cover, he couldn't deny that any fear he felt was accompanied by a real buzz. When Mary had first told him of the possibility of his work being made into a movie, he'd spent many happy hours excited about seeing the characters and places that had come out of his own imagination being represented on screen. This was even better; soon, he'd be heading into one of those locations to meet some of those characters face to face.

'Why is Newman looking so pissed off?' he asked Smith.

'This could be the moment where everything changes. Cassidy has been carefully choosing the moments to involve himself, but now that you're the target, he's sure to be waiting for you. If you kill him, we'll be well on course to stopping the Skeptics completely. However, if he kills you...'

Barney let the words fade to silence. 'But it wouldn't mean you'd lost, would it? Won't you and Newman just find other writers to act as Wardens for? '

'Perhaps, but you don't understand how important you've become. If you take stock of how much disruption you and Charlie have been causing, you might begin to realise how big a problem the pair of you are to them. You're quite a cause célèbre on Ancilla. Your demise would give a new impetus to our enemy. Our position as Wardens would be dangerously fragile.'

Barney was shocked. He'd grown stronger with each Intervention, now regarding them almost as an adventure. Smith's words had brought everything back into perspective. This was obviously why the Wardens weren't sharing Charlie's excitement. He flicked through the pages, then returned to the contents page. Using the chapter headings to refresh his memory, he gave a quick synopsis, occasionally giving way to Charlie, conceding that the younger man's work on the story was much more recent than his own.

Set on the fantasy world of Saipha, *The Sleeping Moon Awakes* was the tale of Bren-Tan, who later becomes the hero of the entire saga. The title of the relevant section said everything that needed saying:

Chapter 17 - The Massacre of the Hillfolk

Barney skimmed the words he'd written many months ago. 'Bren-Tan's family, members of the Lakeside tribe, have been slaughtered by a raiding party of Mustul mercenaries who have taken him prisoner, forcing him to join them. The Mustul's next target is the Hillfolk. Four Wizards from The Guild of Mages have been assigned to assist the Hillfolk. We'll be entering at the point where the Mustul have surrounded the Hillfolk's camp.'

'You can see why the Assassins chose this,' Charlie said. 'In fact, if we'd got to make the movie, Artie was worried about the price tag of all the extras we were going to need to play dead. The gallons of fake blood would have cost a bunch as well.'

Barney glared at the screen, ignoring the comment. 'There's no point hanging around for a knock on the door. How soon can you be ready?'

'Bags packed, tickets bought, passport stamped,' Charlie answered.

Satisfied, Barney turned to the job in hand. The two Scribes began their preparations, each getting ready to greet the other in a different dimension, despite being thousands of earthly miles apart. Charlie would go into the Intervention as Mi-Kall, a mercenary and friend of Bren-Tan, while Barney would witness the battle from the other side, increasing the number of Wizards to five. He took the name of Raven and hoped to have a few useful spells up his sleeve when he arrived.

He opened the book at chapter 17 and began to type.

*Ever since he was a small boy, Bren-Tan had read stories about the Hillfolk's hidden treasures. Some stories become myths, and some myths become truths, and this was one truth that Bren-Tan never had cause to doubt. But now, as part of the preliminary scouting expedition sent to assess the position, he felt uneasy. From his vantage point high on the hill above their encampment, he'd been watching as they went about their business. He could see...*

\*　\*　\*　\*　\*

# Chapter 44: The Ghostly Margins

But something's wrong. Instead of manifesting among the Hillfolk as they prepare their defences, Barney finds himself in Heyton. When he'd been here before, the colours had been dazzling - he remembered them being the bluest of blues and the greenest of greens - but now, everything is monochrome, and it is quiet. Other than his ragged breathing, there are no sounds. No birds are singing, no bees buzzing. Strangest of all, there are no people. The post isn't being delivered, no gossip is being exchanged, and no clinking of glasses is coming from the pubs.

The biggest shock is that he is still Barney Granwell, wearing the same polo shirt and jeans as he had been in his Whitby apartment. Even more bad news - his clothes are covering the same overweight, unfit body that they normally do. If an Assassin comes at him now, it will all be over in seconds. He tries to focus his mind, get it into the returning zone, but nothing happens. Previously, the journey back had occurred naturally, when an Intervention had reached its natural completion, but not this time. This time he's helpless, trapped alone in a potentially hostile world.

Or *is* he alone? Whatever's going on, Charlie should be around here somewhere.

'Charlie,' he shouts, but his voice has none of the power it should have in here. It sounds feeble, even to his own ears. No answer. He makes his way out of the quiet village and heads towards Patford Manor. That was where he'd started last time, so it seems natural to follow his previous path. His breathing grows laboured and his legs are beginning to tire, when he catches sight of the big house. He glances over his shoulder, half expecting the arrival of the Bentley, but still nobody appears. Cautiously, he pushes the front door open. He staggers forward, but not into the entrance hall of the Manor. He's in Valance, standing next to The Berger Palace. Main Street is empty, but three bodies are hanging from The Mercy Tree. He assumes one is Red Rankin, but who are the others? He walks towards them, but before he reaches the tree, his world turns upside down again, and the dusty road of the frontier town morphs into the carpeted interior of an Art Deco building.

Now, he's in the pages of *Deadly Falls The Rain*, in the corridor of The Diamond Club, the same place he'd hidden with Charlie. He drops to his knees, making himself as small a target as possible. If the renegade Chicago cops come this way, they're sure to make quick work of him. Maybe Charlie turned up here? Barney calls out again, but still no answer comes. He climbs unsteadily to his feet. To his left is the room where Tom was killed. To the right is the bar area, the erstwhile slaughterhouse. He chooses that direction, and is nearing the door at the end of the hallway when he stops, hearing the hum of a busy space on the other side of it. What to do? There doesn't appear too much point in walking away from the only sign of life he's encountered since leaving his apartment. He takes a deep breath and, with a shaking hand, opens the door to reveal a crowded courtroom. Instinctively, he steps back, desperate not to be spotted, but no-one has taken the slightest notice of him. He waits for a few nervous moments, then satisfied he can't be seen, moves forward again, curious to witness events unfold.

At the far side of the chamber is the judge, sitting high above everyone else. On the floor below him is a bank of desks. Occupying these is the prosecution team, all smartly turned out in black gowns and barristers' wigs. Barney's heart sinks when he notices some rare patches of colour amongst the greys - the eyes of the judge and the chief prosecutor are a luminescent blue. No-one is presenting the case for the defence, nor is there a jury. The judge silences the crowd with a blow from his gavel.

'Bring in the accused,' he shouts. A door

in the side wall opens, and a group of manacled prisoners - six of them, three men and three women - are led into the dock. Barney's senses are heightened as he recognises Smith amongst them. It doesn't take an Einstein to guess that these are all Wardens. Each of them carries the signs of a recent beating. 'Why so few?' the judge asks. 'I was given to understand there were an extensive amount of defendants in this case.'

'You are correct, sir. This small selection have kindly volunteered to represent the treachery and corruption committed by themselves and their co-conspirators.'

'Let's get it over, then. Chief prosecutor, read out the charges.'

'Certainly, your honour. The accused have been summoned here to answer for the following crimes against the people of Ancilla: treason; betrayal; murder; perfidy, and...' he pauses, ensuring he has everyone's attention, '... genocide.' Hisses and insults replace the previous laughter. 'If I may now present the evidence for the prosecution?'

A clerk sends a signal, and a succession of make-believe characters enter the court, dressed in outfits from a variety of historical periods. Each one is announced in the way VIPs are introduced to the room at a society ball. For what could have been hours, or could have been seconds - to Barney, time at this point seems to possess an elastic property, impossible to measure

- the "evidence for the prosecution" progresses through the courtroom like a solemn cortège at a monarch's funeral.

It is a procession of the dead. Some have surrendered their lives on the battlefield, or drowned at sea; others have been disfigured after dying in bush fires or burning buildings; there are Roman Legionnaires; soldiers from the Napoleonic era; casualties of earthquakes and tsunamis; victims of murderers and brutal dictators; spilled blood, mutilations, lost limbs, blinded eyes. All of which could have been culled from genuine history, but in this case form an inventory of the hideous capacity for pain contained in the minds of human writers.

Barney recognises some of them. A couple are from Dickens' novels - Bill Sikes from Oliver Twist, and Sydney Carton from *A Tale of Two Cities*. *They satisfy the requirements alright,* he thinks. Sikes, shot and left hanging by the neck, and Carton losing his head under the blade of the guillotine. Professor Moriarty, claimed by the Reichenbach Falls while fighting his sworn enemy, Sherlock Holmes; Captain Ahab, dragged below the waves by the whale in *Moby Dick*; Lucy Westenra, cursed to suffer and die in *Dracula.* Most of the others mean nothing to him, but he catches the occasional glimpse of some he's seen during his Interventions in the Margins. There are party-goers in dinner jackets or flapper dresses, and stern-faced cops, all killed in the shootout in Chicago; bedraggled French sailors who had died beneath the hull of Tempest Read's ship; Sir Archibald and his wife, casualties of the shotgun slayer at Patford Manor, and countless more in a relentless march through fiction's bloody history.

When the final spectre has left, the judge speaks.

'There we have it. Some of you may ask, *Where is the defence team*? I will answer that for you; there isn't one, because there can *be* no defence for these atrocities.' A murmur of approval ripples around the room. 'Likewise, there can only be one sentence: Death.' The court erupts in a cacophony of joyous release, as the mob celebrates. Barney is distraught. He is helpless as he watches the prisoners led out through the door by which they'd entered, and on to their fate.

Suddenly, the clamour of the crowd becomes distant and Barney's vision blurs. There follow several flashes, accompanied by a hissing noise, reminding him of the interference on his family's first TV set. He thinks the time has come for his return to Whitby, but instead, yet another familiar scene emerges from out of the miasma.

He's high aloft on *The Dark Angel*, at least eighty feet above the main deck, and clinging on for dear life. He looks down and immediately regrets it as vertigo grabs a hold of him. The sea is rougher than before, and the rolling of the ship is threatening to throw him into its depths. He tightens his grip on the rope, then opens his eyes again and takes stock of his situation. He won't be capable of thinking straight until he's on the closest thing to solid ground available, which is the wooden deck, far below. He reaches down with a foot, searching for the next section of rigging, hoping to use it as the rung of a ladder, but before he finds it, he senses a tremor run through the network of ropes. He glances down and can't believe what he sees - two Assassins have appeared, and are climbing up towards him. The thought comes to him that the rigging is a cobweb, and he is a fly, trapped as the spider scuttles along to devour it. Another one is coming at him from above; he must have been lurking in the crow's nest.

In desperation, Barney wills himself to escape, to get home, but nothing changes. The Assassins will be on him in a matter of seconds. There's no more time to think. Above him is the spar from which the main sail hangs. If he reaches that, he'll be able to crawl along it for a few yards, and then, when the pitching of the vessel coincides with him being directly above the sea, jump off. Drowning seems a less painful way to die than ending on the deck in a pile of broken bones. He forces himself to let go of the rigging, one finger at a time. Another surge of fear gives him the strength to haul himself on to the cross beam, and he straddles it, gripping it with elbows and knees like a rider on a bucking horse. Inch by inch, he crawls away from his pursuers, not stopping to look back, even when he feels the vibration that tells him at least one of them must be close. It's now or never. Struggling to keep his balance, he stands, then runs as fast as he is able to towards the end of the spar and leaps out into the open air. As he falls, something happens that worries him more than anything else he's been through here; an image of Sally's worried face appears in his thoughts for a split second, so quickly he doesn't know if it's a memory or just his mind playing more tricks. A frustrated cry comes from above, while below, the ocean, which up to this moment has been painted in shades of grey, turns an emerald green as he becomes a part of it.

And then, the sound, muffled but unmistakable, of a second body hitting the surface of the boiling waves, seconds behind him.

*   *   *   *   *

# Chapter 45: Whitby/ London

Barney's entire body ached and his heart was racing. Any relief he felt about returning from the nightmare was overshadowed by the fear that had accompanied him from the Margins. Had an Assassin followed him into the deep waters of the Caribbean? If so, did that mean they'd tracked him to Whitby?

But first things first; why was Sally standing nearby, nudging his shoulder with the long handle of a sweeping brush?

'What are you doing?'

The brush fell to the floor and Sally lifted her hands to her face. 'Thank God! I didn't know if you were coming back, or what state you'd be in, and I couldn't touch you, and -'

'- where's Smith?' Barney interrupted sharply. 'I saw him in there. Everything went wrong, and...'

'He just disappeared. Vanished. I don't think he wanted to go because he was struggling and shouting as though somebody was dragging him away.'

A cold shiver ran across Barney's heart. Had the trial really happened, then? If so, had Smith already been executed, either in the Margins, or on Ancilla? Whatever the truth of the matter, any investigation would have to wait until he had time to assess it properly. If an Assassin was roaming around Whitby looking for him, it wouldn't take long for them to discover his hiding place.

'I'll tell you about it later, but I'm pretty sure one of them followed me back. The first thing we have to do is get out of here. I'll contact Charlie once we're on the move, make certain he returned safely; if he ever got there, that is. There's something else. I saw your face; you must have made a connection when you were trying to wake me. If I hadn't seen you in there, I'd have said you ought to run as far away from me as possible, but I reckon it's a bit late for that now. We'd better stick together.'

Despite her shock at Barney's news, Sally wasn't wasting time discussing the situation. She'd left her car parked outside her flat, on the far side of town, so they packed up what they could fit into a suitcase and exited the apartment. Walking out onto the street was as nerve-racking an experience as Barney had ever undergone, including several near-death moments in the Margins. He told Sally to stay out of sight until he scanned the area, ensuring it was Assassin-free. On the way to her place, he suggested that Sally change her appearance. Here in Whitby, her Goth style meant she blended into the background, but wherever they were heading, she would almost certainly stand out. No problem. She had plenty of "civvies" in her wardrobe. As they hurried, she told of her part in the recent events. Smith had been taken just seconds after Barney left for the Margins. If that hadn't been enough to frighten her, she'd known something was wrong by how Barney acted. He'd been agitated and moaning almost the whole time, but it got worse just before his return, when he'd started rocking back and forth, and mumbling gibberish. That's when it had occurred to her to use the brush handle to try to wake him.

Barney did his best to tell his own story, but gave up when he realised even he couldn't make sense of it.

Breathless and bedraggled, they arrived at a quiet road. Barney guessed from the signs outside most of the doors that these had once been family homes, now converted into small hotels or bed-and-breakfast businesses. Sally's car was waiting for them halfway along the street. She stopped beside it and pointed to a top-floor window. 'That one's mine. I won't be long,' she said, disappearing through the front door. Barney sat on the wall, keeping watch as he waited. He was about to follow her inside and hurry her up when she reappeared, carrying a holdall. He couldn't have been more surprised. When he'd first met her, it had taken a while to become used to her appearance as an archetypal Goth. Everything about her, from the mascara down to her boots, and everything in between, had been black. Now that she'd removed the make up and was dressed in jeans, white blouse, and denim jacket, it brought home to him how young she was; the change took five years off her. However, her hair was still raven-black where it strayed from underneath her purple beret. *Other than shaving it off, there's not much she can do about that,* he thought, as he lifted her bag and loaded it into the boot alongside his own case.

Seeing how shaken Sally was, Barney held out his hand for the keys. 'I think I should drive.' She handed them over and climbed into the passenger seat. After one last check to make sure that none of these innocent looking passersby were harbouring any evil intentions towards him, he started the engine, and within minutes they were leaving town.

'Where are we going?'

'London.'

'But I thought you'd decided it was too close to your old home?'

'I did, but it's a big place.' Barney had given the matter some consideration. Even if Cassidy guessed that the capital was where he was heading, then so what? The city was so huge that he now regretted not staying there after the car bomb. He reached into his pocket for his phone and handed it over. 'Try Charlie, will you? We need to know what happened to him.'

She found the Los Angeles number and pressed the call button. 'It's gone to voicemail,' she said. 'I'll leave a message. *Hi Charlie, it's Sally. We're worried about you. Can you get in touch? Bye*.' She made as if to return the phone.

Barney gestured for her to keep hold of it. 'You might as well use it to find somewhere for us to stay.'

'Anywhere in particular?'

'Try the area around Victoria station. It's always busy with travellers, so we can go to ground there.'

By the time they reached Leeds and the M1, Sally had booked two rooms in The Worcester, a hotel situated between Victoria and Pimlico. The monotony of the motorway soon took its hold on her, and Barney was pleased to note that she still had peace of mind enough to fall into a slumber.

Three hours later, they hit the outskirts of London and the never-ending rush hour. Even before his life had taken this peculiar turn, Barney had been a reluctant driver. It was times like this that reminded him why. His nerves, already flagging, were stretched by the continuous stopping and starting, the deciphering of the multitude of road signs, and the abuse he received from other drivers as he endlessly fought his way into the correct lane. The repeated braking and accelerating woke Sally, and when his phone rang from her lap, they both assumed it was Charlie.

'It's not him. It's Robin, your friend. Here -'

Barney waved the phone away, pointing at the busy road ahead, where three lines of interchanging traffic were taking up all his attention. 'You answer it, will you? Take a message and tell him I'll call him back in an hour.'

Sally did as requested. 'Hello? Yes, Barney's here, but he can't talk...sorry, I can't make out what you're saying...I'll ask him to give you a ring...what was that?...oh...he's gone.'

Barney was busy negotiating a right turn against the flow. 'Sounds like it was a poor line.'

'I think he might have been drunk. He was slurring, and I could hardly understand a word he was saying, then at the end, he suddenly sobered up and I could hear him loud and clear. He said to tell you he was sorry.'

\*　\*　\*　\*　\*

# Chapter 46: London

The room was as featureless as he'd expected. After opening his case and looking down at the small amount of clothes he'd brought with him, Barney didn't bother unpacking. First things first; he tried Charlie's number, but once again, there was no answer. No Smith, no Charlie, no means of getting hold of Newman. Not good. Next, he was ready to talk to Robin. He paced the floor as he made the call.

Robin must have been waiting, as he picked up immediately. 'You're not still in Leeds, are you? And who answered your phone before? Can you trust her?' His voice was little more than a nervous whisper. Sally had implied he sounded drunk, but he wasn't drunk. Barney could tell he was frightened.

'Somebody who's helping me with something, that's all. I trust her completely. To answer your first question, I left Leeds a while ago. I've been in -'

'Stop!' Robin's voice wasn't a whisper any more. 'Don't tell me.' Then the real surprise. 'Did you know Cassidy ordered some Assassins to follow you from the Margins?'

Barney was shocked; not about the Assassins, as he already suspected they'd tailed him. The shock came from hearing his friend speak his arch-enemy's name. 'Cassidy? What about him? You didn't believe me when I told you -'

'- and tell your partner he needs to disappear. They've got him in their sights, too.'

'My partner?'

'That American, the one who's been helping you.'

Everything seemed to be accelerating, and Barney had to find a way of applying the brakes. 'Let's start again, beginning with Cassidy. You said I was off my head when I tried to tell you about him before, so what's changed?'

'He's got Cristina is what's changed,' Robin answered shortly, 'and he made me call you. He says if you don't follow his instructions, he'll kill her.'

Barney sat down heavily. Cassidy was holding his goddaughter as hostage? This was a situation he hadn't foreseen. Regardless of how many Interventions he'd been involved in, deep down, he'd always felt there had been a barrier between the two different worlds he'd been inhabiting. A feeling strengthened when Smith had suggested that Lucy should be out of harm's way as long as she stayed away from him.

Robin was close to tears. 'It's because of you she's in trouble, you and your bloody stories!'

'Try to calm down. Take a few deep breaths and tell me what's happened, right from the beginning.'

He heard Robin struggling to rein in his emotions. After a few seconds, he'd regained enough control to say what he needed to say. 'Cassidy sent someone to see me. At first I thought it was some local thug, but then he did something to me, played with my mind, sent me into this nightmare place, and I could sense you were in there somewhere. When he brought me back, he said it was called the Margins, and that he was an Assassin. Then he threatened Cristina; he knew everything about her; her home address in Edinburgh, where she worked, her daily routine. He spelled out what she'd go through if I didn't do it.'

'Do what?'

'Revise a chapter from your book - *The Sleeping Moon Awakes.*'

'You mean *you* were the Shadow Writer?'

'The what? If that's what you call it, then I suppose I was.'

'Did you understand what would happen if you did what he asked?'

Robin emitted a low, cynical laugh. 'There was no asking involved, but yes, I did, because he took great delight in telling me. He said I'd be opening this Channel thing, which would mean he could send someone here to execute you. I was dreading hearing about you being killed on the news. Then Cassidy himself turned up. His plan for you obviously didn't work out as he'd wanted, and now they've taken her; they're holding her hostage until you go back into Valance, that cowboy town you talked about.'

Barney was stunned. *How could he have done this to me?* Even though they'd spent less and less time together as the years passed, they were still The Thompson Twins, weren't they? Or Barney and Robin, the Caped Crusader and his faithful assistant? *On the other hand, would I have betrayed him if Cassidy threatened Lucy? Of course I would, and without a moment's hesitation.* He was angry. Sure, this was partly because Robin had sold him down the river, but there was something else, something much bigger. He felt a rage growing deep in his soul. These bastards had involved his oldest pal in their quarrel and had now kidnapped his goddaughter! His resolve stiffened. Despite this betrayal by his friend, he vowed that he'd do everything in his power to prevent Cristina from being hurt. 'You did what you had to do, I understand,' he said.

'He told me how he intended making you suffer.' Robin asked. 'Why does he hate you so much?'

'It's because he thinks I murdered his wife.'

'But that's ridiculous!'

'I know, but that's not how he sees it. Apparently, she became a character in one of my books, and I killed off the part she was playing, which meant she herself had to die. The damndest thing is I can't even remember which novel her character was in, but because of it, I've put Cristina's life in danger. I'll never forgive myself if anything happens to her.' Another thought occurred to him. 'What about Giuliana? Did the Assassin threaten her as well?'

'No. Her father's in pretty bad shape, so she's gone back to Italy to look after him. She'd already left when all this happened. Her name was never mentioned, so I just hope she's not in danger as well. I called her and asked her to be careful, but I couldn't give her any details, in case she rang the police. Or thought I was mad. Do you think she'll be safe?'

Barney remembered again what Smith had said about Lucy and Jonathan, how their lack of creativity meant they wouldn't register on the Assassin's radar. 'If she was gone before they approached you, she should be alright, but what if she tries to contact Cristina?'

'Cassidy forced Cristina to email her, saying she'd be busy at work for a while, doing loads of overtime, and that she'd be back in touch in a few days.' Suddenly, Robin's tone changed from pleading to accusing. 'So, how are you going to get her away from them?'

'There's only one way, isn't there? I'll go and meet Cassidy in Valance, have it out with him there.'

After a pause, another change in tone,

softer now. 'He'll kill you, won't he?'

'Until my last visit, I got stronger each time I travelled into the Margins, and I'd have been pretty confident about taking him on, but now, things have changed. I can't be sure any more what physical shape I'll be in when I get there, and this'll be on his terms. No doubt he'll have a team of Assassins with him as well, but I'll have my own back up in there to help me.'

'Who? Smith's dead, isn't he? That's what Cassidy said.'

'I...I'm not sure about that.' This confirmation of what he'd feared took Barney aback. Optimistically, he'd tried to maintain the belief that the trial he'd witnessed had been nothing more than a nightmare apparition. Had he been wrong to hope for as much? Probably, unless Cassidy was lying. Whatever the truth of the matter, it was important that Robin didn't sense any pessimism in Barney's attitude.

'He's not the only Warden I can call on.' Barney wasn't going to mention the fact that he couldn't even contact his "American friend", let alone Newman or Taylor, the only other Wardens he knew. 'Anyway, the danger might be closer than that. You said that Cassidy sent some of them to find me. I suspected as much; it's why I moved on. I imagine it's his insurance; he's planning to take care of me on Earth if I don't meet him in Valance.'

'So what happens now?' Robin asked.

'Make sure you do what they tell you to. Leave the... just do as they ask.' Barney had been about to say 'leave the rest to me', but that might be construed as, *I know what I'm doing, and I have a plan.*'

He didn't.

*   *   *   *   *

# Chapter 47: London

*Leave the rest to me.* Had he really been about to say that? What was the point of giving Robin the false belief that he knew what he was doing, that it was only a question of time before his daughter was freed? Without Smith or Newman, he had no means of reaching Valance. No matter which angle he approached the problem from, he could see no possible solution. He felt the need for a drink, and walked down the corridor to Sally's room. She welcomed the diversion and suggested some food would be a good idea as well. There were plenty of eating places in the area, and it wasn't long before they were sitting in a back street Italian restaurant. On the way, Barney told her about his talk with Robin. She became upset when she heard about Cristina's situation, but a double grappa restored her spirits a little, and a plate of pasta aided her recovery.

'So what's next, then? Do you suppose Smith really *is* dead?' She asked.

'It's possible Cassidy was lying to Robin about it, but I think we should assume the worst.'

'And there's no way of making it into the

Margins without a Warden sending you there? A method you haven't told me about?'

'No. I start writing, then Smith lays his hand on me, and I travel into the chapter I'm copying out. Until that last time, of course. So the simple answer is no, I can't do it on my own.'

'What about the other way round? If some Wardens come looking for you, will they be able to locate you?'

'I expect so - they found me and Charlie, didn't they? According to Smith, a writer transmits some sort of signal from his subconscious, and the Warden homes in on it. If I understand this correctly, it's a beacon that's permanently switched on. If I could control it, I'd send out an SOS and hope they picked it up.'

They were at a table for four, eating across from each other. Their plates had just been cleared when one of the empty chairs was pulled back, the legs scraping noisily against the tiled floor. When it was returned to its original position, a strikingly tall woman with shining blue eyes was sitting on it. She was wearing Desert Storm fatigues and suede calf-length combat boots, with long blond hair flowing from underneath a peaked patrol cap. Despite the different outfit, it only took Barney a moment to realise he'd seen her before - she'd been the leader of the posse that had rescued him in Valance. She was still as beautiful as he remembered.

'Hi, I'm Taylor. Looks like you're in need of

my help again, Bill Gardner...' she studied the restaurant and its customers, '...but I suppose you call yourself Barney Granwell when you're here.'

The remaining seat was then filled by the less imposing figure of Newman. He was dressed in the same beach-bum outfit as the last time Barney had seen him, and he still wore the same worried expression on his face.

Barney dragged his eyes away from Taylor and directed his questions at Newman. 'Where's Smith? And what have you done with Charlie?'

Newman shrugged his shoulders. 'I don't know, man, they've just...gone.'

As befitted her combative bearing, Taylor took charge of the situation and recommended they take the forthcoming discussion somewhere more discreet. Barney suggested his hotel room. Knowing that their strange group - a nondescript, bald, middle-aged man, a fresh-faced twenty-something girl, a statuesque woman in military uniform, and a scruffy, bearded rotund ex-hippy - was sure to attract attention, even here in London, he urged caution. Taylor didn't care much for caution, so a compromise was reached. Sally would shadow them from the opposite side of the road, while Newman followed thirty yards behind, keeping a look out for any Assassins. Taylor insisted on striding haughtily alongside Barney, not fearing "the rodents" that she felt obliged to exterminate.

Once they were in the privacy of the room,

they quickly got to the bottom of how they had ended up together inside these four walls. Barney recounted his visit to the Ghostly Margins, the feeling that he'd been followed to Earth, and how he and Sally had fled to London. Newman explained how he'd sent Charlie into Chapter 17 of The Sleeping Moon Awakes - or so he'd thought - when something or someone tried to haul him back to Ancilla. Presumably, the same thing that had happened to Smith, but in Newman's case, the pull mustn't have been as strong, because he'd managed to resist it. However, when he'd gathered himself, there had been no sign of the screenwriter. He'd searched everywhere he knew that Charlie frequented in Los Angeles, and attempted to get in touch with Smith. It wasn't until Taylor turned up that he discovered the terrible truth about his fellow Warden. Barney winced at this verification that the trial really had taken place. It had been Newman's idea to track him down; although Taylor could carry on the fight in the Margins herself, he himself needed a Scribe. Taylor summed up her own recent actions in a simple sentence. Since Tom's demise, she'd been working with her team, killing Assassins. Everyone had now told their story except Sally. She was sitting quietly in a corner of the room, overwhelmed by hearing what was being said, and by who was saying it. The two Wardens assumed that Barney's narrative also covered her involvement, and left her to her own devices.

Barney ended the series of narratives by relating Robin's revelations.

Taylor was puzzled. 'Let's get this straight. This so-called friend of yours did the dirty on you, and now expects you to set off on a suicide mission to rescue his daughter?'

'That's right. He's my best mate, and she's my goddaughter, and I'll do whatever it takes to save them,' Barney said, spiky with aggression. 'All I'm asking is that you help me get into Valance.'

'So Cassidy can kill you?'

'Erm... that's not quite how I've got it planned, but if you can come up with another way of saving Cristina, I'm listening.'

'So, what *is* your plan?'

'That I kill him first.'

Barney couldn't miss the concerned glance that passed between the Wardens. He realised how much his heart was ruling his head. 'Fair enough, it might need developing a bit,' he said, now sounding more doubtful.

'I think we'll be wanting to run through this in a little finer detail. The reason we've come to find you is so that me and you can work together. I've got to admit I thought I'd have more say in where you went, and when, but I guess this forces our hand...' Newman stopped talking as Sally was woken from her reverie by the ringing of her phone.

'Sorry. I'll take this outside.'

'... but if this is what you want to do, then we'll help you.' Newman looked at Taylor for confirmation. She didn't have to answer - the fire in her eyes told Barney she was already primed to go. Details were merely a hindrance to her. 'Cassidy won't be alone in there and you know it's impossible for me to cross into the Margins. All I can do is send you in, then watch over you here until you return.'

'I, however, can,' Taylor interjected. 'I'll try to be there when you arrive -'

'Try? I thought you could travel there whenever you wanted to.'

'I can, but I'm not strong enough to be so accurate. I'll put a team together, but I can't guarantee when we'll get through to Valance. The chances of us manifesting in the same chapter, and at the same moment as you, are pretty small. All I'll promise is that we'll be there when we can. It's up to you to stay alive until then.'

Barney's hopes had been raised by the notion that he'd have some form of back up when he faced Cassidy, and Taylor's admission took the shine off things. However, he had no other choice than to take his chances, with or without her. He was about to say as much when the door burst open and Sally came hurrying through.

'It's Colin.... you'll have to speak to him.' She handed the phone over. Mystified, Barney took it from her.

'Colin?'

'Granwell! Still alive, then?'

'What do you mean?' *Had Sally told him what was going on?*

'I mean, The Writer Killers - they haven't got to you yet? Probably not famous enough for them, but then again, I wouldn't have thought Wylder would have been, either.'

'What are you talking about?'

'I've received an alert from Dulwich Dan, one of my TVV colleagues in London. He's been scanning the police frequencies, as you do, and a suspicious incident was called in half an hour ago. A body's been found, and it's been identified as belonging to one Robin Wylder. I remembered Sally mentioned him when she was taking me home from your place, so I thought I'd let her know. She's just told me you're close to him. Or were. I'd say you ought to be keeping a low profile; if I were you I think I'd -'

But Barney had heard enough. He turned to Newman and Taylor.

'I'm not waiting any longer. I have to go in now.'

\* \* \* \* \*

# Chapter 48: London

Newman needed some convincing about the urgency of Barney's statement. Taylor didn't need *any*. The only problem was Sally. She was adamant about staying, even after Barney did his best to persuade her that distancing herself from him was the only way of ensuring her safety.

'But you said they're already aware of me, so why does it matter where I am?'

It was Taylor who answered. 'We discussed this as we walked here. I believe the Assassins only know of you because you were in the room with him during his most recent journey. This being the case, you should be safe if you distance yourself from him.'

'And as you don't have that creative thing going on in your head, they wouldn't be able to track you down anyway,' Barney added.

'But...I'm a writer too; what about my Internet blog?'

'No offence, but you don't do the actual inventing part, do you? Besides which, you haven't posted anything at all while I've known you.'

Sally still wasn't persuaded, forcing Barney to reluctantly used his trump card. 'I hadn't wanted to say this, but try to think logically about what I'm going to do. I know you've been with me before when I've gone into the Margins, but up until the last time, I felt so strong I was certain I'd get back unscathed. Also, I was taking them by surprise. Well, that failed Intervention shows things have changed. Cassidy will be waiting for me, and he won't be alone. The odds are he'll kill me, and you know what that means. Just imagine it - do you really want to be in here with my...' he faltered, searching for a less brutal way to express himself. He soon realised there wasn't one, '...with my dead body?'

Barney and the two Wardens looked at Sally, watching to see how she reacted. Eventually, they saw realisation and acceptance form in the expression on her face.

'What should I do, then?' she asked, quietly.

'Go home.'

'But some Assassins followed you to Whitby, didn't they? I'm not going there.'

'No, not Whitby. To your parents in Middlesbrough. Tell them you wanted a change of scenery or something. If I don't make it back, Newman will tell you when it's safe to return to your flat.' Barney understood how shocked Sally had been by the phrase, "my dead body", because it had had the same effect on his own mindset. Saying those words had shone a light on the perilous position he was putting himself in. Sally went to her room to pack.

The new plan comprised three simple steps. Step 1: Taylor would set off immediately, gather her team, and find a way into Chapter 5 of Zach's book, hopefully getting there in time. Step 2: Newman would send Barney into the same story. Step 3: Barney would hope and pray that he arrived with the skills and strength he'd need if he was to have any chance of survival. That was it. *Three steps to heaven or the road to hell?* He wondered.

When Sally returned to deliver her reluctant farewells, she found that Taylor was already en route to the Margins, bringing home to her how quickly things were moving. Barney handed her the keys to her car. She disconsolately accepted them and took her leave with a minimum of fuss. She hated leaving, but the idea of being alone with his corpse left her in no doubt she was doing the right thing.

Newman's pessimism showed no signs of letting up. 'Just so we're both clear about this - after I send you in, I'll stay here as long as I can, but as soon as I see you going under, I won't be hanging around. By then they'll have a beam on you, and I don't intend to be sitting here twiddling my thumbs when they come through that door.'

*As soon as I see you going under.* Barney thought. *Not exactly up there with, "We shall fight them on the beaches"*. Not that it mattered; saving his goddaughter was all the inspiration he needed. 'Thanks for the warning,' he said, 'I'll bear it in mind.' He sat at the desk and lifted the lid of his laptop. His copy of *The Angry Sun* lay next to it. There was no reason to writing himself in as Bill Gardner, Bernoff Lund, Giles Bishop or any of the other pseudonyms that he'd used on previous visits. No more hiding behind a made-up character with a made-up name. He'd had enough of all that, and anyway, Cassidy knew he was coming.

He meant to finish the job as Barney Granwell.

Newman didn't seem to have anything else to offer him, at least nothing constructive, so he could think of no excuse for any further delay. Despite the probable outcome, this thing had to be done if Cristina was to be made safe. He turned to Chapter 5 and, after confirming with a glance that Newman was ready to play his part, began the process.

*The blazing Arizona sun was at its highest when the riders pulled up outside The Berger Palace, hot, thirsty, and bedraggled after their hard ride through the arid landscape. Scoot and Frenchie had been following Red Rankin for nearly two weeks now, determined to reclaim both their losses, and some of the pride they'd lost after the card sharp had made fools of them back in Tucson. Almost as embarrassing, the gambler had killed their friend Curly...*

\* \* \* \* \*

# Chapter 49: The Margins - Valance, Arizona, 1882

Barney sits astride his horse, facing the sign for The Berger Palace. He twists in the saddle, checking up and down Main Street, searching for any sign of Cassidy. It is another hot day, but whereas the last time he'd been here, the heat had been desert-dry, now there is moisture in the atmosphere. A thunderstorm is coming. The sky is darkening, and the huge black clouds that fill the horizon are edging closer. Townsfolk are gathered in groups on the boardwalks, all of them staring in his direction. *Why?* He is wearing a Stetson, a heavy trail jacket, grubby shirt with a blue neckerchief, and dark work trousers. All that might distinguish him from any other cowpoke are the Colt single action revolvers he's carrying, but these are out of sight, hidden beneath his coat.

Shrugging off the feeling of paranoia, he dismounts, ties the reins to the hitching post, and walks across the wooden boardwalk and into the saloon. There are around thirty people inside, most of them men. If the place had quietened on his entrance, with everyone turning to confront the newcomer, that would be one thing, but he senses they were already silent and staring at the door before he'd entered. They'd been expecting him. He's about to speak when it's as though an unseen hand flicks a switch, signalling that everybody should get back to business as usual. In the space of a second, he's gone from being the centre of attention to an ordinary cowboy, thirsty from his last cattle drive and desperate for a drink. He walks to the counter, orders a whisky, and turns to face the room.

In the corner, a well-dressed man is sitting alone, oblivious to the clamour and rowdiness taking place around him as he plays a game of patience. It's the scarlet waistcoat that Barney recognises first, then the fiery hair and equally colourful Vandyke beard. *Will Red still die in this chapter if I defeat Cassidy?* he wonders. *Or if Cassidy emerges victorious, will he then waste his time stringing up a character from an old potboiler like The Angry Sun*? Barney has a thought; should he warn the gambler about his fate? *If it puts a spanner in the works and creates some chaos, why not?* He walks over to the table.

'Red Rankin?'

Red answers in a slow Texan drawl. 'Mr Barnaby Granwell, I declare...'

Barney's hands move instinctively towards his revolvers. He's half expected an answer, maybe even a general conversation, but he hadn't been prepared for Red to call him by name. Even if some sort of residual memory from his previous visit still lingers in the air, wouldn't he be known here as Bill Gardner?

'How do you know my name?' Barney asks as he sits down.

'Why, you're famous around these parts, sir; everybody in town understands the reason for your presence.'

'Okay. Why don't you tell me exactly what it is you think they understand.'

Red gathers up the pack. He shuffles them dexterously, a lifetime spent at the gaming tables of the Old West contained in his nimble fingers. 'Look about you, Mr Granwell, and consider this question - who are these good people? To you, they - along with myself - are merely characters in a book you wrote, and you have decided that not all of us will survive to see tomorrow.'

'Hold on!' Barney interrupts. '*I* didn't write this story.'

'No, sir, you did not, but you've written plenty like it, haven't you? And every time you get to the end, there are a few less Ancillans around. Everyone knows who you are and why you're here, Cassidy made sure of that. You see those fellows?' He points over Barney's shoulder. 'I reckon they've already decided whose side they're on and I regret to tell you it will not be yours.'

'And what about you?'

'Me? Well, same as everyone else in here, I usually have no choice but to go where I'm sent, but this little scene that we're playing out today isn't of the usual variety, and there are times when I prefer not to follow the herd. It may surprise you to know that I am the only friend you have in here.'

Once more, Barney considers telling Red how things are due to end for him, but he is speaking again.

'I guess you are wondering why I should take this stance when you presume to be aware of my fate?' Red smiles at the puzzlement on Barney's face. 'Yes sir, somewhere outside of this saloon a noose awaits me, and I know I have two executioners: the creator of this sorry tale, and Cassidy. However, this is no longer the original story, is it? Now that you've interfered with it, there are thousands of possible outcomes. So who knows? In this version, and with your assistance, perhaps I'll live to be a hundred years old?'

Barney is about to reply when the room suddenly reverts to the same eerie quiet that had greeted him on his arrival. He's the focus of attention again. He stares at Red. 'Is this it, then? Is this where I find out if I get out of here alive?'

'I believe your question is about to be answered.'

Cautiously, Barney stands up. No sooner is he on his feet than the switch is flicked again and the silence is broken by angry shouts as several pairs of hands grab at him. He lowers his head and tries to shield himself, but he is helpless as the mob hauls him to the swing doors and pushes him through. Once outside, the throng, with Barney an unwilling member, moves as one towards the churchyard.

They're taking him to the Mercy Tree.

Three lifeless bodies are already hanging from it, facing away from him, swinging in the strengthening breeze. They arrive at the tree and his hands are tied behind his back. A fourth noose is waiting for him. Someone fits it around his neck, and two heavily built men take a hold of the other end of the rope. They brace themselves and heave. Barney feels the noose tighten, and his feet leave the ground. He is losing consciousness when, through the thudding of the blood in his ears, he hears a voice shouting.

'Stop!'

The rope is freed, and Barney falls to the floor. He lays still, coughing, gathering his wits, then struggles upright, ready to make a desperate run for it. Then the same voice sounds again. 'Leave him to me.'

Cassidy has arrived.

Barney's heart sinks even further when he sees he is accompanied by three Assassins. The throng parts for the newcomers, who dismount and form a semi-circle. One moves forward and cuts Barney's hands free. As the rain lives up to its earlier promise, the audience standing near The Mercy Tree joins those enjoying the spectacle from the shelter of the covered board walk. Barney massages his wrists, willing the blood to return. There's no hope. Each of his opponents is armed with a pair of deadly pistols. It's their eight weapons against his two. *Perhaps he can even things out to some extent by shaming the chief Assassin?* He raises his voice, making sure everybody in the street hears him over the gathering storm. ' "Leave him to me", you just said. Don't you mean, "Leave him to *us*"? Four against one; those are the kind of odds you favour, isn't that so, Cassidy? Have you ever taken anybody on when you weren't standing behind these goons? Or is that too dangerous for a worm like you?'

Cassidy laughs and gestures at the watching audience. 'Nobody here cares about a fair fight, Granwell. They all want to see you swinging up there next to your friends, but personally, I'd rather watch you bleeding out at my feet, with my lead in your belly.'

*Friends? What is he talking about?* Barney keeps his eyes fixed on Cassidy as he takes a few wary steps backwards, giving himself a clear sight of the hanging bodies; the bodies that once belonged to Smith, Charlie, and Robin. Barney gazes on their lifeless faces as a torrent of thoughts flows through his mind. He hasn't asked to be involved in any of this. All he'd ever wanted was to provide for his family, and fate had dictated that the path for him to do this was to give him a talent as a writer. He'd always assumed that, by using this gift, he'd helped his readers to escape from the drudgery of their own existences for a few hours. Not for a single second had he considered that what he did caused anyone any harm. Now here he is, being punished for his naivety. In desperation, he struggles to think of a way of beating the overwhelming odds he's facing, but he quickly realises that not only can he not find a solution, he's also lost the will to do so. He's exhausted every possible avenue, and now he's finished. Before coming here, he'd known that only with Taylor's help was there any chance at all and without her, there's none.

His time's up.

He considers one last act of defiance. If he's going to die, then maybe he can take at least one of Cassidy's minions with him. The thought passes when he recognises the way the strength has drained from his hands. They wouldn't reach the butts of his revolvers before he'd be gunned down. He waits for the final blow with arms limp at his side and his gaze low.

'Before I kill you, I've got a question,' Cassidy says. 'Do you remember Gillian Cresswell?'

Barney shakes his head.

'No, why should you? She was just another character you created so you could murder one more Ancillan for your own enjoyment. Where you messed up was that this particular Ancillan was my wife. I've waited a long time for this, Granwell. I guess this isn't how you thought things might play out? And you know what? It's not over yet. After I've finished with you, I'll be having some fun with this feller's daughter.' He looked up at Robin's body. 'She'll pay extra for the trouble you've caused, as will that little girl who's been helping you. I can't really let her go unpunished, can I?'

And now Cristina and Sally will be made to suffer for his own unwitting actions, and there's nothing he can do to stop it. Perhaps if he makes it easy for Cassidy, the Assassin might lose interest in his vendetta and forget about the two women? Barney straightens his back and faces his tormentor.

He opens his arms wide to show he's no longer a threat, and waits for a welcome end to his misery.

\* \* \* \* \*

# Chapter 50: London

Already nervous, Newman's anxiety had grown now that he had no-one to share it with. All he could do was wait for Barney to come back, or watch him die as a result of being killed in the Margins. He desperately wanted to return to Ancilla, to be amongst his own kind, but he'd promised to oversee the Scribe during what would doubtless be his final Intervention. He was considering trying to contact Taylor when he became aware of their presence. He stopped pacing and crept towards the window, taking care to stay out of sight. The sky had suddenly darkened. Four of them, standing on the opposite side of the road, staring directly up at him, impervious to the heavy rain that bounced around their feet. Cassidy's fall-back plan should the unexpected happen in Valance, and Barney somehow came out on top. They disappeared from view as they crossed the street, walking over to The Worcester's main entrance, down below. He estimated he had less than a minute to act before they reached the fourth floor. There was no way he'd be able to take on even one of these trained killers by himself, and he wouldn't last more than a few seconds against this many.

He rushed back across the room and took hold of Barney by the shoulders. 'Barney, can you hear me? They've found us. I'm sorry, but I think I've done as much as I can.' No response. Despairing, Newman stepped away. The beat of hurried footsteps echoed in the corridor. If he left now, he'd live to fight another day. If he stayed, he'd surely die. 'I have to go. I'll do whatever -'

But something was happening, something new. Barney's hands had taken on a life of their own, and hovered above the keyboard, hesitatingly, as though deciding how to start the next sentence. All at once, the dam of indecision burst, and his fingers became blurred, dancing over the keys in a desperate frenzy. Newman couldn't understand; Barney hadn't typed a single word since he'd left for the Margins, so this surge of activity was totally unexpected. The inside of the door handle turned. Once, twice, someone confirming it was locked. They were here, and it was time for him to leave. He took one last look at the Scribe and then he was gone, on his way home. The door crashed open, and the Assassins burst in to find their prey alone and defenceless.

Barney had stopped typing, and his hands were still again.

\*   \*   \*   \*   \*

# Chapter 51: The Margins
# - Valance, Arizona, 1882

With his defences down, Barney waits helplessly, expecting these to be the final few moments of his story, both here and on Earth. But nothing happens. He looks up to find that Cassidy and his group are standing motionless, like pawns on a chess board waiting to be moved. And then he hears a new sound above the noises of the brewing storm - a distant tapping, a rhythmic pulse that sounds almost like someone using a keyboard. In fact, that's what it is; somebody's typing, and he understands at once who - it's Barney Granwell, writer of stories, creator of worlds.

Scribe.

Somehow, a crack has appeared in the intangible boundary that lies between his two lives, and the Barney he'd abandoned in London is helping him here in Valance! He can almost hear the Earthbound version of himself saying the words as he writes them in that distant hotel room, telling his story...

*... enough is enough. Cassidy has to be stopped,*

*and the task has fallen to him. Barney feels a new power surging through his body. His muscles grow stronger, his reflexes swifter. It's like his first time in the Margins. He stares at Cassidy and every pore on the killer's face, every globule of rain dripping from the rim of his hat, appears to Barney as though he's studying his enemy through a magnifying glass. He sees clearly the coldness in this executioner's eyes, and he hears the rapid beating of his dark heart. With his raised perception, he can't miss the minuscule movement of Cassidy's head, the signal for his companions to gun down their powerless target. But Cassidy might as well have held up a placard with the word "Now" written on it. The Assassins appear to him to be moving in slow motion as they reach for their weapons. He is barely aware of the actions of his own hands as they draw his pistols at superhuman speed. A quick rattle of gunfire - eight bullets, two for each of them - and then a moan of dismay from the gathered townsfolk. The few deadly seconds of action are over...*

...the typing stops, and Barney's moment of supernatural clarity is over. Three Assassins lay on the ground, dead. They have all reached the grips of their revolvers, but that had been as far as they'd got before falling under the fusillade of high-speed shots he'd sent their way. Cassidy, though, is still alive, down on his knees and covering the wound in his stomach with his hands. 'Well, who'd have thought it?' he groans, bubbles of blood escaping from the sides of his mouth. 'You *do* know how to fight. But I won't be cheated, not now; I still aim to kill those women.' With a struggle, he raises his right hand, ready to snap his middle finger and thumb together. 'All I have to do is -'

A shot rings out, and Cassidy's eyes fill with shocked surprise. He turns, trying to figure out who fired the bullet that is now lodged in his skull, but before he can do so, he falls face down into the muddy streets of Valance. He will never know that the coup de grâce was applied by a flame-haired Texan gambler.

Red drops his pistol. 'I apologise if you wished to finish this rat off yourself, but you seemed intent on standing and listening while he signalled his wishes to his comrades on your world. I assume he was talking about someone of importance to yourself, and as such, I deemed it necessary -'

'Red - stop talking. You're right. I should have shut him up earlier.' Barney studies the bodies lying at his feet. Only Cassidy means anything to him. He looks closer and tries to see how this lifeless figure ever had the power to cause so much suffering. That triggers a thought about the pain that he himself has unknowingly caused over the course of his writing career. Cassidy must have truly loved his wife to have sought vengeance so ruthlessly, but this is not the time to worry about the rights and wrongs of the past. Alongside the exhilaration of victory, he feels a rush of sadness. Through some mysterious alchemy, he is aware that the vessel of flesh and blood which carried him through his fifty years on Earth is no longer alive. The bond between himself and his now dead body in London has been broken.

Barney shows his appreciation to Red with a gesture. 'You realise you've made an enemy of the Assassins?' He looks towards the crowd, but even as he does this, he sees they are fading away. The world is shifting, changing shape before his eyes. The wooden buildings of Valance are disappearing behind a rolling bank of fog - the equivalent of the curtain coming down in a theatre so the scenery can be replaced. The thunder and rain quietens as the fog wraps a blanket of silence around him. He realises he isn't alone in the heavy mist. Red is still with him.

'Why haven't you gone with the others?'

Red's eyes are wide in wonder. He stares down at his fists as he opens and closes them repeatedly, as if ensuring he still has control of them. 'I don't know. However, one thing I *do* know is that in another version of this story, that rattlesnake we just killed was fixing to take great delight in stretching my neck on those gallows.' Red turns to where The Mercy Tree had been standing until a few seconds ago, but like the frontier town itself, it too has vanished, taking the three bodies with it. 'Well, I guess it's out there somewhere, waiting for me. I can only assume that my future is now connected to you, Mister Granwell.'

Then another fresh development occurs. The temperature has dropped and the sultry heat of an Arizona thunderstorm has disappeared. After a moment, the fog clears, revealing a grassy valley surrounded by high, rugged hills under a grey sky. In the distance lie snow-covered mountains. Barney notices a change in the way he is dressed. He's now wearing camouflaged combat trousers, fur-lined jacket, and a soft peaked cap covering a woollen balaclava that he is grateful for. In his gloved hands, he is holding a C8 carbine. As he's come to expect in this place, not only is he able to identify the weapon, but he also knows he has the skill to use it. Red still wears the lightweight clothes of a Southern card player, and has his arms wrapped around himself, struggling to get warm.

They each pick up the throbbing of the motor engine at the same time. Bouncing over the uneven terrain, a military truck appears through the last few wisps of fog. As with his new weapon, Barney instinctively recognises it. It's a Jackal, the nickname given to this type of light patrol vehicle when utilised by the British Army in the early twenty-first century. *My own period,* he thinks, *...or it used to be.* The big brother of an old-fashioned jeep, the Jackal contains a unit of six soldiers, all in the same uniform as himself. One is standing in the back, using the heavy mounted machine gun he is manning to keep his balance. The truck comes to a stop and the soldier sitting beside the driver jumps out and lowers her bandanna.

'You made it!' Barney shouts. '...Eventually.'

Taylor smiles grimly. 'Yeah, we got diverted into another story and had to deal with a few Assassins somewhere in Siberia. Those Cossacks are as tough as they come. I have to admit, I wasn't sure you'd still be alive, but it's good to see you. I take it that Cassidy's dead?'

'Him and three of his thugs.'

Taylor is impressed. 'Then congratulations are in order. Now that's done, what's next? Are you heading back home?'

Barney shakes his head. 'I guess this is my home now, so I'll tag along with you, if that's okay?'

'We never turn a volunteer down. If you think you're up to it, we'll have you.'

'I'm up to it, don't you worry.' He scans the area, looking for clues as to their location. 'Where are we, and what year is it?'

Taylor gestures at the landscape. 'The year is twenty-oh-six, and we're in Afghanistan. To be more specific, the highlands above a small town called Aranas. I've had a report that a team of Assassins are hiding out near here.'

'Good. What book are we in, and who's the writer we're looking out for?'

'No idea.' It's plain that not only does Taylor not know, she doesn't care. Barney knows she has her own reasons for killing Assassins - reasons she keeps to herself - and saving human writers isn't among them. While she's speaking, another two Jackals have appeared on the scene. Barney does a quick head count. Including Taylor and himself, they are a seventeen-strong unit.

'Let's go, then. Which one am I riding in?'

'Aren't you going to introduce your friend first?'

'Bloody hell, I almost forgot. This is Red Rankin. I think he wants to join us.' Red, still shivering, signals his agreement. 'I'll vouch for him,' Barney adds, seeing the doubt in Taylor's eyes.

She gives Red the once over, taking in his unsuitable clothing. After a moment's thought, she says, 'If that's what you want. You'll ride with me. Rankin, you're over there.' She points to the central vehicle of their mini convoy. The moment Taylor accepts his involvement, Red's outfit changes from Old West gambler to operational member of the SAS. He's busy examining the C8 that has replaced his Colt when the vehicles set off.

Barney climbs into his appointed Jackal and sits next to Taylor. She nudges him in his ribs and grins. 'This is the life, hey?'

But Barney is quiet. His mind is on those he's lost - Robin, Smith, Charlie; even Tom Jefferson, and the one's he's left behind - Lucy, Sally, and Mary; Cristina and Giuliana; the network of family and friends he's built up over his lifetime. He thinks about the message he'll soon be sending to Sally, giving her a list of passwords and asking her to delete every draft copy she can find of *Death is the Currency*, his almost-finished fourth instalment of *Seven Hells*. If Mary gets her hands on it he knows she'll find a way of publishing it, causing more unnecessary mayhem. Then there's the Lucy and Jonathan Carpwell-bloody-Higgins situation; who would have thought that, at the same time he'd been irritating Barney with photos from their tour, he was unwittingly keeping Lucy safe from Cassidy?

And what about Newman? Have the Assassins killed the Warden? Did he leave Barney alone in the hotel to look after himself? No doubt he'll find out the truth in good time. He studies his surroundings again and senses the millions of other stories that exist beyond the hazy boundaries of those mountains, and the locations in which they take place: the foggy Victorian back streets and the skeletons of shipwrecked liners; bombed-out city ruins and alien concentration camps; stately drawing rooms and floating cities in distant galaxies. Places where Assassins lurk, standing by for a Shadow Writer to open the Channel so they can carry out their deadly orders on Earth.

Places where he will hunt them down and

kill them.

After a second or two, he smiles back at Taylor and answers her question.

'It is now.'

\* \* \* \* \*

# Epilogue: England, Present Day

Most days, Guy Tibbs would emerge from his post-prandial nap alert and refreshed, ready to add another few hundred words to the thousand or so he'd struggled to write in the morning. He rarely dreamed during his hour's sleep, but today he'd been coughing and spluttering as he came to, frantically clearing his lungs of the imaginary sea water that he'd felt himself to be drowning in. He'd never dreamt about any of his own stories before, so why has he just had one based on his own novel - *The Battle of the Deep* - about the fictional *HMS Argon*, a British submarine escorting Atlantic convoys during the Second World War? On its third transit across the ocean, an enemy torpedo hits the Argon. In the book, she goes to the bottom, lost with no survivors.

In the dream, events had taken a different turn...

*...by some miracle, Captain Graham has brought the sub to the surface. Guy is the first man up top, sent to assess the damage. He's climbing through the*

hatch of the conning tower when someone - someone who had no right to be on the deck of a surfacing submarine - grabs him and throws him over the side. He lands heavily on the deck, stunned, and he can't stop himself from sliding into the cold sea. His mouth fills with water and he knows he is drowning; but before he loses consciousness, a strong pair of hands haul him back to safety. As he regains his composure, something catches his attention; it is his attacker, laid lifeless on the deck in front of him. Guy staggers backwards as the body begins to disintegrate, becoming translucent, then transparent, before disappearing completely. Before he can process this, his rescuer approaches, and looks him in the eye, checking his recovery. His face is encircled by flaming red hair and a peculiarly old-fashioned beard. Satisfied that Guy will live, he shouts out to yet another newcomer, his voice battling against the clamour of the wind.

'Time to move on, Mr Granwell. I believe that's the last assassin we'll find here.' Then, more impatiently, 'Come on, Barney - let's go!' Another voice speaks, this time from close behind him. 'Someone will be in touch, Tibbs; take care.' Guy spins around three hundred and sixty degrees, seeking out this third stranger; but when he completes the full circle, he finds himself completely alone. His attacker and both of his defenders are gone, disappeared as if they'd never existed...

...he woke up in the warmth of his house, with

the smell of ozone in his nostrils, and the taste of salt water on his lips. That had been a hell of a nightmare. He'd genuinely felt as though he'd been about to drown. Who the hell was the red-haired chap who yelled some nonsense about assassins? And those names he'd shouted - "Barney" and "Mr Granwell". He'd met a Barney Granwell once at a publishing event, a fellow writer, but hadn't they found his body in a London hotel room a few months ago? Guy didn't believe in ghosts, and to him, dreams were just tricks played by an over-active mind; maybe Barney's name had been mentioned on the radio while he'd been sleeping, and that had caused his brain to go into overdrive? And what was the phrase, "*... someone will be in touch...*"?

It would take a psychoanalyst to explain that little lot.

He sat down in front of his computer and glanced at his watch. He didn't have time to waste pondering the mysteries of his subconscious; he had stories to write, plots to invent, locations to describe.

Characters to create.

Printed in Great Britain
by Amazon

77287902R00199